MW01118253

bythepeople.gov

bythepeople.gov

A Novel

Jim Gilmore

iUniverse, Inc.
New York Lincoln Shanghai

bythepeople.gov

Copyright © 2007 by Jim Gilmore

iUniverse books may be ordered through booksellers or by contacting:

iUniverse
2021 Pine Lake Road, Suite 100
Lincoln, NE 68512
www.iuniverse.com
1-800-Authors (1-800-288-4677)

Because of the dynamic nature of the Internet, any Web addresses or links contained in this book may have changed since publication and may no longer be valid.

This is a work of fiction. All of the characters, names, incidents, organizations, and dialogue in this novel are either the products of the author's imagination or are used fictitiously.

ISBN: 978-0-595-47407-3 (pbk)
ISBN: 978-0-595-71085-0 (cloth)
ISBN: 978-0-595-91685-6 (ebk)

Printed in the United States of America

For the girls

The basis of our political system
is the right of the people
to make and alter
their constitutions of government.

—*George Washington*

P R O L O G U E

—————————— ▼ ——————————

On the opposite side of our galaxy, some 80,000 light years from our solar system, shines a minor yellow star, one of a hundred billion stars in the Milky Way that is identical to our sun.

This very average star, which lies in the direction of Sagittarius, and is too faint to be seen as anything but a pinpoint of light by our largest optical telescopes, has a planetary system identical to ours, consisting of nine planets and their satellites, an asteroid belt, and an erratic collection of orbiting comets, giant snowballs, and interplanetary dust. Circling the minor star at an average distance of some 93 million miles is the system's third planet. If we could see it, the planet would appear to be blue and is orbited by a single large moon.

The blue planet has a diameter of 7,916 miles; its thin atmosphere is 78 percent nitrogen, 21 percent oxygen with trace amounts of argon, carbon dioxide, neon, helium, krypton, xenon, hydrogen, methane, nitrous oxide, sulfur dioxide, and carbon monoxide. Water vapor and dust are suspended in the atmosphere, forming distinct bands and swirls of clouds. The surface of the planet is divided into seven seas and seven continents. The seas, which cover about 70 percent of the surface, account for the planet's blue color and abundance of life.

The dominant land species of the blue planet's varied life forms is a two-legged being that stands erect, has two hands with four fingers and opposable thumbs, and views the world with binocular vision that enabled the creature to make tools. This being calls itself man. Man named his planet Earth.

This other, very distant Earth is an almost identical mirror image of our Earth. Its time is our time and our time is its time: the first decade of the 21st century. While I sit at my word processor here on my Earth, there, 80,000 light years away, sits another Jim Gilmore working at his word processor on his planet Earth. We appear to be identical, but like most identical twins we are merely mirror images of each other, not alike in every detail of our lives. I've been married to the same woman for more than 50 years, while he's been divorced five times and is now living with a nubile young lady of 19.

By the People.Gov is the title of the book the other me is writing. The title of my book is *bythepeople.gov.* Similar titles, to be sure, but as one can plainly see, not the same. Both books are about the evolution of democracy in the 21st century of the two nearly identical worlds. If the characters and events in this book are similar to the characters and events in the other book, it's not coincidental, nor is it coincidental if they're not. I simply don't know which book you are reading or on which planet.

What follows is not science fiction, but it is fiction, for what is fiction other than asking, "What if?"

THE BEGINNING—MICHIGAN

CHAPTER 1

▼

If there's anything I'd hate, it would be for future historians to claim that I was a psycho like Caesar or Napoleon or Hitler or any of the other megalomaniacs of history. My motives were far different from any of theirs. I did what I did for love.

You see, there was this girl, Melanie Schultz. She worked in Programming, and I used to see her during coffee and lunch breaks in the company cafeteria on the twenty-sixth floor of the United States Satellite TV building in Southfield, Michigan.

Now that I look back, I can't help thinking the designer of the cafeteria chairs was just as much to blame for what happened. The chairs, like everything at USS-TV, were very modern for the time, cleverly molded from a single lump of Lucite to perfectly conform to the curves of one's back and bottom, enfolding the sitter with a disarming gentleness. But comfort, unusual as it was for plastic chairs, isn't the only reason I considered the chairs to be masterpieces of design; it was the wonderful effect their seats had upon a woman's skirt. I have no idea what the designer's secret was, but whenever a woman sat upon one of the chairs her skirt magically hiked halfway up her thighs.

On my first day on the job at USS-TV, the day after I walked at Michigan State University, I was totally blown away by what I saw while enjoying my first morning coffee break in the company cafeteria. Melanie Schultz got a cup of coffee, headed for a table, and when she sat down, her skirt hiked up revealing her knees, the most fabulous pair I'd ever seen. I've always been a knee man, but Melanie's were truly masterpieces of patellar construction. There were two little dimples above each cap with little curving creases below them, creating two smiling faces. You know, like the *Have a Nice Day* faces you see at the end of road construction delays.

Melanie's knees became my obsession.

For the next couple of days, trying not to be too obvious, I ogled them each morning, lunch, and afternoon break. It wasn't until the second week that I had any desire to look above her waist. When I finally did, I discovered how perfectly matched her top and bottom halves were. And that was it. My heart was fatally pierced by Cupid's arrow. I knew I had to have Melanie Schultz.

But being the way I was at the time—a wild and crazy guy, yet completely lacking in self confidence—I realized this conquest could take time. Like lots of guys my age, I spent more time on line than I did in social intercourse, so I was lacking a few interpersonal skills. And I was sort of a late bloomer physically. My pecs and abs were a bit underdeveloped, and I was too skinny, almost to the point of scrawniness, with an Adam's apple that bounced up and down like a yo-yo whenever I tried to talk to a member of the opposite sex. Then, too, I'd recently had the collection of body art removed from my ears, eyebrows, nose, nipples, and belly button, so my skin was still a little pocked and raw. Aware that I wasn't exactly the kind of stud a hot-looking chick like Melanie would totally want to be into, I decided to play it cool and bide my time before I made my big move.

I studied Melanie for almost a week, observing her carefully from a distance at the morning, noon, and afternoon breaks, noting she always took them with the same friend, and that they always sat at the same table, one in the far corner, completely across the cafeteria from me. That's how I spent the following week, just sitting there, observing from afar, and taking detailed notes of her cafeteria habits. The next Monday I began to move in, slowly, patiently, the way a cat stalks its prey, sitting at a new, closer table each break before abandoning it for the next nearer one, until the ten-fifteen break that Friday, when I quietly slipped onto one of the empty chairs at their table, arriving so casually they didn't seem to notice.

Once there, I simply sat, nonchalantly sipping my morning Starbucks, munching a ham and cheese sandwich for lunch, sipping a can of Pepsi every afternoon break, listening to their every word, hoping for some opening.

I learned Melanie's friend's name was Cheetah. If ever a chick lived up to her name, it was Cheetah. She had the eyes and body of a cat, sleek and sinewy, a long, swan's neck curving up to a sleek head topped with tightly braided cornrows, a Masai princess in tight, stonewashed Wrangler Jeans and gray cotton UCLA Athletic Department T-shirt. Can you believe it? The chick wore the same T-shirt every day as if it were a uniform or something. That's so uncool it's actually cool. Like, you gotta have a really great bod to wear a UCLA T-shirt in Southfield, Michigan. I'm sure she did it just to bug all the MSU and Michigan alums at USS-TV.

Now I suppose you're wondering why I'm spending so much time talking about Cheetah when it was really Melanie I wanted. Actually, it was Cheetah who gave me the opening to enter Melanie's life. Like, if Cheetah hadn't been there, Melanie would've probably just sat there, like me, not saying a word. But the chicks loved to schmooze about their jobs and all, so I quickly learned they were into programming. Since I was a programmer myself, that gave us something in common, giving me the courage I needed to break the ice.

"Yo, word up!" I finally managed to blurt out at the afternoon break.

Cheetah blinked her golden cat's eyes at me as if she'd seen me for the first time, and then turned back to Melanie. "Hear something?"

Melanie giggled. "Think he wants to talk to us?"

"Yo! I'm down with that," I shot back.

"Cut the shit!" Cheetah snapped. "If you ain't ghetto, speak fucking English."

"Okay," I said.

"You have a name?" Melanie asked, obviously interested in me.

"Andrew. But my friends call me Andy."

"Andrew what?" she pressed.

"Cohan," I said. "Like George M."

"Who's he supposed to be?" Cheetah asked.

"He wrote 'I'm a Yankee Doodle Dandy,'" I said.

"TV show?" Melanie asked.

"Song," I said.

"Hum a few bars," she urged.

I began to hum the chorus.

"Oh, I know that one!" Cheetah began to sing, "Yank my doodle it's a dandy, yank my doodle do or die—"

"Not the exact lyrics," I stopped her.

"Whatever. That's how I learned it," she said.

"You should hear her version of the *Star Spangled Banner*," Melanie said. "Go ahead, Cheetah. Sing it for him."

"Oh, say can you see," she began, "any bed bugs on me ..."

"Oh, wow! That rocks my world!" I interrupted.

"Scared of bugs?" Melanie asked.

"No way! It's just that … well, that's how I learned it, too, when I was a little kid. I still sing it that way at baseball and football games. Know what that means?"

"You're a massive tool," Cheetah said.

"Cheetah!" Melanie scolded. She smiled at me. "Sorry, tell us what it means."

"We have a lot in common."

Cheetah sniffed. "We've zip in common."

"Not true, you're both in programming and I won the Kensinger Prize and all." They exchanged puzzled glances, so I quickly added, "You know, the Kensinger Prize for Web Page Design? I won it just before I walked at MSU. I was in the College of Communication Arts and Sciences. Got a B.S. in Virtual Reality Programming. Now I'm in Computer Graphics here, so I'm a programmer, too."

"We're not programmers," Cheetah hissed.

"Whoa!"

"We work in *Programming*," Melanie explained.

"With a capital *P*," Cheetah added.

∗   ∗   ∗   ∗

It wasn't until lunch break the next day that I learned the difference between programming and Programming with a capital P. Melanie and Cheetah worked for the station's Programming Department. They spent the entire break explaining how Programming departments drive the world of broadcasting.

"TV is really, really nothing without great programming," Melanie began my education.

"The guts of the business," Cheetah agreed, licking up the shaft of a bread stick.

Melanie nodded. "Our bread and butter."

"So, what do you do? I mean, actually." I squeezed a packet of mustard on my sandwich and bit into it.

Cheetah said, "This morning, we each made over fifty phone calls."

"Oh, wow! Your ears must be sore!" I said.

"Some mornings we make even more," Cheetah said.

"Why?" I asked.

"We need to know what shows the viewers are watching," Melanie said.

I shrugged. "Like, that's important?"

"You're such a geek!" Cheetah exclaimed.

Melanie explained, "The most important thing anyone in broadcasting can know is what shows which target markets are watching."

"Target markets?" I said.

"If you'd taken your mouth off your bong for a few minutes at MSU, you'd know what we're saying," Cheetah said.

"Sorry." I felt like a real dork. "I don't get all your jargon."

Cheetah said, "Melanie, honey, the geek don't get where we're coming from. Speak more plain, know what I'm saying?"

"Target markets are people, the kinds of people the advertisers want to reach." Melanie went on. "Reach and frequency are the name of the ratings game. Ratings can make or break a network and its affiliates. Broadcasting's all about CPMs—Cost per Thousand—bottom line stuff like that. If USS-TV wins the ratings game, the costs of our commercials and profits go up. If we lose, they go down."

"It's all about the Benjamins, dude," Cheetah said.

"Yeah, right. I knew that! Money's what America is all about," I said, not exactly lying. I'd seen stuff like that surfing blogs and *My Space* on the Net, but I'd spent so much time looking for naked chicks, I hadn't bothered to dig into the bean-counting side of broadcasting. "Guess knowing what people are watching is sort of important, huh?"

Cheetah crouched forward, cat's eyes narrowing. "You got it, white boy. It's fantastically important. How'd you think Harmon P. Harper made it to the top?"

I took a bite from my sandwich, and slowly chewed it, stalling, hoping to avoid answering her question. Like, I didn't want to appear really stupid and I had no idea who she was talking about.

"Well, come on with it!" Cheetah demanded an answer.

I washed down the bite of sandwich I'd been chewing with a swig of Pepsi, cleared my throat, and took a totally wild shot in the dark: "Like, the head of your department?"

"You serious? How long you been here?" Cheetah growled.

"Since May Day."

"And you don't know shit about Harmon P. Harper?"

My bad. They knew I was clueless, so I decided to be honest, and shook my head in defeat.

"Oh, Lordy!" Cheetah howled at Melanie, "What a geek!"

"So? You can't expect me to know everyone around here. Not yet," I defended myself.

Melanie sighed deeply. "Harmon P. Harper is only the President of United States Satellite TV."

"HP's rise to the top is legendary," Cheetah purred. "Seven short years ago, he was a mere mail boy at NBC in New York—"

"Can you imagine?" Melanie asked. "A mere mail boy!"

"But he had this talent," Cheetah said, "this totally wild talent. HP didn't just wonder what TV shows people liked. HP *knew*. You feel me?"

Melanie said, "Harmon P. Harper didn't even have to watch TV. He was so fabulously perceptive he could thumb through a copy of *TV Guide* and predict the coming week's ratings winners and losers."

"His mind is just off the hook!" Cheetah said.

"A really, real genius," Melanie agreed. "He became a giant of the industry when he was twenty-four. Just a year older than I am now!"

"HP even predicted the exact week *Seinfeld* reruns would start slipping in the ratings," Cheetah went on, "when all the other industry know-it-alls were predicting the target market would love *Seinfeld* forever."

"Boffo!" I exclaimed to impress them, using a show biz term I remembered seeing on *variety.com*.

For the first time, Melanie reached across the table and put her hand on mine. "Can you imagine what power, what charisma, such a genius can generate?"

I felt the power her touch generated in me. "Megagigs!"

Cheetah said, "They say, women stand in line to hit it with HP, longing for just a taste of his power."

"Oh, wow!" I said.

Melanie pulled back her hand to finish off her granola bar. "You understand?"

"Kinda," I said, feeling the power she'd generated in me drain away.

"He could put his kicks under my bed any time," Cheetah purred.

Melanie ignored her. "Right after the millennium, Harmon P. Harper left NBC to take over United States Cable TV. And he realized the future of broadcasting lay with digital HDTV."

"He digitized the whole country, practically overnight," Cheetah said.

"Filling the heavens with birds," Melanie said.

"Satellites," I put in, showing off the industry jargon I picked up on the Internet.

She flashed me a smile, apparently pleasantly surprised. "And he changed the company name from 'Cable' to 'Satellite.' We beam over nine hundred channels of entertainment, sports, and news down to every corner of the globe!"

Cheetah licked her lips. "Including six channels of hard core porn."

"Balanced with six Christian gospel channels," Melanie quickly added.

"That's what Programming's all about," Cheetah said. "Giving people what they want."

"Porn and gospel!" I agreed.

"Exactly!" Melanie said. "And that's why Harmon P. Harper's the programming giant of the industry. He's a people person. He knows what people want and how to keep them happy. He's always picking our brains for really, really big ideas. Like, just this morning we got an e-mail from him, addressed to all Programming Department employees, offering huge bonuses to anyone who comes up with a big blockbuster reality TV idea that will beat the ratings of the other reality blockbusters."

"Like?" I asked, wondering aloud how big the bonuses would be.

"*Who Wants to be a Millionaire*," Melanie said.

"That much?" I said.

"It's a reality TV *show*," Cheetah said. "On ABC."

"I know that." I never watched reality TV. Like most guys, I thought they were more or less chick shows. Like, I mostly watched football, basketball, hockey, wrestling and baseball. And I was more into computers and the Internet than I was into TV anyway. "So what other shows does he want to beat?"

"*Survivor*," Cheetah said. "It's been in the top ratings since the beginning of the millennium. And it's still hot, hot, hot!"

"A really, really super blockbuster!" Melanie added.

"What's the plot?" I asked.

"That's the beautiful part. There is no plot," Melanie said. "And CBS doesn't have to pay any writers or actors. They just dump a bunch of unknowns in some godforsaken place and see who survives. It's real people doing real things. That's why they call it reality TV."

"Who'd watch stupid shows like that? Like, if there's no big names or story."

"Because of the suspense. The last survivor wins a million dollars," Melanie said.

"So it's just another millionaire show," I said.

"No way!" Cheetah roared. "*Who Wants to be a Millionaire* is a quiz show. *Survivor's* a contest of who can outwit, outplay, and outlast the competition."

Melanie said, "Each week the contestants are given a really, really big challenge they have to survive or else. Like, on one show the contestants all had to stand on a log in the ocean until one of them lost their balance and fell off and was eliminated."

"Eaten by sharks?" I asked.

"The water's only knee deep," Melanie said.

"That's a load, man! The ratings would really go up if the losers were ripped to pieces by sharks!" I said.

Cheetah sniffed. "Where you been, boy? People love reality shit. 'Specially the kind of shit they loved or hated when they was little kids. Know what my all-time favorite blockbuster is?"

"Camp Retard?" I said.

"Oh, brother!" Cheetah said. "Melanie, tell the geek. It's your favorite, too."

"*Big Brother*," Melanie said. "What a great show! Very deep and Orwellian. They lock a bunch of twenty-somethings up in a house on the CBS lot in Hollywood that's rigged with lots of little TV cameras, so the target market can watch them do whatever they do. You know, like Big Brother's watching you."

"Yeah, right. I saw it on the Internet," I said.

"Liar!" Cheetah shot back.

"It's never been on the Internet," Melanie said.

"Has too," I said. "It's called *Voyeur Dorm*."

"Not the same," Cheetah said. "*Voyeur Dorm*'s just another Internet peep show. Soft porn. All girls. No guys. Only attracts computer geeks like you. *Big Brother*'s a unisex show. Aimed at TV's prime target market: twenty-somethings, like us."

"That's so lame!" I said.

Melanie said, "No, it's really, real. Like, I love to view young people like us in their most intimate moments, hearing them discuss important issues of their daily lives."

Cheetah leaned closer to me, curled a hand to her mouth, and in her most intimate tone, said, "We've got a friend at an ad agency who talked to one of the producers. Our friend says they've already taped a sequence where one of the guys asks the women who they'd rather go out with—a male model with a one inch dick or a geek with a ten-inch dong."

"A geek like me?" I asked.

"Oh, *playa please!*" Cheetah snorted.

Melanie giggled. "Do you?"

"She said it, I'm a geek," was all I admitted.

"With delusions of grandeur," Cheetah chortled. "Let's bounce to another table. He's just a big ol' nothing! Upstairs and downstairs!"

"Don't be mean," Melanie rushed to my defense.

"She hasn't seen my SATs," I said.

"Ha, ha," Cheetah laughed.

"If you saw my scores, you wouldn't laugh" I told her. "I just wasn't into grades and all that shit."

"You're sooo full of it homey!" she shot back.

"There's a way to prove you've got a great brain." Melanie smiled and touched my hand again. "Come up with a really, really big blockbuster idea for a new reality TV show, to help us win one of Harmon P. Harper's blockbuster bonuses. You'd do that for *us*? Wouldn't you?"

"You know it!" I exclaimed.

"No way!" Cheetah told her. "The geek's only been at USS-TV a month and a half and he's gonna win us a blockbuster bonus? What a freaking space cadet!"

Right then and there I vowed to prove to Melanie that I was really great upstairs and downstairs.

CHAPTER 2

▼

Cheetah took off an extra day to recover from the Michigan Marathon she ran on Memorial Day, so Melanie and I had the cafeteria table all to ourselves for once, which I thought would make it easier to talk. In a way it did and in a way it didn't.

"We're finally alone," I told her.

"Andy, there's something I really, really need to tell you."

I smiled. It was the first time she'd called me Andy, so I thought she finally considered me her friend. "I'm down with that. Shoot."

"You're driving me crazy."

"Awesome! You drive me crazy, too."

She shook her head. "Not *that* way, you know. Not in a good way."

"Whoa!"

"Actually, you drive me really, *real* crazy."

"Like, nuts? Bananas? Cuckoo in the coconut?"

She lowered her eyes, staring into her cup of Starbucks. "Believe me, Andy, I don't want to hurt you. I've never purposely hurt anyone."

"Go ahead. I can take it."

She looked up from her coffee cup, stared at me, her big brown eyes glistening. "I don't know if I can or should say this. Not to your face, you know. And I could be really, really wrong."

"Say it."

"Well ... um ... I think you've got a thing for me—"

"Duh?"

"And I want you to know—or need you to know—the feeling's not exactly mutual." She let out a big long sigh of relief, smiling as if she'd just finished the SATs. "There. I said it and I'm glad I did."

Suddenly I wished Cheetah hadn't taken the day off. "Like, you don't have a thing for me?"

"Sometimes you even bug me."

"Like?"

"All you ever say is *why* this? *Why* that? *Why* whatever? Your *whys* and *whats* really, really drive me up the wall."

"My *whys* and *whats*?"

"I hate questions."

"That's sooo lame! *Whys* and *whats* are how you learn. Like, I want to learn more about you, so I ask lots of questions. What's so wrong about that?"

I guess it was my last *what* that broke the camel's back, so to speak, because she totally lost it. "Oh, God, it's just like Cheetah says! You *are* a geek! A total freak!"

I didn't know what to say. I felt like a little kid again, you know, being ragged on by my best friend, so I taunted back, "If I'm a freak, you're a freak!"

"No way! I'm a really, really normal person who thinks really normal thoughts."

"Yeah, right. Actually, you're not as normal as you think."

"What?"

"Did I hear you ask *what*?"

"Only because you said I wasn't normal. Why would you say a terrible thing like that?"

"You just asked *why*."

"What's your problem?"

"Whoa! Now you're *why* and *whating* me! Like, if I'm a freak, you're a freak!"

"If I am, it's all because of you! Sickos like you can be contagious."

"Since when was asking questions a disease?"

"Since ... when ... well ... ah, I don't know! And it's really none of your business."

I could see she was totally upset. Something in her past had obviously turned her against questions. She needed help, so I sat back, the way my shrink always did, and said, "Tell me about it."

"About what?"

"Why you are the way you are. Something in your past made you hate *whys* and *whats*. You'll feel much better if you get it off your chest."

For a long two or three minutes, she just sat there, staring at her hands. I began to think she'd never speak to me again, but she finally looked up and started to talk, slowly at first, then faster and faster, beginning to verbalize what her problem was.

"I wasn't brought up to ask questions or even wonder why," she admitted. "It's probably genetic or something, you know? I was born and raised in Michigan. I was taught not to question anything, except maybe, myself. People who aren't born and raised here may not understand that. But my mom and dad worked at GM, and so did all my other relatives, except a couple of funny uncles who were at Ford's or Chrysler's. Oh, God! Did you hear that? Only a Michigander would talk about Ford and Chrysler as if they were family friends.

"Anyway, everyone I knew believed in the Autoworker's Code—actually, a kind of unwritten code—that it's not smart to question anything. Like, when I was a little kid, and I'd forget and begin a sentence with *why*, I was told either to shut up or to stop asking so many questions, so I learned not to. It was the same with all my friends. We grew up believing ending a sentence with a question mark just wasn't cool. I mean, if you had to ask *why* or *what* it proved you didn't know everything. Right? So whenever someone asked why something was or wasn't the way it was, we'd cut them off by saying *Hello?* or *Oh, really?* or *Whatever* just to prove we weren't interested in listening to questions."

She paused to catch her breath, and I nodded again, asking, "And how do you feel about that?"

"Oh, God! Now you've added *how* to your *whys* and *whats*."

"So?"

"Sometimes, Andy, I think you must have been born in Lower Slobovia or someplace just as freaky."

Yeah, right. Like, Minnesota."

"I knew you weren't a true Michigander! You *tricked* me into telling you things about me—things I never really, really never understood about myself, because you want to learn more about me. Correct?"

"Guess so."

"Most guys just want to get into my pants, but you want to get into the really *real* me."

"Don't be pissed."

"Know what I think about you now?"

"Not really," I said, thinking she was going to say I was a pervert or something.

"You're not the geeky geek Cheetah says you are. You're just different."

"That supposed to be good or bad?"

"I'm not sure. It does make you a little more interesting. What about me first attracted you?"

"Your awesome knees," I admitted.

"My knees? That's totally wild! Why my knees?"

Now that we were finally beginning to communicate, I decided to tell her the truth, the whole truth and nothing but the truth. "Your knees have these smiley little happy faces," I said. "They really turn me on."

"Oh, my God!" She began to laugh, so hard the tears were rolling down her cheeks.

"It's not *that* funny," I said, thinking she was laughing at me.

She gave my hand a reassuring squeeze, suddenly becoming serious. "You're so right. It's not funny. It's just that I've never had a guy tell me he has the hots for my knees before."

"Well, like you said. I'm different."

"And kinda sweet," she said, giving my hand another squeeze. "Just like my mom. When I was a little kid, she used to kiss my knees and tell me they were such happy little knees."

"I'd love to kiss them."

"Oh, you!"

"I am totally into you, your knees, your upstairs and downstairs, all of you."

"What can I say?"

"I'd do anything for you. That's why I was up all night last night."

"Doing what?"

"Designing a new virtual reality software program to help you and Cheetah win a blockbuster bonus."

"I love it!" She leaned forward, so she could speak to me more intimately. "It really, really feels good when a guy, even someone as different as you, says he'll do anything for you, like helping you win a huge blockbuster bonus! Does that make me sound like a money hungry bitch?"

"No, you deserve it. You're terrific."

"You know, I try to be. I've always taken good care of myself. I exercise regularly. I eat all the right food groups. I drink only bottled water or Starbucks Coffee. Rent all the Netflix *Abs* and *Buns of Steel* DVDs. TiVo Oprah religiously. And I shave my legs every time I take a shower, under my arms, too. I even follow the Biore Three-Step Plan for More Beautiful Skin. So, who am I to argue if you want to put my knees and me on a pedestal?"

"You're sooo cool!"

"What do you call your new program that's going to win us lots and lots of money?"

"*Decision Tree.*"

"What does it do?

"I feed it real problems and it comes up with real decisions."

"It's a decider. How does it work?"

"It's kind of hard to explain, like, I'm still creating it, but if it's okay with you, I can give you and Cheetah a sneak preview tomorrow."

"I'd love to see it and I'm sure Cheetah will, too."

CHAPTER 3

▼

I confess I was exaggerating a little when I told Melanie I'd created a new software program—Decision Tree—that would make her and Cheetah rich and famous. But she'd seemed so happy and laughed so hard that she began to cry, so what could I say? I stayed up all that night, letting my fingers race across my MacBook's key pad, running a race with the clock. In just one night, I came up with a program so awesome and mind-blowing I couldn't believe I'd dreamed it up all by myself. Like, it wasn't just any old program you can pick up at Best Buy or places like that. Even Bill Gates or Microsoft or Bill Jobs couldn't have dreamed it up. Decision Tree was all mine, a program that could change America forever.

The next morning at the ten-fifteen break, I slid onto the chair opposite Melanie, opened my MacBook, and, bleary-eyed as I was, happily blurted out, "It works! I've got an idea for a great new reality show!"

"Yeah, sure!" Cheetah snorted.

"Give us the plot line," Melanie said.

"It has no plot."

"That's a plus," Melanie said.

"Yeah, sure," Cheetah said again, not quite snorting this time, but sniffing just the same. "So what's it about?"

"I call it *Highway to Happiness*," I said. "It's sort of a road trip."

Melanie said, "Another *Road Trip*?"

Cheetah yawned and said, "It's been done before."

"No way. This is a really different kind of road trip show," I said.

"Boring, boring," Cheetah said. "So where's the suspense? Reality blockbusters gotta have suspense. And interaction. Lots of interaction. And a big reward at the end."

"*Highway to Heaven's* got it all!" I told them.

"Tell us about it," Melanie urged, wanting it to be a good idea, I guess, because of the bonus.

"Keep it short," Cheetah warned. "Like Harmon P. Harper says, if you can't write your idea on the back of my business card you don't have an idea."

"Did Harmon P. Harper say that?" Melanie asked.

"According to Google, it was a guy named Belasco," I said.

"Whatever," Cheetah said. "Just don't take all day. We've got more important things to do than listening to a geek like you."

"We have to make fifty more phone calls before noon," Melanie said.

I nodded. "*Highway to Heaven* is a competition. A competition between four couples in a car."

"Same car?" Melanie asked.

I had to think about that for a moment before saying, "I guess."

"Gets a little crowded in there, doesn't it?" Cheetah asked. "I mean, with eight people and all."

I quickly said, "It's an SUV. A big one."

"Got to be a top brand," Melanie told me. "Product placement is a very important revenue producer in this business."

I said, "It's a Mercedes."

"Not good," Cheetah said. "Should be American. This is a country of patriots."

"Okay!" I agreed. "A Ford Explorer?"

"Too tippy," Melanie said.

"Jeep?" I asked.

Cheetah shook her head. "DaimlerChrysler makes Jeeps. Same German company that makes Mercedes."

"No way. America invented the Jeep," I said.

"Doesn't matter," Cheetah said. "It's a Kraut car now. Don't want to offend the Jewish target market."

"Should be a GM model," Melanie said, still loyal to her heritage. "My mom and dad worked at GM."

"Okay," I agreed. "How about a Chevy Suburban?"

"Acceptable," Cheetah said. "The burbs are TV's primary target market for SUVs. So where does this Suburban go?"

"Nobody knows. That's the beauty of it. The contestants have no idea where they're going. The couple who figures it all out and gets to the mystery place wins a million dollars," I told them.

"But if they're all in the same car they all get there at the same time," Melanie pointed out.

"Not if we eliminate them one by one," I said.

"Yeah, sure," Cheetah sneered. "Like, *Survivor* on wheels."

"*Highway to Heaven's* more like a scavenger hunt," I explained.

"The game we played as kids!" Melanie said. "Good! Totally good. Viewers love to see grownups playing the same games they played as kids. It gives them relatetivity."

"You mean relativity?" I asked.

"No, no," Melanie informed me. "Relatetivity. Six syllables. You know, *relate* with *tivity* added. Like, relating to something the way you did when you were a kid."

"It's Programming Department jargon," Cheetah explained. "Relatetivity was the secret of *Seinfeld's* success—the reason why people could relate to Jerry, George, Kramer, and Elaine."

"Because character-wise, they were all selfish little kids in grown-up bodies, so we could visualize ourselves in them," Melanie added.

"So *Seinfeld* really wasn't about nothing," I said.

"You've got it," Melanie said.

"So where's the relatetivity in *Highway to Heaven*?" asked Cheetah.

"Well," I began after another long, thoughtful moment, "at the beginning of the show, each couple's given a list of clues about where they're going."

"Good. Viewers like clues." Melanie said.

"But they can't be too hard," Cheetah added. "And I still don't see any relatetivity."

"The clues are to places. Where when the contestants get there they can ask directions to the next place. And here's the twist. Like, you know how guys are?" I said.

"Tell us," Cheetah said with a sarcastic smirk.

"Guys don't like to ask directions. So maybe they can figure out a couple of clues, but when they get there, they won't ask for directions, so only the chicks can go on and become winners."

"You said this was a couple show," Cheetah said.

"It is. But the couples are paired up guy-to-guy and chick-to-chick. Didn't I tell you that?"

"Nooo," Melanie said, unable to hide the disappointment in her voice.

"It'll never fly," Cheetah said.

"Why?" I asked.

"Viewers don't like shows about gays," Melanie said.

"They're not gay," I disagreed. "Unisex is in. It's cool."

"Gimmie a break! TV is visual. What people see is everything. And what the audience will see on *Highway to Heaven* is four gay couples taking a joy ride in a Chevy Suburban!" Cheetah got up, snatching her tray from the table. "This morning has been a complete waste of time."

*   *   *   *

It went that way for the next couple of days. Every morning I'd come up with a new show idea, and every morning they'd shoot me down, and I'd just sit around and sulk during the lunch and afternoon breaks, racking my great brain, trying to work out the bugs in Decision Tree.

Looking back, I have to say some of my ideas weren't all that bad. But Cheetah wouldn't buy anything I came up with, not without some research to prove the show would appeal to the target market and Harmon P. Harper.

"Give up!" Cheetah snapped at me after I told them another of my ideas. "I'm tired of listening to your crap. Once an idiot always an idiot!"

"Oh, yeah?" I said. "How about you? You're so fake."

"Me? *Fake*?" Cheetah snarled. "There's nothing fake about me!"

"Yeah, right" I said. "Like, Cheetah's not a fake name!"

"Motherfucker!" she yowled like a cat in heat. "My mama named me Cheetah! When you insult my name, you insult my mama. Know what I'm saying? So take all your stupid blockbuster ideas and shove' em up your big fat a-hole. I can't take any more of your dumb ass Decision Tree BS!" She sprang from the table and slinked out of the cafeteria.

"That wasn't nice of you to tell Cheetah you didn't like her name," Melanie told me after she was gone. "She's a very sensitive person."

"Like, I'm not? Like, I'm supposed to enjoy being called a *geek*?"

"That's different. Your mother didn't name you that."

"So? She's so full of it. I don't have a big ass."

"I know, I know," she soothed. "And you're just trying to help us win a big blockbuster bonus. But you have to understand it's hard for people like Cheetah and me to visualize concepts we've had no part in creating. We're not loners like you, you know. We're team players."

"You're saying my Decision Tree needs Cheetah's and your input?"

Melanie nodded. "To prove you're not a loner. Loners are bad. The F.B.I. profiles on serial killers, rapists, and kidnappers say they're all loners. Totally bad people always are. Good people are people people. Team players, you know? Creating TV shows is a team sport—like all great American sports. That's where Cheetah and I are coming from. It takes input from the other team players to come up with big blockbuster ideas."

"I guess."

I think Melanie could see by the way my shoulders sagged that she'd hurt me, because she put her hand on mine and said, "I see where you're coming from, too, Andy. Making decisions isn't what computer programming's about, is it? I mean, programmers are total loners. Right?"

"That's *so* bogus. I like working with you. We're a team. But Cheetah drives me up the wall.

"Be nice to her, Andy. She's very fragile."

"Yeah, right. Fragile as a bowling ball. And I'm getting a little pissed at all the strikes she keeps throwing at me and my ideas."

She squeezed my hand. "Listen to me, Andy. Cheetah's not as tough as she seems on the outside. Inside, she's very frail. She's been diagnosed as bipolar, you know."

"Like, she's crazy?"

"Not really, really crazy. She just has major highs and lows."

"Oh, wow!"

"So like I said, be nice to her. She's pretty stable now. But if you put her down, and frustrated her, it could tip her over the edge. Understand?"

"Word. How can I help her?"

"Stop being such a loner. Don't just tell her your ideas. Make her feel like she really, really belongs to the team. Ask for her input. Make her part of the creative process."

"Yo!" I closed my MacBook and got up from my chair. "Tomorrow, I'll prove I'm not one of those loners the F.B.I profiles. I *am* a team player."

CHAPTER 4

▼

The next day Melanie took a sick day, and I was afraid to sit at our regular table, because I knew how pissed Cheetah had been when I'd told her that her name was so fake. So I tried to hurry past her, heading for a table across the cafeteria, but she reached out a hand, digging her claws into my arm, snarling, "Sit, A-Hole!"

As I sank onto the chair next to her, I said, "Yo. Word up. Sorry I hurt your feelings yesterday. Like, I didn't know your mama named you Cheetah."

"Okay, geek. I'm going to level with you. I thought a lot about what you said yesterday. And Melanie told me if we're going to be teammates, and win a big blockbuster bonus, we gotta be completely honest with each other."

"I'm down with that. It's another thing we have in common. We talk the same language."

"Shut up and listen, geek!" she snapped, and she suddenly switched to pure ghetto. Like, what she was saying came straight from her heart. "Mama didn't name me Cheetah. It's my family name. My given name is Placenta. Placenta Cheetah. How'd you like that on yo birf certificate? Now, you's probably axing, how da fuck'd you get hit wit some names like dat? Mama would always be telling me, 'You weren't no easy baby to bear, Placenta.'"

"My birf certificate confirms dat. It say I was ten pounds four ounces when I popped out dat womb. Mama say she birfed me going on nineteen hours. Dat whole time she was cursing my Daddy for not buying some of dem Magnum condoms dat night, and den for bouncing with her little sister, Henrietta, on top of dat. Sos da whole time I was being birfed, Mama was screaming, 'cheetah! cheetah! cheetah!' She were actually screamin' *cheater*, but mama be talking funny. She never went to college like me, sos she never learnt to speak good as me. That's what education does for you. In the hood, I speak ghetto. When I'm with upscale white suburban people I articulate good as Oprah.

"Anyway, Mama screamed *cheetah* so often, and so loud, the delivery room nurses thought it was her mantra or someting. After I finally popped out, the nurse filling out my birf certificate axe Mama what da baby's daddy's name was, and she screamed, 'Dumb ass cheetah!' So, dat's what da nurse put down as my Daddy's name, Dumas Cheetah, and while Mama was still layin' dere on da delivery room table, feet in da stirrups, legs spread-eagled, da way women had to deliver babies in dem days, da nurse axed, 'What's her given name?'

"Mama was still panting and puffing, like one of them old steam locomotives, but still she managed to grunt, 'Ain't thought up no girl name. Was hopin' for a boy.'

"Just my luck, at dat exact moment da doctor's head popped up from between Mama's legs and he say, 'Placenta's coming!'

"Mama claim hearing dat suddenly made her feel real good. 'Placenta! Dat's soo beautiful! Girl's name's gonna be Placenta!'

'You can't name her *that*!' da nurse say.\

'Any law agin' it?'

"The nurse say, 'Well, no, but—'

"'No buts,' Mama say. All she knew da word *Placenta* meant was dat a huge wave of relief swept over her da second she hear it. 'My Placenta's gonna be a joy to da world!'

"When I was a little kid, I did seem to bring joy to a lot of grownups. Whenever dey'd hear my name dey'd grin, and laugh, almost bustin' dey sides. But by the time I was three or four, I began to know da difference between people laughing because deys happy, and when deys laughing at you. Didn't know yet what Placenta meant myself, so's I thought dey was laughing at me because I were funny looking or sometin'.

"It was my kindergarten teacher, Mrs. Keyster, what changed my life. Mrs. Keyster look like a giant chocolate Pillsbury Doughboy, or Doughgirl, know what I'm saying? Whatever. On da first day of kindergarten, when I handed her my school registration card, she read it and look at me, very serious, sayin', 'Placenta Cheetah?' I kinda wonder why she didn't laugh like da rest of da grownups when dey first hear my name. Mrs. Keyster just smile and say, 'Those are very unusual names. Especially your last name. Cheetah. Do you know the cheetah is the world's fastest animal? Cheetahs can run seventy miles an hour. That's fast as cars go on the expressway. Least, that's fast as they're supposed to go.' She smiled at me again, and sort of bowed her head, looking at me over da tops of her glasses. 'Cheetahs are sleek and graceful with bright, golden eyes just like yours. They're very beautiful. So maybe that should be your only name. Know what I'm saying?'

'No, ma'am.'

'Ever heard of Cher?'

'She sings.'

'That's right. Is Cher her first or last name?'

'I dunno.'

'Nobody knows. That's a fact. But in French, Cher means dear. So using just one name makes it easy for everyone to love her. That's why I think you should use just one name—like Cher—to make it easier for people to love and remember you.'

"She picked up her pen and scratched out the first name on my card. 'From now on, you just be Cheetah. You'll be sleek ... and graceful ... and work very, very hard to be the best at anything you do. Promise?'

'Uh, huh.'"

Just as suddenly as Cheetah switched to ghetto, she switched back to straight English. "And that's what I've always tried to do. I worked my butt off in school to stay ahead of my class. Like a cheetah, I was a natural born runner. I won a track scholarship to UCLA when I was sixteen, and the next year I was an alternate hundred-meter dasher at the Olympics. Then, I blew one of my knees, and my track days were over. But the Athletic Department let me keep my scholarship, and I graduated at the top of my class with a B.A. in drama. My dream was to be a TV star like Oprah. So why am I telling you this? So you know why I'm not about to take any shit from an MSU fuckhead like you."

*   *   *   *

The day after Cheetah had more or less spilled her guts to me, I sauntered up to their table, still believing I could help her, plopped down my MacBook, and said, "We're all team players. One for all and all for one. Right?"

Cheetah grabbed Melanie's hand. "Time to bounce!"

"Wait a second," Melanie said, pulling away from her. "I think Andy really, really needs us."

"No way!" Cheetah said. "I think the geek's gonna flash us or something!"

"You're not being a team player," Melanie scolded.

I had my MacBook up and running. "Let's brainstorm Decision Tree!"

"Excuse me?" Cheetah said.

"Decision Tree*'s* that new program Andy's been working on," Melanie said.

"You can't brainstorm with a geek with no brain!" Cheetah shouted so loud everyone in the cafeteria turned to look at us.

I simply flexed my fingers, like a concert pianist, and rested them on the key pad. "Decision Tree helps team players solve problems. Ask it questions and the program comes up with the answers."

"Oh, like Twenty Questions!" Melanie exclaimed.

"Sort of," I said. "We input the seeds and the program uses logic to help us grow big blockbuster ideas."

"Like, from little acorns grow giant oaks?" Cheetah said.

"Yo! We're connecting!" I exclaimed.

"Bullshit!" Cheetah said.

"Give him a chance," Melanie insisted.

"Decision Tree is rule based, like brainstorming," I went on. "The most important rule of brainstorming is not to step on an idea before it has a chance to grow."

"That *is* an important rule," Melanie agreed.

"If we're a team we have to play by the rules. Right?" I said, trying to get everyone on the same page.

"We are a team, aren't we?" Melanie asked Cheetah.

"The A-Hole Team," Cheetah said.

"Yeah, right." I ignored her jibe, lifted my hands from the keypad to crack my knuckles. "What's the first thing we need to know if we're going to create a new blockbuster reality show?"

"Too easy," Cheetah humored me. "The demographics of our target market."

"That's really, really important," Melanie agreed.

I ran my hands across the keyboard. In less than a millisecond the answer popped up on the screen:

MALES/FEMALES TWENTY TO THIRTY.

Cheetah said, "We already knew it was twenty-somethings. We gotta have more focused data."

I typed. The computer shot back:

THE Z-GENERATION

"Right on!" Melanie said.

"Innovators or survivors?" Cheetah asked, trying to get hard data about the target's values and lifestyles.

NO NEEDTO KNOW. VALS DO NOT APPLY. TARGET CAN BE OVER/UNDER EDUCATED, HIGH/LOW INCOME. JUST ONE CONSTANT: TARGET MARKET 100% REALITY FREAKS.

"Like, wow!" Cheetah said. "That's hard data we never knew before."

"Go for it!" Melanie said. "What kind of reality shows do male targets like to watch?"

33% LIKE WATCHING SHOWS INVOLVING MALES. 33% LIKE WATCHING SHOWS INVOLVING FEMALES. 33% LIKE WATCHING SHOWS INVOLVING MALES AND FEMALES.

"Doing what?" Melanie wanted to know.

FIGHTING

"Big deal," Cheetah said. "I don't need a computer to tell me men like to watch wrestling and boxing!"

"No, no!" Melanie exclaimed. "You're not interpreting the data right. Look at the screen. It says thirty-three percent of the target males like to watch *women* fighting. The networks aren't into that and neither are we!"

"Half the crap on our porn channels is girl-on-girl," Cheetah disagreed.

"But they're not really, really *fighting*." Melanie disagreed.

"Where you been, Girl? Women are boxing on TV now, too." Cheetah said.

"The fighting part is still important data. Now we need to know what kinds of reality shows female targets like to watch."

"Yo!" I agreed, entering Melanie's question. Decision Tree came back with:

FIFTY-NINE% LIKE WATCHING WOMEN. THIRTY SIX % LIKE WATCHING MEN. TWENTY-THREE %LIKE WATCHING MEN AND WOMEN.

"Doing what?" Cheetah wondered.

FIGHTING!

Obviously, Melanie was impressed. "That is sooo cool! I'd have guessed sex was more important than fighting to both the male and female targets."

"That's probably why the network news shows are so totally into war and political infighting. They know more about entertainment than we do," I said.

"Yeah, sure," Cheetah agreed.

You're not going to believe this: In less than twenty minutes we created a decision tree that evolved into a big blockbuster reality show idea. We called it *Coliseum*. The core idea was to build a replica of Rome's Coliseum where TV evangelists could battle World Championship Wrestling superstars for million dollar purses. But when the computer insisted the losers be thrown to the lions, the team agreed to shelve the idea. Like, it was an election year, and all the candidates of both parties and the religious right were calling for the networks to cut back on TV violence, so the timing wasn't right. Timing is everything when it comes to TV ratings. We agreed to save the idea in case the target's tastes changed after the election.

One of the best reality blockbuster ideas we came up with that week was *Devil's Island.* The idea was super simple. USS-TV would buy a small island somewhere in the Caribbean and build this totally authentic prison set on it. Like, the one France built on their island Devil's Island. And just like France, we'd recruit America's most dangerous convicts and ship them to our Devil's Island.

Decision Tree told us most American convicts would jump at the opportunity to join the cast, because the show would give them a chance to escape. Of course, there were real challenges and risks involved. Risks that only totally desperate men would be crazy enough to take. Like, they'd have to break out any way they could. Of course, most of them would end up being shot dead for trying. Really dead, you know, with no special effects or computer animation. There'd be real blood splattered everywhere. Only the bravest and luckiest would somehow make it to the water and swim for freedom. The water, for real, would be totally shark infested. Lots of freedom swimmers would be eaten alive, torn limb from limb in bloody feeding frenzies, churning the water into a crimson tide. The lucky few that weren't eaten, or didn't drown, would be hunted by patrol boats and machine gunned, making the water even bloodier. Talk about reality TV! And the winner takes all. Every thirteen-week TV cycle, one cunning, lucky prisoner would win his or her freedom and the million dollar grand prize!

We all agreed that *Devil's Island* was a totally big blockbuster idea. But in the end, the team and Decision Tree decided the show, like *Coliseum,* was probably a little too violent for the times. So again, we filed the idea away, hoping the country might buy more gore after the election. But like I said, *Devil's Island* was totally a big blockbuster idea.

We kept on working on new show ideas the next couple of weeks, and we still didn't have an idea we thought was a big enough blockbuster to win one of Harmon P. Harper's prizes. Almost totally discouraged, Melanie asked me to ask the computer what our team really needed to come up with a winning idea. So I typed the question into my MacBook, and Decision Tree came back with:

BOUNCE ONE TEAMMATE.

"That's a totally great decision!" Cheetah screamed, leaping up from her chair. "Peace out! I'm jumping this geek ship of horrors!"

At the morning break the next day, Melanie tearfully told me Cheetah had suffered a breakdown, the result, her shrink claimed, of a conflict between her manic and depressive selves. That may have been true—who am I to argue with a shrink—but I suspect Cheetah's discovery that I'd been using her to get to Melanie was the cause of her breakdown. Anyway, by the time Cheetah returned to work a week later Melanie and I had become close friends. I tried to be nice to the returning former mental patient, inviting her to rejoin us at our table, but she insisted, quite loudly, that her shrink forbid her to sit with us.

Much to my delight, Cheetah moved on to the next table, leaving Melanie and me to create by ourselves. Being so young and naïve, I actually thought Cheetah was doing us a favor. I should have remembered that famous quote from the Bard:

> *The venom clamors of a jealous woman*
> *Poison more deadly than a mad dog's tooth*

CHAPTER 5

▼

"Geek!"

"Lousy rat-fink!"

"No good cheaty punk!"

"Moron!"

"Stupid intellectual!"

"Jerk!"

"Stinky idiot!"

"Rotten egghead!"

Those were the venom clamors Cheetah poisoned the air around me with for the next week whenever I went to the cafeteria. Each time I sat down at the table with Melanie, Cheetah would scream out another of her insults: "Cohan's a big fat pain in the you-know-what!"

I'd been called all those things before—even worse, if you can believe it—so I'd learned the best way to deal with such insults is to ignore them. But poor Melanie never had the opportunity to learn that lesson.

"Are you a man or a mouse?" she asked me one Friday during the afternoon coffee break.

"Why do you ask?" I asked.

"Mickey Mouse man!" Cheetah screamed from the next table.

"How can you sit there day after day and let her make fools of us?"

"She's only making **a** fool of herself."

"Sappy sadist!" screeched Cheetah.

"Oh, God help us!" Melanie cried.

"She's got to be running out of things to call me."

"Squinty-eyed squirt!" Cheetah shouted.

"I can't stand it!" Melanie sobbed. "I really, really can't stand it any longer. Andy, you don't know how embarrassed I am."

"Now, now," I comforted her, "why be embarrassed? There's no one here but the three of us." As you might imagine, everyone at USS-TV seemed to be avoiding the cafeteria. We'd had the place to ourselves for days. "So who's to hear?"

"Sawed-off runty runt!" Cheetah shrieked.

"I can," Melanie said, "and so can you."

"It doesn't bother me."

"Dumb, dumb bunny!" shrilled Cheetah.

Melanie said, "If I'm ever going to respect you as a man"—her emotion-choked voice went up a full octave—"you've got to shut that bitchy bitch up!"

"Putrefied pervert!" Cheetah squawked.

I could tell by the set of Melanie's jaw that she meant what she said, so as much as I hated to acknowledge Cheetah's venom clamors, I turned to her and icily said, "Sticks and stones may break my bones, but names will never hurt me."

Cheetah's mouth opened; like she was going to shout another insulting epithet, but much to my surprise, the gaping hole in her face slowly tightened into a thin smile. She leaped to her feet, letting out a terrifying yowl, and ran from the cafeteria.

"She's gone," Melanie said.

"My clever sarcasm was too much for her."

"You hurt her feelings."

"I did?"

"I know you did."

"Like, I did it for you."

"You didn't have to hurt her."

"You asked me to shut her up."

"She's my friend, you know. My very best friend."

"I know—"

"Why did you hurt her like that?"

"My bad."

"Being sorry isn't enough."

"Suppose you're right. I—"

"Of course I'm right. The poor thing. It was terribly cruel of you, Andy. Terribly cruel, you know. I mean, she's my really, really best friend. Go find her and apologize."

"But—"

"No *buts*, Andy. If you ever want me to speak to you again, find that poor girl and tell her how sorry you are."

After all the time it took me to build a relationship with Melanie, I certainly wanted to remain on speaking terms with her. So I excused myself and got up from the table and went to find poor Cheetah to tell her how sorry I was. But I never got the chance. As I passed through the cafeteria door, I heard that wild yowl of hers, again, and a little sort of pop. A bright burst of light went off in my brain, then everything went dark, the way it does when a light bulb burns out.

*   *   *   *

The next thing I remember was a far-off angelic voice repeating over and over, "My poor Andy! My poor, poor Andy!" Everything was still all dark, and my brain felt as if it were sloshing around in my skull like so much wet slush. It took all my strength just to open my eyes, and when I did, all I saw was this weird, spinning blur. Then that far-off angelic voice cried out again, "Oh, he opened his eyes! That's a good sign, isn't it doctor?"

"Could be," I heard a man's voice say. "Let's take a look in there." The beam of what seemed like a million candle power searchlight stabbed through the spinning blur. "His eyes are clear. No sign of hemorrhage. Of course, his skull might be fractured, but I rather doubt it. More likely, it's a concussion."

"He won't die or anything, will he?" the angel said.

"We all have to go sometime, now, don't we?" the man's voice said jokingly. "But I think it's safe to say his time hasn't come yet."

"Thank goodness! My girlfriend never would get over it if she killed him."

"I doubt your friend here would either," the man's voice joshed.

By then the spinning had slowed, and I could see the angel was Melanie. Her sweet face still seemed a little blurred, like the way you see when you open your eyes under water and look up at an object just above the surface. But I could still tell it was her.

"What happened?" I asked.

"Cheetah hit you with a stick."

"What kind of a stick?"

"Nightstick. She borrowed it from the twenty-sixth floor security officer."

"Ow!" I said, and everything started to spin again.

*   *   *   *

It was four days before I began to see things clearly, and another two days before I was allowed to leave the hospital. I'd missed a full week of work. But you can always find some good in any misfortune. Like, it was fortunate that Cheetah chose to strike her blow on a Friday afternoon, since it meant two of my days in the hospital fell on the weekend, making it possible for Melanie to visit me without taking time off from work.

Like, I can't remember her actually being there, though I'm sure she was. I imagined her visits were wonderful, with her holding my hand and gently stroking my forehead, perhaps even kissing me on the cheek before she left each day. It was lucky, too, that the attack took place on a Friday, because I was in the hospital until the following Thursday with orders not to return to work for at least another day, so it gave me another weekend to rest and recover.

That second weekend seemed an eternity. The loneliness of our separation made me utterly miserable. Yet as much as I longed to be near her, at the same time I was terribly afraid of what might happen if we continued to see each other. Cheetah was sure to drop the second shoe so to speak. After all, I'd told her what sticks and stones could do, and so far she had only tested my stick theory. I was sure it was only a matter of time before she tried her skill with a stone. Not that I was afraid for myself, but there was no way I could be sure of Cheetah's throwing accuracy. What if she hit Melanie instead of me?

As it turned out, when I walked into the cafeteria during the Monday morning break on my first day back at work, I was hit by a stone, but hardly the kind I expected. Cheetah had thrown him at Melanie while I was in the hospital. But I knew nothing of that then. I simply saw this overgrown Ivy Leaguer sitting in my chair.

Surprised, I blurted out the first thing that came to mind, "Hey, what are you doing in that chair?"

He turned and smiled up at me with one of those toothy boyish smiles they seem to teach all Ivy Leaguers to grin and said, "Sitting."

"But it's my chair," I said.

"Get lost, Geek," Cheetah said, who had moved back to Melanie's and my table during my absence.

"Assassin!" I snarled.

"Is he all there?" the Ivy Leaguer asked Melanie, tapping his temple.

"He was hit on the head last week," she answered, her voice filled with concern.

"Ha!" Cheetah laughed. "He sure was!"

I barely managed to keep my self-control. "Please get out of my chair," I pleaded.

He slowly rose to his feet, and for the first time I saw just how big and overgrown he was, standing at least six foot three.

"Didn't you hear the young lady suggest you leave?" he asked me.

"Get lost, Geek," Cheetah snarled.

"Oh, let him stay," Melanie said, rushing to my defense. "He's harmless."

"Ha!" Cheetah said. "Hit him, Rock!"

"Don't!" I cried out, protecting my head with my arms. "I just got out of the hospital and I'm wearing glasses."

He looked down at Cheetah and said, "I can't hit him."

"Why?" Cheetah asked.

"He's wearing glasses."

"So?"

"I could cut my hand on them and get blood all over my blazer."

"What's a little blood?" Cheetah asked. "I'll foot the cleaning bill."

"But he's your friend," he told her.

"Ha!" Cheetah snorted.

I ignored her. "Yeah, right. We're friends and team mates. So sit and join us."

"But it's your chair," he said.

"Consider it a gift from me to you. I'll take this chair on the other side of the table. You down with that, friend?"

"Call me Seymour," he said.

"I thought Rock was your name."

"Cheetah calls him that because his last name is Stone," Melanie told me.

"Like, a stone's a rock, you know," Cheetah said. "Even a geek like you should dig that."

Melanie sighed as Seymour sat next to her. "Isn't he a dream, Andy?"

Suddenly it dawned on me. She liked him.

I knew if I wanted to keep her I'd have to do something to prove I was a better man than Seymour. Probing for a weakness, I asked, "Like, how long have you been at USS-TV?"

"A week. I'm a trainee."

"Don't you just love the way he talks?" Melanie asked Cheetah.

"I've never heard such a beautifully masculine voice," she agreed. "He's too smooth and smart to stay a trainee forever." She looked at him, giving him a come on smile. "Bet you're going to be president someday."

"I suppose so," he said with a yawn.

"What department are you in?" I asked.

"Research at the moment," he answered. "The first step in the Talking Head Training Program."

"He went to Yale," Cheetah said.

"Yale, really?" I said.

"I have a Masters in Fine Arts from the Yale School of Drama," he said.

"And he did his undergraduate work at the Haas School of Business at Berkeley," Melanie said.

"Berkeley?" I said.

He yawned. "University of California. I have a B.S. in Business."

"You can research me anytime," Cheetah told him.

"What kind of research do you do?" I asked. It was the first I knew there was a Research Department at USS-TV, and with my B.S. from Michigan State I thought there might be an opportunity for me there.

"I sit in on focus groups and study the results of program pre-testing," he said in a bored way.

"What's a focus group?" I asked.

"We set up discussion groups with respondents—ordinary people we invite off the streets—to tell us what kind of shows they want the Programming Department to create," he answered.

"Like, you're into what Melanie and Cheetah do?" I asked.

"Boy, are you dense!" Cheetah said. "We already told you, Geek, the most important thing anyone at USS-TV can know is what TV shows people like."

"TV shows are our bread and butter," Melanie said.

"That's why my talking head training director started me out in research," Seymour said. "Knowing what TV shows people like is the guts of the business."

"It is?" I said, wondering if they were teasing me or something.

"Oh, brother!" Cheetah said with a sarcastic laugh. "Listen to the geek;"

"Andy, remember what I told you about Harmon P. Harper?" Melanie asked.

"Yeah, right. Like, anyone can become president of USS-TV if they're as smart and talented as him. Only there's one thing about that I don't understand."

"What?" the three of them asked at once.

"If Harmon P. Harper's a mere boy—and with all his brilliance and talent—how can anyone at USS-TV ever hope to become president of the company?"

"That's the beautiful thing about USS-TV," Melanie said.

"It's corporate policy to reward genius," Cheetah said.

"No one stands in the way of progress at USS-TV!" Seymour declared. "That's the first thing we trainees are taught."

"USS-TV is always looking for ways to improve itself," Melanie said. "Harmon P. Harper showed anyone can work his way up to be president of this network—even a mere mail boy. No one stands in the way of true genius at this company."

"Like, if someone proved he was better at picking TV shows than Harmon P. Harper, that person could become president of the company?" I asked.

"Exactly," Melanie said. "Harmon P. Harper would gladly step aside."

"So anyone at USS-TV can become president. Down with that, Geek? Cheetah said.

"Even me?" I said.

"Yeah, sure," Cheetah said with a snort.

"I think I can do it," I said.

"Do what?" Seymour asked.

"Pick better shows than Harmon P. Harper. Like, it should be easy to find out the kinds of shows people really want."

"Ha!" Cheetah laughed. "No one can pick shows better than Harmon P. Harper. It takes years and years to develop a talent like his."

"But it didn't take him years and years," I pointed out.

"You don't understand, Andy," Melanie said, soothingly. "No one in the world has Harmon P. Harper's special kind of talent. He's a genius. A true genius."

"But you said anyone could become president of this company," I said.

"Listen to him!" Cheetah said. "The geek's got delusions of grandeur."

"Andy, it's only a figure of speech," Melanie said. "Sort of like saying anybody can become president of the United States. You know things like that really, really don't happen."

"But it happened to Harmon P. Harper," I said.

Melanie sighed. "There's only one Harmon P. Harper."

"There's only one Andrew H. Cohan, too," I said.

"Thank God for that!" Cheetah said.

I took one of Melanie's soft hands in mine. "If I become president, well, will you? Ah, I mean, will you?"

"Do what?" she asked."

I always had trouble finding just the right words to say what I wanted to say, but I somehow managed to blurt out, "Marry me?"

She laughed. "Is that a proposal?"

"It's insane!" Cheetah exclaimed.

"Will you?" I asked Melanie again.

She lowered her eyes for a moment as she thought my proposal over, then she raised them to meet mine and said, "Andy, I'd marry anyone who was president."

As sometimes happens to a young man who seems to have no real ambition, once I was practically engaged a great change came over me. Now I had somebody to work for, a goal in life worth going after. The challenge stimulated my brilliant but lazy brain into action. Little did I know that my innocent quest would eventually allow me to control the destiny of the entire world!

CHAPTER 6

▼

The next day at the morning coffee break, Cheetah apparently decided to have a little fun at my expense. "Well, well, if it isn't Boy Wonder," she said as I sat down at our table. "Moved into Harmon P. Harper's office yet?"

"Not yet."

"Not ever," she scoffed.

"No, not yet," I said, firmly. "And it may be sooner than you think."

"Listen to the geek," Cheetah said.

"Have you come up with a big idea?" Seymour asked.

"Yo," I said. "I created it with my Decision Tree."

"Decision Tree?" Seymour said.

"A stupid program the geek uses to come up with ideas," Cheetah told him.

"Is it a really, really big idea this time?" Melanie asked with a nervous tremor to her voice, no doubt worrying about the wedding, what with all the planning involved.

"I admit it's not your average big idea," I said. "Actually, it's humongous! The ultimate reality TV program—*America's Dream City of the Year*."

"Yeah, like that's real humongous," Cheetah snarled.

"What's the narrative thread?" Seymour asked.

"Basically it's an awards show. Like, you know how the National Civic League hands out All America City awards to the ten best cities in the country each year? Well, my show's sort of like that."

"That's an old hack idea," Cheetah said. "Harmon P. Harper's looking for new ones."

"Yeah, right," I said. "But here's the twist. Instead of looking for great cities, we'll have the audience nominate and vote for America's ten worst cities."

Seymour shook his head. "I'm not sure Americans will want to give awards to the country's ten worst cities."

"That's what's really different about my show. If a city's voted into one of the top ten, we give it a million dollars to fix its streets or schools or whatever. When the audience finally picks the worst city in America, we'll blow it up, you know, like get STRATCOM to drop an atomic bomb on it."

For a moment they just sat there staring at me.

"That's a really, really crazy idea," Melanie finally gasped.

"No way," I insisted. "It a total blockbuster. Think of it as urban renewal. Every Fourth of July we'll blow up that year's worst American city—"

"Killing all the people living there?" Seymour asked.

"No. We'll evacuate them the day before we blow it up. Then they can sit and watch the fireworks on TV like everyone else in the country."

"The geek's totally freaked out," Cheetah said.

"Really, really far out," Melanie said.

"What about the radiation?" Seymour asked.

"America's got clean bombs now. I read about them on the Internet. So radiation won't be a problem," I explained. "And the day after the fireworks' grand finale, the country rallies all its resources to completely rebuild the city. Like, within a year it'll rise again as a great new All America City. Think how it could stimulate the nation's economy—"

"You're a total sicko," Cheetah hissed.

"Andy, you've only been out of the hospital for a week. Does your poor head still hurt?" Melanie asked.

"You don't like my idea?"

"*American Dream City* is a nightmare," Seymour said. "It'll never fly."

I could tell by the looks on Melanie's and Cheetah's faces that they agreed with him, so I laughed and said, "Just kidding. That's not what I actually dreamed up last night."

"I really, really hope not," Melanie said.

Seymour yawned and said, "So what's your big idea, I mean, for real?"

"Well, I don't like to brag," I modestly said. "But last night I came up with the most revolutionary advance in programming research since the invention of TV."

"Oh, God!" Cheetah said. "Here he goes again. Let's bounce."

"No, wait a minute," Seymour said, grabbing her arm as he checked his watch. "We've got time to hear what he came up with."

I knew the word research would get to him. "It's a simple idea. So simple I'm surprised no one has thought of it before."

"Simple thoughts come from simple minds," Cheetah taunted.

"Okay. Let us in on your little secret," Seymour said. "But make it quick."

"Yes, please tell us," Melanie said.

"I don't think I should tell anyone yet," I told them.

"Ha!" Cheetah laughed. "The geek hasn't come up with a thing. He's just stalling."

"Andy, if you really have come up with a really, really big idea you must tell us about it." Melanie said, giving me a reassuring smile

"Why?"

"Because we're your dearest friends."

Cheetah laughed." Ha!"

"Melanie's right," Seymour said, putting his heavy arm across my shoulders. "We are your friends, Andy. And your teammates. Tell us all about it."

"No. You might tell someone."

"Real friends never tell each other's secrets." He looked at Melanie, and then at Cheetah, giving them both sincere winks. "Right, ladies?"

"We really, really are your best friends," Melanie said. "If you can't trust your best friends, Andy, who can you trust?"

"God, can you trust us," Cheetah said.

Seymour gave my shoulders a friendly squeeze. "Okay, Andy, tell your friends your secret."

"Well," I started, secure in the knowledge that my secret would get no further than my three friends, "I invented a way to tell exactly what channel a TV set is tuned to the instant it's turned on."

They sat in stunned silence for a moment before Cheetah exclaimed, "God, what a genius! He invents something every TV set has had since the beginning of time!"

"A channel indicator," Seymour muttered.

"Is that all?" Melanie said.

"What a geek!" Cheetah grumbled.

"Channel indicator? You mean the light that tells you what channel you're tuned to?" I asked.

"Brilliant!" Cheetah said. "The geek catches on fast!"

"I didn't invent that," I protested.

"We know that!" Cheetah said.

"Wonder who did," Seymour said.

"Who knows?" I said. "But my invention's revolutionary."

"Are you trying to tell us your invention is more than just a way to tell what channel a TV set is tuned to?" Seymour asked.

"Much more."

Seymour leaned a little closer, making sure no one from another table could overhear, and asked, "Just exactly what does it do, Andy?"

"Like I said, it does tell what channel a TV set is tuned to. But not just one set."

"How many?" he asked.

"Oh, roughly, one or two hundred million."

"You mean—" he started, and his jaw dropped open.

"That many!" Melanie said.

"God! All at once!" Cheetah cried.

"Shh," Seymour cautioned, "we don't want everyone in the cafeteria to know about it."

"With my device," I whispered, "you can tell at any given moment exactly what TV shows everyone in the country is watching."

"Unbelievable!" Seymour said.

"No way!" Cheetah snapped.

"Oh, Andy," Melanie cried, and for the first time she kissed my cheek in public.

"How does it work?" Seymour asked.

"That's my secret," I said.

"Of course it is," he said, "a secret we must guard with our very lives. You don't know, Andy, what lengths some people would go to to steal an invention like yours."

"You've got to start thinking of things like that, Andy," Melanie said.

"God, people have been murdered for less," Cheetah said.

"Let us share your danger," Seymour said. "There's safety in numbers. Tell your teammates how your invention works and we'll all be in this together."

"One for all and all for one," Cheetah said.

I said, "I can't do that. I mean, like, I wouldn't want to endanger you."

"We're not afraid," Seymour said. "Tell us."

"No way. I'll bear the burden of this alone."

"My poor brave Andy," Melanie said kissing me on the cheek again.

"Of course, you'll need an agent," Seymour said.

"An agent?" I said.

"Someone to protect your interests," he said. "Someone who knows the ins and outs of company politics. Now, it just so happens I have someone in mind."

"You do?" I said, gratefully.

"Me," he said.

"What a true friend you are," Melanie told him.

"God, what a friend!" Cheetah said.

"I don't know," I said.

"Andy, a creative genius like you has to have an agent," Melanie told me.

"Why?"

"Because you're creative," she said. "Everyone knows creative people are shy and impractical. Creative people have no business sense. They need someone to protect them from themselves."

Seymour said, "Now, if I'm going to be your agent, you've got to tell me how your invention works."

"Electronically," I said, thinking fast.

He took out his iPhone and thumbed in that fact.

"How much will it cost?"

"I haven't made any firm cost predictions yet," I told him. "But it shouldn't cost more than a dollar twenty-five."

"A buck twenty-five?" Seymour gasped.

"Per unit," I added quickly, not wanting it to sound too cheap.

"I see," he said, entering that in his iPhone. "And you say it would take somewhere between a hundred and fifty and two hundred million units to cover the entire country?"

"More or less," I said.

He did some fast figuring. "That means we could do the whole bit for something like two hundred and forty-eight million."

"Too expensive?" I asked.

"Quite reasonable, actually," he said, pocketing his iPhone and rising to his feet. "Anyway, I'll see what Harm says."

"You're going to see Harmon P. Harper?" Melanie gasped.

"Might as well go right to the top," Seymour said.

"God, you've got guts!" Cheetah said.

"Aren't you glad you've got someone like Rock for an agent?" Melanie asked me.

"Sure am," I said.

Now, I suppose you think I must have gone back to the Data Processing Center feeling wonderful, knowing Seymour was going right to the top to sell my idea. But if you want to know the truth, I was feeling a little upset to my stomach again, because my invention was little more than an idea at that stage. It was, of course, beginning to take shape in my mind. Like, I already knew it worked electronically, and that it cost a dollar twenty-five cents a unit to manufacture. But there were still a few problems I had to solve; and what if Seymour came back with an order for two hundred million of my devices before I knew how to produce them?

And I was a little upset that Seymour was taking my idea right to the top. Like, I dreamed up my device to get Harmon P. Harper's job, and it just didn't seem fair, using him, so I could force him to step aside for the good of the company.

CHAPTER 7

▼

Shortly before noon that same day, I was sitting at my computer console, thinking how wonderful it would be when I was president of USS-TV, married to Melanie and all, living in one of those fancy mansions in Bloomfield Hills, with maybe two or three little kids and a Dalmatian at my knee, when the telephone on my console surprised me and everyone else in the computer room by ringing. No one had ever called me at work before.

When I recovered from the shock, I picked up the phone and discovered it was Seymour. "Yo, word up?" I asked, trying to act nonchalant with all those ears listening.

"Andy, you have no idea how much excitement that little invention of yours is causing at old USS-TV."

"Mr. Harper liked it?"

"Well, I haven't taken it quite that far yet. But believe me, Andy, I'm really giving it the old hard sell. The right people are starting to hear good things about you."

"Like, who?"

"Like, Hedda Nichtwahr, for one."

"Hedda who?"

"Nichtwahr. My department head. Brilliant researcher. She has all kinds of degrees from places like Heidelberg and the Sorbonne. They're not Yale, of course."

"I thought you were going right to the top with my idea."

"I was, Andy, believe me. But then I decided against it. I mean, there's a right way and a wrong way of doing something like this—"

"There is?"

"Right. I could have gone right to Harmon P. Harper. He's a Yale man, too, you know. And a Yale man is never afraid to talk to another Yale man. But it really wouldn't be politically correct."

"It wouldn't?"

"Heck, no, Andy. In an organization like USS-TV, you never go over anyone's head with an idea."

"You don't?"

"Never. People at USS-TV welcome good ideas. Ideas are our business, you know. They're gold, Andy, pure gold. So you don't go over someone's head with a good idea. That would be like robbery. Now, this idea of yours is big, Andy, totally big. And we have to do this thing right, or not at all. You with me?"

"I'm very lucky to have a friend like you," I told him.

"True, true," he agreed. "Now, since this idea of yours falls into the research area, I thought we should get a little advice from an expert. So I told Hedda about it, and you should have seen how excited she got. Why, she wants to have lunch with you today, Andy, to sort of get the story right from the horse's mouth—"

"Oh, but I couldn't do that," I said, lowering my voice to a whisper, so Cheetah, who I knew was sitting right on the other side of the computer, would not overhear.

"But you've got to," Seymour insisted. "I went to a heck of a lot of trouble to arrange all this, Andy. You can't let me down."

"What would Melanie think?"

"Who cares what she thinks?"

"I do," I said, coolly. "She would be absolutely furious if she saw me eating lunch with another woman in the cafeteria."

"You've got to be kidding. Andy, you're dealing with management now. Management never eats in the cafeteria. Actually, think what it would do to morale if common, ordinary employees saw their leaders eating eighty-five cent lunches in the cafeteria, rather than dining at The Melting Pot, the Whitney, or Sweet Lorraine's on expense account. I ask you, where would the incentive to get ahead be?"

"I never looked at it that way before," I admitted.

"Well, you never went to Yale," Seymour said, pityingly. "But believe me, Andy; the cafeteria is strictly for peons. Today we're moving up to the foxiest place in town."

"Like?"

"Machus Red Fox. That's where we're having lunch today. It's got a real history—the last place where Jimmy Hoffa was seen the day he disappeared. Hedda loves the atmosphere. So don't worry about Melanie seeing you. Just get over there as fast as you can. Hedda and I are leaving right now. We'll meet at the bar."

"Bar?" I asked, suspiciously. "Do they serve liquor?"

"They sure do!" Seymour said, happily.

"Well, then, I can't go," I told him. "I'm from a good Baptist family, you know. And good Baptists never—"

"Andy, I don't want to knock your religion or anything like that. But you've got to be practical. Hedda is really big at USS-TV—one of the real old pros. Actually, she's been at USS-TV almost three years. Believe me, she's got connections."

"I believe you. But if they serve liquor—"

"Don't let me down, Andy. This could be my—our big break. You do want to be president of USS-TV, don't you, so you can marry Melanie?"

"Of course."

"Okay. If you ever want to get to the top, you've got to forget your principles. Only until you do get to the top, mind you. Then you can have principles the Baptists never dreamed of."

Even a good Baptist can have a little Machiavelli in him, and I saw at once that the end in this case certainly did justify the means, so about twenty-five minutes later I met them at the bar at Machus Red Fox. If you think I was surprised when my telephone rang in the computer room that morning, you should've seen me when I saw Hedda Nichtwahr. She was totally not the woman I expected her to be. Like, if you're going to meet a female research department head from Milwaukee with a name like Hedda Nichtwahr, you'd probably expect her to be a little Wagnerian too, with fat, blond braids wrapped around her head, and a figure like an Aryan Amazon.

Hedda Nichtwahr was not like that—no, not at all. She did have blond hair, the blondest hair I have ever seen, but it was parted in the middle, and falling in long waves, framing her lovely face in spun gold. Her features were delicate, almost angelic, with high, sensitive cheekbones accenting almond-shaped eyes that were clear and blue and sparkled like cool wavelets in the morning sun. And her figure—well, to tell you the truth, if it were not for the fact that I was already betrothed, I would've fallen in love with her right then and there.

"So this is your young Mr. Cohan," she said to Seymour after he had introduced us. "I like him. He is very cute."

"So are you," I blurted out. I know that's not like me, acting so bold and forward, but I totally meant it.

"And so charming," she said, holding her hand out to me. I suppose she wanted me to shake it, so I did, and she laughed lightly, winking at me as she did, and said, "Oh, and you're a shy boy, too. Really, Mr. Cohan, I just adore shy boys."

It's strange, the effect I was beginning to have upon women. There seems to be some tropistic attraction that draws them to me like moths to a flame. Here Hedda had only known me for a matter of minutes, yet she already adored me. Ah, *recherché talent* as the French say.

"I like shy girls," I said, returning the compliment.

She looked up at me with those cool, blue eyes of hers, and said. "It's Andrew, isn't it?"

"As a matter of fact, it is." I hoped I sounded totally suave.

"Come, Andrew," she said, patting the red leatherette of the booth seat, "slide in next to me."

As I slid in next to her, Seymour said, "He's just like I described him, isn't he?"

"Absolutely," she agreed.

"I am?" I asked.

"But of course," she said, putting a friendly hand on my knee. "You have the look of a true genius, and I just love true genius."

"How many geniuses have you known?" I asked.

"Only one other," she said. "Harmon P. Harper."

"Already a living legend at Yale," Seymour put in.

"What sort of legend are you about to spin, my little genius?" she half-whispered, giving my knee a sincere squeeze.

"Tell her how your invention works," Seymour urged from across the booth.

"Now, now, Seymour, dahling, do not be so impatient. Let our poor little genius relax and have a drink before we talk business."

"Andy doesn't drink."

"Oh, no?" she said, her mouth turning into a small, round 0 that matched the big, red polka dots on her floppy hat and white silk dress.

"I drink all the time," I quickly lied, too embarrassed to admit the truth.

"Good," she said, prodding Seymour to signal for a waitress. "What would you like?"

Well, I'd never had hard liquor before, so I had no idea of what the names of any special drinks were. But I shrewdly noted she was drinking what looked like a glass of water with a little lemon peel in it, and, compared to the dark, amber liquid in Seymour's stein, it looked perfectly harmless, so I pointed at her glass and said, "One of those."

"Double Stoli on the rocks for Mr. Cohan here," she told the waitress with a pleasant smile. After the girl left to get my drink, Hedda moved even closer and began to rub my leg with one of hers, so I could feel her nylons scratching against my corduroys.

"Do you have an itch?" I asked.

She laughed. "Andrew, you are absolutely priceless."

"A real gem," Seymour put in.

She placed a hand on my shoulder and began to tickle a small circle of hair on my neck with her finger. "Now, dear boy, tell Hedda all about that marvelous invention you've come up with. Seymour reports you've discovered a way to tell exactly what program every living soul in the country is watching—"

"All at the same time," Seymour added.

"Brilliant!" Hedda said.

"True," I said as the waitress brought me my first drink. I took a sip from the glass, and found it both warm and cold at the same time.

"Exactly how does it work?" Hedda wanted to know.

"It reads information from a TV set," Seymour informed her.

"Like what programs people are watching?" she asked me.

I took another sip from my glass. "Right."

"And how much does this little device of yours cost to produce?" she asked.

Seymour took out his iPhone and checked his numbers. "Dollar twenty-five."

"Installed?" Hedda questioned.

"Installed," I agreed.

"Absolutely brilliant," she said.

I stirred the chips of ice in my drink with my finger. With each sip, I found it became more and more agreeable. "Amazing," I said, holding up the glass. "It's cold, yet it makes me feel so warm inside."

Hedda pressed her thigh against mine. "Very warm, I hope," she whispered. "Does your device work electronically?"

"Absolutely," Seymour said.

"Positively," I added. Now, a strange thing began to happen. The more I had of that drink, the clearer the picture of the device became in my mind. "Actually, it works by intercepting the free ions that are radiated from any TV screen."

"Does the TV have to be connected to the Internet?" Hedda asked.

I took a moment to picture the device more clearly in my mind. "No. It's a totally new technology."

"Exactly how does it work?" she asked.

"Andy's not prepared to divulge any design details yet. Not until the device is patented," Seymour stepped in.

"Can you tell me how big it is?"

"I think it's safe to reveal that," Seymour advised me.

I was looking down at the front of Hedda's dress, and I saw all those beautiful polka dots. Touching one of them with my finger, I said, "No bigger than one of those."

"No bigger than a bosom," Seymour thumbed into his iPhone.

"Polka dot," I corrected him.

"That small?" Hedda' asked.

"Small as a polka dot," Seymour confirmed.

"Can I have another of these?" I said, holding up my glass.

Seymour signaled the waitress that I needed another double Stoli on the rocks, and Hedda looked into my eyes, whispering, "Now, Andrew, you must tell me everything."

"You can call me Andy,"

"Tell me everything, Andy" she urged.

"Everything?" I asked.

"Everything," Seymour said.

"Well," I began, slowly, thinking back to the beginning, "I was born in Albert Lea Minnesota about a hundred miles south of the Twin Cities, you know. In nineteen-eighty-five. So I'm a member of the Y-Generation—"

"Really?" Hedda asked. "You're just a boy."

"You might say," I went on, "that my electronic ability is genetic. Like, my dad was a NASA radar technician, and my mom wired smart bombs at a defense plant—"

"I think everyone would agree your genius for electronics was genetic," Seymour said, making a note of the fact.

"Please do go on," Hedda said.

Just then the waitress brought me my second drink. "I'm a Baptist, you know," I told them, taking a swallow from the glass. "We never drink. It's against our religion."

"Beautiful," Hedda said, and she ran her hand up under my suit coat and began to gently rub my back. "Now, about that device of yours—"

"You're very pretty," I told her.

"Beautiful," Seymour agreed.

"Thank you, dahlings," she said. "But please do go on, Andy. I'm absolutely fascinated by it and you."

"It works electronically," I said.

"You already told us that," she said.

Scratching my head, I tried to remember. "I did?"

"You did," Seymour confirmed. "As your agent, I advise you not to reveal any of your invention's secrets—"

"Seymour, dahling," Hedda cut in, her cool, blue eyes turning to ice, "why don't you be a good boy and go back to work? I think our poor genius needs the afternoon off to relax his brain."

"Sure?" Seymour asked.

"Absolutely," she said.

"If you say so." Seymour got to his feet and disappeared into the sort of white blur that seemed to be rolling in around me like a bank of swirling fog.

After he was gone, she snuggled up to me and began to nuzzle my neck. "Now, Andrew, you dear, shy boy, wouldn't you like to go someplace where we can relax and talk more freely?"

"Where?" I asked, holding onto the table with both hands to keep it from spinning off into the fog like Seymour.

"How about my apartment?" she asked.

CHAPTER 8

▼

The next thing I remember was smelling this wonderful fragrance, heavy but sweet, like the scent of orange blossoms; and having this satisfying sense of well-being, with every-thing touching my skin feeling soft and warm and silky. It was so pleasant, just lying there on my back, smelling and feeling, that at first I was afraid to open my eyes, thinking I might be dreaming, and not wanting to end the beauty of it all by waking up. But then it occurred to me that to feel so good I had to be in heaven, and I always did wonder how the place looked, so I opened my eyes and saw everything above me was a misty white and silky, like a cloud with a silver lining, just as I had always pictured heaven.

Thank you, Lord, I said to myself, humbly, really thankful to Him for not sending me to that other place as my punishment for drinking liquor. I turned my head and felt this sharp pain stab me right between the eyes, and it made me realize one has to die before he goes to heaven.

"Hedda!" I cried out, suddenly worried that the two of us had been killed in some horrible accident while we were drifting around in all that fog.

"I'm right here," I heard her sweet voice whisper.

"Are we dead?" I asked.

She giggled and I felt her bare leg rub up against mine. "Do I feel dead?"

I had to admit to myself that her leg definitely felt very warm and healthy, so I guessed we were still alive, and if that were true, we could hardly be in heaven.

"Where are we?" I asked.

"In my bed."

I sat bolt upright. "Your what?"

"My bed," she said, innocently, smiling up at me with those cool, blue eyes of hers.

You should know that when I sat up so suddenly, the gold satin sheets covering us fell away, exposing the top half of her body, enough for me to see she was stark naked. I practically dove back under the sheets, pulling them up to my neck, trying my best to cover her at the same time, so she wouldn't be embarrassed at my seeing her that way. "What happened to your red and white polka dot dress?" I asked in a state of near shock.

"You took it off."

"I must've been out of my gourd."

"On the contrary, you were absolutely wonderful. So bold and masterful." She snuggled next to me, and by the feel of her body pressing against mine, I could tell I was naked, too.

For more than a moment, I simply lay there, too embarrassed to talk, staring up at the white and gold chiffon canopy over the bed that only a few minutes before I'd mistaken for a heavenly cloud, trying desperately to think of something to say that might alleviate what was most certainly a rather awkward situation. "You know," I finally said, hoping to ease her embarrassment by pointing out I was more or less in the same boat, "I don't have any clothes on either."

She giggled again, seeing the humor in it. "I know."

"Why would I take off my clothes?" I asked.

"Well," she said, rolling over on her side and propping herself up on one elbow, "I think you were hot."

"That makes sense. But why did I take yours off?"

"I was hot, too. Are you still hot?"

"Well, I do feel totally warm. But I've got a bad headache. Maybe you shouldn't get too close to me. I may be contagious."

"Don't be silly. Hangovers aren't contagious. But you do look flushed. Why don't we throw off the sheets?"

I clutched them to my neck. "No way. Like, I don't mind being hot. Not really."

"Neither do I," she said in sort of a throaty, animal voice. "Let me kiss your headache away." She kissed me on the eyes and nose and mouth.

"What are you doing?"

"Letting you make love to me."

"You are? Why?"

"Because it is the only way."

"It is?"

"But of course, dahling." She threw herself on top of me. "Once you make love with me you'll have to tell me the secret of your device."

"Wait. I can't tell you—"

"Don't talk so much," she whispered, kissing me on my mouth.

"I've got to be back at work by one-thirty."

She laughed. "Then there is nothing to worry about. It's not quite midnight."

"Midnight!" I cried. "I'm over ten hours late!" I started to climb out of bed. "Sorry, Hedda, I gotta jet—"

"Don't be ridiculous, dahling," she said, pulling me back. "There won't be a soul in data processing this time of night."

"Like, I'll be fired."

"Impossible," she said, wrestling me down on the mattress.

"Impossible?"

"Absolutely. Andrew, you are a genius. It's strictly against company policy to fire a genius." For no reason, she suddenly bit my ear lobe.

"Ow!" I cried.

"My, you are a very tender genius," she whispered, kissing the hurt.

"Please, Hedda, like, I know I'm a genius, and you know I'm a genius. But no one else at USS-TV does. I'll be totally fired!"

She put a finger to my lips. "Don't worry, my dear little boy toy. If I know, that's all that matters. No one would dare fire you. Come now. Make love to Hedda."

Like a playful cat, she rolled over on her back, releasing her grip on me to spread her hair on a plump, gold-satin pillow.

I thought I saw my chance to escape. "But we're not married!" I shouted, leaping out of bed and, while on the fly, wrapped myself in a white satin comforter I grabbed from the foot of the bed.

"So?" She leaped after me. "What does it matter? We are both consenting adults. No one can possibly be hurt by what we do."

"But I'm saving myself!"

"For what?"

"Melanie Schultz."

"And who is this Melanie?"

"She's going to be my wife. As soon as I become president of USS-TV."

"Ha!"

By now, the playful cat had become a tigress, literally stalking me, and suddenly she sprang, grabbing one corner of the comforter. For an instant, I thought the game was over, but then I let the comforter go, throwing her off balance just long enough for me to run into the bathroom and lock the door.

"Coward," she shrieked. "Come out and make love to me!" She began to pound on the door with her fists. "Come out, Andrew, or I will see to it that you never marry this Melanie Schultz. I can have you both fired."

"You can?"

"Do you wish to put me to the test?"

"No, no," I told her, stalling, trying to think the situation out calmly. But it's hard to think calmly while locked in a bathroom with a beautiful, stark naked female research director outside, practically breaking the door down with her bare hands. "If I come out," I said, slowly, trying to make some sort of a deal, "will you help me become President of USS-TV, so I can marry Melanie?"

"But of course."

"Cross your heart?"

"And hope to die."

"Really?"

"Absolutely. I give you my word."

I was still skeptical. "How can you help me?"

"How does the mama sheep help her little lamb?"

"But you're not my mom."

"Isn't that lucky for us?"

"Lucky or not," I said, standing my ground, "I want to know exactly how you're going to help me."

"After you tell me how that marvelous device of yours works, I will suggest ways you can improve it. Then, when it is absolutely perfected, I will personally take it to Harmon P. Harper. I promise you that, Andrew. Now, please, be a good boy and open the door for Hedda."

"How can you improve it?"

"I can't. Unless you tell me how it works."

"I'm down with that."

"Now, please open the door."

"Give me a minute to think about it."

I waited for more than a minute with my ear to the door. It was absolutely silent on the other side, so quiet that I began to worry that she had gone to get an ax or something to break down the door. Then she whispered, "Andrew, do you like me?"

"You're cool," I told her with complete honesty.

"Am I'm pretty?"

"Beautiful."

"And you like my figure?"

"Right, right."

There was another short silence before she asked, "Then why don't you want to make love to me?"

"It's not that there's anything wrong with you," I said, not wanting her to take it personally or anything. "I just can't."

"Why? Is there something wrong with you?"

"Like?"

She laughed a mocking laugh. "Do you have E.D.?"

"What's that?"

"Erectile Dysfunction."

"No way!"

"Then prove it," she taunted.

"I can't! Like, I'm saving myself for Melanie Schultz."

"I give up!"

"You do?"

"Absolutely. You can come out now. I will not force you to do anything you don't want to do."

Fearing some sort of trickery, I said, "Not until you put some clothes on."

"Very well."

I heard her move away from the door. After about five minutes, she came back and said, "All right, my shy, little genius. I have a robe on. Unlock the door."

"Bring me my clothes," I said.

"Promise to tell me and no one else how your device works?"

"I'll tell you everything," I promised. "Just bring me my clothes."

＊   ＊   ＊   ＊

After I was dressed, I kept my promise over a cup of black coffee in Hedda's kitchen. "It's a small, black device," I told her, picturing it clearly in my mind, "no bigger than a polka dot. It works wirelessly with any HDTV."

"I know," she said with a yawn. "And it costs only a dollar twenty-five per unit. But exactly how does it work?"

I had to think quickly. "It captures and focuses the video output radiation signal."

"The what?"

"The digital picture radiates light waves."

"But of course, everyone knows that."

"Yes, but not everyone knows that radiation can be intercepted, decoded and sent back into the TV set."

"It can?"

"If you know the secret."

"How very interesting," she said, pouring me another cup of coffee.

"Yeah, isn't it?" I said, beginning to believe myself. "Laymen call the signal radiation. Like, the radiation can be turned into an electrical impulse by stripping ions from the radiation atoms. That signal can be picked up by a special ion receiver built into the master computer. The computer merely computes the signal strength to determine how many TV sets are tuned to a channel—the stronger the signal, the greater the number of sets that are tuned to it."

"I see," she said. "Of course, it is very simple. But I don't exactly understand how it can determine what channel a set is tuned to."

I had to think again for a moment. "Easy," I finally said. "Since each channel is receiving a different video input signal, the radiation for each channel has to be different, too. The computer is programmed to differentiate between signals to discriminate between TV shows. In other words, it knows exactly what show every TV set in the country is tuned to at any given time."

"How brilliant!" she cried.

"Yes, I know."

"But practically useless as a research tool, you know."

"It is?"

"But of course, dahling. It is not enough, Andrew, to know what channel a TV set is tuned to. We must know if the people who are watching the show like it, and what they think of the commercials. And to do that, we must be able to ask questions and receive answers."

"Like, that's a good point."

"Absolutely. So now I'll tell you how to improve your device. What it needs is yes and no buttons so we can ask the viewers simple questions. Surely a genius like you can figure out how to do that."

After a little more thought, I said, "Well, I suppose I could install yes and no buttons."

"Ah, good," she squealed, clapping her hands like a happy child. "See? I have already improved your device."

"You totally improved it," I admitted.

"Now, there is one other little problem I would like to help you solve."

"I'm lucky to have someone like you to help me," I said.

"For your device to be absolutely perfect, we must be able to tell who we are questioning. For example, we should know if the respondent is male or female, his age and occupation, and things like that. Could you make your device do that?"

"Like, that's a humongous order."

"But you are a genius, Andrew. Surely such a challenge should be no problem for you."

For once in my life, I really had to strain my brain for an answer. "Would it be good enough to know the social security number of the respondent?" I asked. "It would be easier to build in a digital readout than an alphabetical one—less characters, you know."

"Absolutely brilliant!" she squealed. "The government has already classified everyone by their social security numbers. Andrew, you truly are a genius!"

"I know," I said, modestly.

"Make love to me," she cried, practically leaping across the table.

"I can't," I said, dodging her and running for the door. "I'm saving myself for Melanie Schultz."

I made it into the hall, slamming the door behind me and I ran down the hall to freedom.

CHAPTER 9

▼

This next part may seem a little unbelievable. I include it to show you the ends some people will go to in their efforts to stand in the way of progress when progress threatens profits.

I'd just left Hedda Nichtwahr's apartment, and was still running down east on Big Beaver Road, happily congratulating myself for having enticed her into helping me perfect my device the way I had, when a long, black, Lincoln Town Car screeched up to the curb and two swarthy little men wearing gray Borsalino hats, dark gray Gucci check stripe three-button business suits, black Beckley loafers, and Princeton school ties jumped out waving furled Huntsman's Gents Walking umbrellas at me.

"Get in," the black bearded one requested, motioning to the open rear car door with his umbrella.

"Yeah, we're taking you for a ride," the gray bearded one said.

"Thanks but no thanks," I said. "My mom told me never to accept rides from strangers."

"Look, buddy boy, we're not fooling," blackbeard warned, jabbing me sharply in the ribs with the tip of his umbrella.

"Nor I," I said, defiantly.

"Yeah?" graybeard said, hooking my arm with his umbrella handle. "Don't you know you can get hurt running around on the streets this time of night?"

"You can?" I asked, never before having been out jogging on the streets so late.

"Don't you watch TV or read the papers?" blackbeard asked, helping me into the back seat of the limousine. "There are all kinds of freaks out this time of night. We're doing you a real favor."

"Thanks," I said.

"You're welcome," graybeard returned, climbing behind the wheel.

"Sit back and relax and enjoy the ride," blackbeard said, pinning me to the back of the seat with his umbrella shaft.

"Where are we going?" I had to ask.

"To a theater down near Cobo Hall," graybeard informed me.

I looked at my watch. "But isn't a little late to see a show? It's after one-thirty and I have to go to work in the morning."

"This place is open all night," graybeard said.

"I'm really tired," I told them, trying to get up from the seat. "Why don't you go on without me?"

Blackbeard caught me by the coat collar with his umbrella and yanked me back into the car.

"We wouldn't think of allowing you to walk home this time of night, buddy boy," he said. "Right, Mo?"

Mo was apparently graybeard's name, because he turned around and smiled a broad, toothy grin, and said, "Indomitably."

"Indubitably is the word," blackbeard said.

"Sorry, Al" Mo said, his grin disappearing. "You won't tell the Wizard on me, will you?"

"Just shut up and drive, stupid," Al said.

"Who's the Wizard?" I asked.

"The boss. He's putting on the show tonight," he answered.

"A magic show?" I asked.

"You might say that," Al grunted.

"Then, like, I am glad you invited me," I said. "I've always been fascinated by magicians."

*   *   *   *

A few minutes later, the black limousine pulled up in front of a small theater a few blocks north of Cobo Hall. Somehow, it seemed strangely out of place in that particular neighborhood. Where the other buildings on the block were enjoying a state of middle-aged depravity, unkempt and slovenly, with flashy neon signs blinking out a visual cacophony of monosyllabic words, it was cleanly modern, constructed from poured concrete that glistened with the look of alabaster. As Al and Mo hustled me from the car to the lobby, I noted that instead of the usual theater marquee there were merely three giant, stainless steel, *sans serif* letters attached to the antiseptic facade—GYP.

"What does GYP stand for?" I asked.

"I donno. I just work here," Mo returned, humorlessly.

"Jezz, you're in broadcasting, buddy boy, and you never heard of GYP?" Al asked, his pockmarked face showing utter disbelief.

It was the first time they mentioned that they knew that I was in broadcasting, and since I hadn't mentioned it before, I began to think that our meeting had not been serendipitous.

"Can't say I have," I said, tensely, suspecting they could be from USS-TV human resources.

"Thought all you TV finks knew about GYP," Mo put in, allaying my fears. No one at USS-TV would ever refer to a fellow employee as a fink.

"Our PR must be slipping," Al said, shaking his head.

"PR and GYP are aberrations," Mo started to explain.

"Abbreviations, stupid," Al corrected.

"Yeah, abbreviations," Mo said, knotting his beetle brow in dismay.

"For what?" I asked.

"For what?' he asks," Al said, giving Mo a knowing wink with his one good eye.

"You'll find out," Mo told me with a happy giggle.

"Yeah, you'll find out," Al repeated, and the two of them escorted me through the stainless steel doors into the theater itself. I must say, the interior surprised me. Mo had described it as small, but of course my mind was working in the lexicon of USS-TV, so I had expected it to be the size of one of our pilot screening rooms, with seating for perhaps four or five hundred. But once inside, I discovered there were no more than fifty or sixty seats, all in the orchestra, each of which looked more like a dentist's chair than a theater seat.

"Exactly what kind of a theater is this?" I asked as they led me down one of the two side aisles. "Legitimate?"

For some reason, the word legitimate seemed to anger them. "You ask too many questions," Al snapped again, giving my arm a small twist.

"Yeah, you ask too many questions," Mo grunted, curling his protruding lower lip, adding a small arm twist of his own.

"I'll try not to ask any more," I said, quickly, not wanting to offend my hosts. "But I must warn you, I have a very inquisitive mind. I'm a genius—"

"Shut up!" Al cut me off.

"Yeah, shut your face," Mo sneered, showing his uneven, yellow teeth.

For a moment, I feared they might change their minds and not let me see the show, but apparently they were not the kind to hold grudges, for they led me to what had to be the best seat in the house, exactly fifth row center, and Mo graciously helped me into it, fastening me down snugly with the nylon belting attached to the arm and foot rests. My inquisitive mind had questions I wanted to ask, like, why were they strapping me to the seat?

But knowing they hated questions, I resolved to ask no more, and simply commented, "This is a totally unusual theater."

"That's what everyone tells us," Al mumbled, connecting what looked like a sphygmomanometer to my right arm.

"Hope we haven't missed the last show," I said, looking round the empty orchestra. "There doesn't seem to be much of an audience."

"Hold your stupid head still!" Mo ordered, struggling to tape some sort of electrodes to my temples.

"Sorry." To make his job easier, I stared straight ahead at the purple velvet curtain with the gold letters GYP outlined upon it in ten feet-tall sequined letters. When Al and Mo finally completed all the various connections they had to make between the seat and me, they politely removed their hats and took the seats next to mine.

There was an exciting trumpet fanfare, and the purple velvet curtains slowly drew apart, revealing a giant-screen, closed-circuit HDTV picture of the title GYP projected digitally on it.

"I was hoping it would be a live show," I whispered, disappointed.

"Don't complain, buddy boy," Al warned.

"Yeah, you're lucky to be alive," Mo added.

As I watched the screen, the title suddenly dissolved in a puff of white smoke, and an enormous image of a man's face appeared. The face had a definite Middle Eastern look to it, with dark and leathery skin, deeply etched lines running from the inner corners of the small, narrow-set, glinting eyes down to his sagging jowls. Although it was plainly an old man's face, his brows were black and thick. The ocher lips below the bulbous tip of the nose were cruelly thin, turning down at the corners, giving the mouth a perpetual sneer of contempt. Dangling from the distended lobe of the left ear was a large, gold ring. I'd seen only one other face like it before, at the county fair in Albert Lea, when I had my fortune read by the great Madame Solmar, a Gypsy fortune teller. It was Madame Solmar who first told me I would grow up to be a genius. I've had nothing but the greatest respect for Gypsies ever since.

To my complete surprise, the giant face smiled at me with an enormous ten foot smile. In a deep, rumbling voice, the face said, "Welcome, Mr. Cohan, to the GYP Preview Theater. I am your humble host, Ray Solmar, the Wiz—"

"Hey," I interrupted. "Are you related to the Great Madame Solmar?"

"Madame Solmar is my twin sister," the face admitted, laconically. "What makes you think she was so great?"

"She read my fortune when I was ten."

"Oh?" the giant face said, raising its eyebrows about three feet. "I imagine she told you that you had a great future?"

"She said I would grow up to be a genius."

"That is great!" the face said with a knowing snicker. "I see you have also met my esteemed associates, Mr. Fulain and Mr. Basared."

"Al and Mo?" I said.

"Oh, good!" the face exclaimed with a jolly sneer. "I'm delighted the three of you are on a first name basis. It makes things much friendlier, don't you agree, Mr. Cohan?"

"Suppose so," I said. "Call me Andy. That's what all my friends call me."

"Very good, Andy," the face said. "You can call me Wizard."

"That's what all his friends call him," Al said under his garlic breath.

"Yeah, it's his name da plum," Mo added.

"*Nom de plume*," Al corrected.

"Pen name?" I asked.

"More like a nickname," Al said.

"What's his real name?" I asked.

"Rahan Solmar," Mo said.

"Raymond Solmar," Al corrected.

"Gentlemen, gentlemen," the Wizard interrupted, pleasantly enough, although I noticed his smile had shrunk to less than five feet. "The hour is late, and I do wish to get on with the business at hand." The camera pulled back, and I saw he was sitting at a table fondling a crystal ball with the letters GYP engraved upon it. "Shall we proceed?"

"Okaydonkey," Mo agreed.

"Okaydoaky," Al corrected.

"Mo is one of my most trusted associates," the Wizard told me. "But frankly, he confuses some words."

"I've noticed that," I had to admit.

"You see, Mohammed?" the Wizard scolded, shaking his head. "Even he noticed it. Really, my boy, you must try harder."

"I do try!" Mo cried, pulling a dog-eared pocket dictionary from his inside coat pocket. He wildly thumbed it. "I read a hundred pages of this crummy book every day. A hundred stinking, lousy pages! But it don't do no good. No good at all. Guess I'll always be illegitimate."

"Illiterate," Al snapped.

"What's the difference? You always know what I mean," Mo said.

"See what a trial legitimacy can be, Andy?" the Wizard said with great compassion. "We traded in our casual Gypsy garb years ago for business suits and bankers' umbrellas. But some of us—" he gave Mo the evil eye— "don't easily adapt to the Global Economy."

"Like, he's trying," I said.

"And now that we are respectable," the Wizard continued, "can you think of any other group of businessmen more suited for their profession? We Gypsies have been considered great fortune tellers for centuries simply because we tell our clients what they want to hear. Our reputation as clairvoyants was unshakeable. When it comes to marketing, my people have always been considered shrewd and cunning. As door-to-door peddlers, we were the first to discover the techniques for selling people things they didn't want or need. And we have always been the world's foremost jugglers, dancers, knife throwers, and magicians, so when it comes to the entertainment business, who could be more expert at judging popular tastes? Last, but not least, since we have never had a nation of our own, or, for that matter, been part of any body politic, we retain a completely objective view of politics. So by our very nature, we are the perfect pollsters and market trend analysts, offering a complete line of predictive services. Today, instead of merely telling fortunes, we predict future business trends. We no longer go door-to-door, selling people things they don't want or need. Now we simply advise advertising agencies how to do it. Our inside knowledge of the entertainment world has made us invaluable consultants to the networks. And our objective political outlook makes us the ideal political pollsters. Believe me, Andy, we Gypsies have at last found our true calling. And as you can imagine, it's turned out to be very lucrative, very lucrative, indeed. Why, last year GYP grossed almost five hundred million dollars."

"Oh, wow!" I said.

"Predictions are our bread and butter, Andy," the Wizard said, "with a capital P. That's what GYP stands for—Guarantee Your Predictions. GYP gathers more information and makes more predictions than any other organization, including Homeland Security, the CIA, FBI, Department of Labor, GAO, Department of

Defense, UNESCO, USIA, NSA, even the White House, all of whom are on our client list."

"Awesome list," I admitted.

"Sort of gives the lie to everything you've been led to believe, don't it?" Al put in.

"Yeah, right," I answered.

"Give him a couple of examples of how our predictions help the Musketeers," Mo urged.

"Marketers," Al corrected.

"When you look at the average Mrs. American Consumer and ask yourself, 'Does she or doesn't she?' you probably assume she does, because decades of advertising repetition has made it part of the American lexicon. Right?" the Wizard asked.

"Doesn't she?" I asked.

"GYP focus groups have discovered it's more of a she does and she doesn't kind of thing, depending on her mood," he said. "We also predicted that giving female consumers a goose could jump sales of insurance."

"Aflac," I said.

"Exactly. And we predicted giving consumers a real headache could boost headache relief product sales."

"Like, Head On," I guessed.

The Wizard nodded his giant head. "Correct. And we even predicted Detroit could sell bigger and bigger SUVs and pickups."

"Because American's are getting bigger and bigger?"

"No. Because baby boomers are the 'me' generation. They want to drive 'kill the other guy' cars."

"Oh, wow!"

"Those are the kinds of predictions that have made us indispensable to every advertising agency, television network, and politician in the nation. Have any idea how much it costs to gather all the facts it takes to make our predictions, Andy? Have any idea of the investment we Gypsies have made in our facilities throughout the world?"

"Afraid, I don't," I said.

"Literally millions," he informed me. "The investment in this preview theater alone is over five million dollars, what with all the special effects we've installed. For example, seats like the one you're sitting on cost as much as a Cadillac equipped the way they are with polygraphs, electroencephalograms, and Pavlov shockers. And this is but one GYP Preview Theater. We have seven others scattered across America in key target markets."

"Like, what do you preview in all these theaters?" I interrupted, anxious to get on with the show.

"TV commercials," the Wizard answered.

"Just commercials?" I said.

"Well, sometimes we do show an old TV pilot film," he admitted. "You'd be surprised at how they spice things up for the respondents. Respondents really appreciate the commercials more when we throw in a little entertainment."

"Who would pay to see TV commercials and old pilot films?" I had to ask.

"Oh, they don't pay," the Wizard quickly replied. "We just open the doors, put up a sign that says 'free,' and the respondents swarm in."

"We got a real cross section of America's middle class," Al added.

"Yeah," Mo said. "They're mostly indigents."

"Right," Al agreed.

"Homeless people?" I asked.

"Yeah, that's what they are," Mo said with a toothy grin.

"That is why we purposely built each GYP Preview Theater in a marginal neighborhood like this," the Wizard pointed out. "So we always have a never-ending supply of cooperative respondents waiting at our doorsteps."

"But is that fair?" I asked, naively, not yet fully understanding the problems facing modern marketing research, "showing commercials to helpless indigents?"

"Why not?" the Wizard demanded, pulling at his gold earring. "Commercials are perfectly harmless to people who have neither money nor credit."

"Look at it this way, buddy boy," Al said with a refined burp, "we keep the bums off the streets."

"Yeah, and we feed them hot coffee and doughnuts after every show," Mo added. "It's better than the Salvation Army. We don't make them pray or nothing like that."

"You don't understand," I said. "Like, is it fair to test your clients' commercials on the homeless? They can't afford to buy anything."

"The purpose of consumer research, Andy, is not to be fair," the Wizard went on. "It is simply to gather facts. And how, may I ask, could we gather facts if we had no audience to test our clients' commercials on? Why, no normal person would ever sit through an hour-long showing of test commercials, let alone answer some one hundred and fifty questions after the show."

"Even with homeless bums, we got to strap them into the seats to get them to stay," Al said.

"Yeah, and give them a good jolt with the Pavlov shockers once in a while to keep them awake," Mo said, gleefully.

"But why did you bring me here tonight?" I questioned. "I'm perfectly normal."

"We want to make you a little, ah …" the Wizard smiled his twisted smile, "shall we say, business proposition? You see, Andy, I have been authorized by the Supreme Council of GYP to offer you ten thousand dollars—"

"Ten thousand dollars?" I gasped.

"Cold cash," Al said.

"Yeah, in unmarked bills," Mo added.

"What for?" I asked, thinking the offer was kind of high for one interview.

The Wizard chuckled sinisterly. "For the world rights to your little device, of course."

"My device?" I said. "You know about it?"

Music began to swell and fill the theater.

The Wizard's voice boomed over the music, "The GYP Crystal Ball sees all and hears all!"

And right before my amazed eyes, a scene of Hedda Nichtwahr chasing me around her bed dissolved and came into focus within the giant crystal ball.

"We saw and heard everything that went on in Miss Nichtwahr's apartment!" the Wizard shouted.

"Everything?" I asked, horrified as I sat and watched.

"We really got her place bugged," Al sniggered.

"Yeah, with digitalis video recorders," Mo said.

"Digital," I corrected.

"Yeah, that's what I meant," he continued. "We sure taped some hot show tonight. Just like a regular stag movie—"

"You had quite a night," Al interrupted, leering at the screen where the completely naked Hedda stood twenty feet tall, pounding on the bathroom door.

"Please, please," I said, wishing my hands were not strapped to the Truth Seat, so I could blacken his one good eye. "Show no more."

"Then you agree to accept our offer?" the Wizard asked with a malevolent snigger, and the camera moved back until I could see his vicious face full screen again.

"I need time to think," I said, embarrassed by what I had seen.

"Maybe this will help you think faster," the Wizard chortled, and his eyes glinted like cold steel as he pushed a button built into the top of the table he was sitting at.

A million needles seemed to prick my skin all at once as a surge of electricity jolted my body rigid.

"You fiend!" I shouted, straining at the seat belts.

"You are the fiend!" the Wizard shouted back, giving me a stronger jolt. "You and your diabolical device could destroy overnight what it's taken us generations to build! We cannot allow you to do that. Accept our generous offer, or take the consequences."

"What consequences?" I demanded.

"Accept," Al urged, "or we show the tapes to Melanie Schultz."

"You know about her?" I asked.

"The GYP Crystal Ball sees all and hears all!" the Wizard's voice boomed again.

"Yeah, so don't push us too far," Al warned.

"I'll never accept your offer," I said, defiantly. "Melanie Schultz could never respect a man who bowed to blackmail."

"How about a hundred thousand dollars?" the Wizard asked, raising the voltage of the Pavlov shocker as he raised the price.

"Never!" I cried again.

"A million dollars is our top price." The Wizard upped the stakes and the voltage until my hair stood on end.

"I'll die before I sell out!" I screamed.

"You may do that," the Wizard said with a ghoulish sneer.

"Fry him," Al suggested.

"Yeah, incarcerate him," Mo advocated.

"Incinerate!" I screamed.

"Shut up!" Al snapped, apparently angered by my usurping his privilege, and he gave me a sharp jab with the metal tip of his umbrella. There was a searing blue flash. To my complete horror, I saw Al's beard burst into flames.

"Yow!" he screamed, unable to release his grip on the umbrella handle. Instinctively, Mo jumped up and tried to knock Al's umbrella away from me with his. There was a second, more brilliant, blue flash.

"Yowee, yow, yowl" Mo shrieked.

Then everything happened at once. There was a loud zapping sound and a puff of acrid smoke from the seat beneath me. The HDTV picture of the Wizard's terror-stricken face flickered and shrank to black nothingness. The nylon belting at my wrists began to melt away, and the current stopped surging through my body. I leaped to my feet just as the Truth Seat burst into flames, setting off a chain reaction of blazing seats. Grasping the senseless Al and Mo by the collars of their smoking Gucci suits, I somehow managed to drag them through the almost suffocating heat and smoke to the nearest emergency exit.

"What happened?" Al groaned, dazedly, as I deposited him and Mo safely on the sidewalk outside the inferno that had once been a GYP Preview Theater.

"You shouldn't have jabbed me with the metal shaft of your umbrella." I explained the electrical phenomenon in layman's terms to Al: "It short circuited me."

"Yeah, stupid," Mo moaned.

"A curse on you!" I heard the Wizard's voice shout.

I saw him run out of the smoke, all his clothes burned away save for his charred Jockey shorts and T-shirt. "Curse you! You monster, you devil!" he screamed, flailing his fists against my belt buckle.

"Did anyone ever tell you that you look smaller in person than you do on HDTV?" I asked, fending him off with one hand on his forehead, the way a grown man holds off an angry child.

"You accursed incendiary!" he panted, jumping up and down and flailing the air with his fists. "You burned everything!"

"Everything?" I said.

He looked up at me wildly, tears of anguish streaming from his small, narrow-set, glinting eyes to his slightly singed jowls. "The theater, the Truth Seats, my beautiful purple GYP curtain, and all that HDTV equipment—"

"Even the tapes?" I said.

"Every last tape," he cried, sinking down on the sidewalk as the fire engines pulled up.

"Like, it's been an interesting evening," I said, edging away. "But it's late, and I'm tired. Hope you don't mind if I run along now."

I turned and started running north on Woodward heading for my apartment in Southfield.

"You can't escape!" the Wizard shouted, waving a sooty finger after me. "The Gypsy curse will follow you wherever you go!"

"We'll get you!" Mo shouted.

Fortunately, I had in my pocket my lucky rabbit's foot that protected me from all evil. I gave it a few extra rubs just to make sure it still worked and sprinted until I got home and went to bed.

CHAPTER 10

▼

The clock radio on the floor beside my bed turned itself on at precisely six forty-five, and I awoke to a new day with my usual sigh of relief. Unless you happen to be a genius, subject to dreadful dreams as I have always been, you can't possibly appreciate what a pure delight the simple act of waking up can be.

No matter what terrors the night has held for you, the rosy warmth of the sun's rays peeping through the holes in your window shade always tells you there's nothing to fear. Even the harsh voice of a news announcer crackling over the clock radio can be music to the ears as it soothingly reports the latest wars and floods, civil riots and murders, an airliner crash or a new famine in India—all the wonderful, ordinary, everyday things of the real world that put the horrors of your dreams behind you for another day. And, as you might imagine, after the nightmare I had just been through, waking to discover it had indeed been just another of my dreams was especially pleasurable.

But my pleasure was short lived. Almost at once my confidence that the events of the previous day and night had been merely a dream began to wane. First, as I started my morning ritual of Qi Gong exercises, I discovered I had a tired, dragged-out feeling. I know many people, ignoring all the common sense rules of good health, wake up every morning of their lives feeling that way. But I never wake up tired and dragged-out, thanks to my mom, God rest her soul, who was a great believer in preventative medicine. She taught me the value of eight full hours of sleep every night and a good breakfast every morning. Now, as I stood there on one foot, my arms flexed above my head, I distinctly remembered having taken my One a Day vitamins at breakfast the morning before, so I reasoned my tired, dragged-out feeling could hardly be due to tired blood or iron deficiency anemia. I concluded it was caused by a lack of sleep. With a fresh supply of blood rushing to my head from my elevated feet, I at once saw that lack of sleep is usually caused by not sleeping, and, if that's true, it meant I'd been awake at least part of the night, leaving open the possibility that what I'd simply passed off as just another nightmare could have been an actuality.

But once my sleep-dulled brain had been fully refreshed with a new supply of refreshed Qi blood, I had to laugh at that ridiculous possibility. After all, I mused, going into a leg-cross and balancing on my knees, I'd dreamed of waking up and finding myself in bed with a naked woman at least a hundred times, yet I certainly had never actually done such a thing. So why, after so many years of complete self control, would I suddenly go off the deep end? And what about Al and Mo and the Wizard? Surely, something as absurd as a group of Gypsies banding together to bring humanity the benefits of consumer research had to be something out of a bad dream.

With renewed confidence, I switched to the Qi squat and flexed the muscles of my index fingers vigorously. But with all due respect to the great Chinese martial artists, I should have plugged them into my ears, for just as my confidence returned, it was suddenly shaken again when I heard the news announcer report over the radio that there had been a four alarm fire at the GYP Preview Theater downtown during the night. Could there be more than mere coincidence to that? I asked myself. According to all logic the answer had to be yes. But that's one of the great things about being a genius. You don't have to be logical all the time. I remembered I had often dreamed of having lived through events that had actually happened before my lifetime. Like, once I was trapped on the sinking Lusitania. Another time I was executed for the assassination of President McKinley without having participated in the episode in a physical sense. So instead of allowing my mind to panic, I stretched out, my body supported only at two points—the back of my head, which rested upon the crate I used for my writing desk, and my heels, which I had placed upon my one window sill. Making my body completely rigid, I suspended all physical activity, and withdrew my mind from all external influences to concentrate the entire being of my soul on the universal truth that life is but a dream.

After ten minutes of this, all the time it took for me to attain a state of profound well-being, I allowed my bodily functions to resume. Falling limply to the floor, I rose again, completely refreshed, and went into the bathroom ready to began a new day. It was while I was in the bathroom, washing my face as a prelude to shaving, that I received the jolt that was to finally make me realize my nightmare had truly happened. As I gazed at my reflection in the mirror above the sink even my myopic vision told me something wasn't quite right. The blur that stared back at me was not the same blur I'd observed staring back at me every other morning of my life.

With a mounting uneasiness, I went to my bed and got down on my hands and knees and groped around on the floor beside it for my glasses. When I finally found them where I'd left them the night before, on top of the clock radio, I rushed back to the bathroom and put them on to take a closer look at myself the mirror. Instead of seeing my image sharpen, it became even more diffused, as if I were seeing it through smoked glasses.

"I'm going blind!" I shouted. With trembling hands I removed my glasses and held them up to the light.

Imagine my relief when I discovered the lenses were simply clouded over with some form of carbon, oddly enough resembling pure lampblack. I wiped them clean with a piece of toilet paper and put them back on. Taking a long, close look at my face, I found most of my features were unchanged. That good old straight Roman nose was still there. So was that delightfully dimpled jaw. My eyes, enlarged as always by the lenses of my glasses, were still the same, friendly Cocker Spaniel eyes they had always been. Yet, something was different. What could it be? My large but endearing ears were sticking out right where they ought to be. Opening my mouth, I checked my teeth one by one and found they were all still there, excepting, of course, my wisdom teeth, which I'd had removed the summer before. Quizzically, I raised my eyebrows, and immediately I saw what was missing. They were gone! My eyebrows were gone! Dumbstruck, I ran the tips of my fingers across my naked brows, discovering as I did that the few hairs that remained were badly singed. Then it hit me. My poor eyebrows had been burned away during the night.

But how could that have happened? I never smoked, so I knew I could not have gone to sleep with a lighted cigarette and accidentally set my bed afire. Besides, a thorough examination of my bedding proved there had been no fire there. Yet the fact remained, my eyebrows weren't there.

Frantically, I began searching my apartment from top to bottom, starting by getting down on all fours to scrutinize every square inch of the floor at close range. Then I methodically explored the darkest reaches of my one, crammed closet, carefully removing and then replacing all the bits of memorabilia I had collected since my arrival in Southfield.

I hunted beneath the cushions of the under stuffed wing chair I had picked up at the Goodwill for five dollars and eighty-five cents that I've had people tell me would have been a bargain at twice the price. I even sifted through the contents of the five gallon ice cream carton under the sink that served as my combination wastebasket-garbage can.

"Truth! Like, why must you be so naked?" I screamed, plugging my ears upon hearing Hedda's giggle as a remembrance of my visit to her apartment flashed on in my brain like a giant, closed-circuit TV picture.

In one, last, desperate effort to free myself from such agonizing truths, I rested my head upon the crate I used for my writing desk, and attempted to raise my heels to the window sill. But no matter how I strained and struggled to make my poor trembling body rigid, it remained limp and flaccid. The power I had always enjoyed of withdrawing my mind from all external influences to concentrate the entire being of my soul on the universal truth that life is but a dream was impotent. So I sank to the floor and assumed the fetal position and cried like a baby for ten minutes, all the time it took me to realize that I had better get up and wash and shave and dress before I was late for work.

CHAPTER 11

▼

By the time I left my cheery fourth floor walkup for work that fateful morning, I'd finally resolved to tell Melanie everything—the truth, the whole truth, and nothing but the truth—and I would have, had it not been for the demonstration in the USS-TV Plaza, a totally unfortunate incident that eventually led me to glamorous Hollywood.

It started at three minutes to nine as I unsuspectingly trotted up to the Satellite City Plaza, still panting from the fifteen block jog from my apartment, a practice I'd made part of my keep-in-shape-on-the-way-to-work program. I was surprised to see the entrance was blocked by a mob of demonstrators. There was really nothing out of the ordinary about that by itself. Back in those days, the *Good Morning World Show* was broadcast from Studio A on the ground floor of the USS-TV Building Monday through Friday from seven to nine a.m. And the highlight of the show came during the last three minutes when the director turned the cameras from the set to the studio windows where crowds of visitors seeking their ten seconds of fame stood shoulder to shoulder, some sticking out their tongues, others thumbing their noses or flipping the bird at the cameras, while others held up humorous signs of greeting to the worldwide TV audience like "Get No More Getmos," "Come Clean America," "Go Go Global Warming," and "U.S.A. You're Gonna Pay!"

So, there was a never-ending daily gathering of protest groups from all over the world, each group trying to outdo the others to bring its particular cause to the attention of the world audience. I for one actually enjoyed seeing the protests as I arrived at work each morning. Like, they started my day off on a high note by bringing important world issues to my attention.

But the demonstration that morning was unusual. Like, it was much bigger and far better organized than any I'd seen before. Instead of the usual gathering of twenty-five or thirty protesters, I estimated the crowd to number over a thousand demonstrators that formed a double picket line that completely surrounded Satellite City Plaza, blocking every entrance to the building. And unlike previous demonstrators, the crowd wasn't made up of divergent groups of protesters trying to promote their own cause. This time they were totally together, carrying the same signs and singing the same songs of protest, like, all for one cause.

A great throng of my fellow employees had also gathered in the Plaza to cheer the protesters on. As tall as I was, I couldn't see the signs the protesters were carrying or recognize any of the tunes they were singing, so they didn't trigger a sense of apprehension in my great brain, they simply aroused my curiosity.

I did recognize the beat of the songs. It seemed right out of burlesque. From that and the way the crowd was cheering, I reasoned the demonstrators were strippers and burlesque comedians protesting the demise of their art.

I pushed and shoved my way deeper and deeper into the crowd. With all the cheering and shouting going on around me, I wanted to join in with a few shouts and cheers of my own. Like, it's kind of lonely standing mutely by, in a madly rejoicing crowd, totally in the dark about what was going on. And I'm not the kind of person who lends his voice to a cause he knows nothing about. It was a totally frustrating experience. Like, I was just about to lose my self control and start shouting my lungs out simply to relieve the tension that was building within me, when the most wonderful thing happened. I felt an acorn bounce off my head.

You may ask what's so wonderful about an acorn bouncing off your head. Like, it probably happens to at least a million people every day, what with all the oak trees in the world. But that's my point. If an acorn falls on your average person's head, he or she thinks nothing of it. But when something falls on the head of a genius, he wonders about it, you know. I mean, look what happened when an apple fell onto Newton's head.

So I had to wonder: why would an acorn fall on my head? I looked up and saw a chubby old man sitting on one of the lower branches of an oak tree growing out of a concrete tub. He was clad in a bright Day-glow orange skydiving jumpsuit loaded with pockets that zipped, and on the suit's back USS-TV was lettered in bowing shirt script. He wore a white scarf around his neck, and patent leather army boots on his feet.

"What are you doing up there?" I called up to him.

"Har! Har! Har!" he laughed, looking down at me. He wore a black patch over his left eye. "What are you doing down there, laddie?"

"Trying to see the demonstration."

"What a coincidence! That's what I'm doing up here."

"Can you see it?"

"Of course! Didn't I just tell you that's what I'm doing up here?"

"Like, I wasn't totally sure."

"Good. You should never be too sure about anything, laddie. For all you know, I could be a tree surgeon performing a brilliant operation."

"Yeah, right."

"Why would you suppose anything so ridiculous?"

"Did I say I did?"

"You're confused, laddie, aren't you?"

"No. I'm a genius, so I'm not sure of anything."

"Another coincidence. I'm one, too. Why do you think I wear this orange suit?"

I had to think about that for a moment before I said, "To show everyone how brilliant you are."

"Har! Har! Har! Good! No one's ever guessed that before. You're a true genius. No doubt about it."

"I see you work for USS-TV," I said.

"You deduced that from the letters on my back. Right?"

"Yeah, right."

"Forget the *yeah*. Just say, *right*. Everyone says 'right' when I say 'right.'"

"So what do you do for us?"

"You're not playing my little game. You didn't say right the last time I said right."

"Right," I admitted.

"Say it again, two more times. I said it two more times than you did."

"Right. Right."

"You catch on fast, laddie."

"So what do you do for USS-TV? You a maintenance man or something?"

"You might say that. Cleaned the place out a few times in my day. Needs a good cleaning out again, too, if you ask old Roger Jolly. Yes sir, rebob, that's what this ship needs—clean sweep down, fore and aft. Now hear this: Sweepers, man your brooms!"

"Were you in the Navy?"

"Bet you figured that out from the way I talk. Right?"

"Right."

"Only half right. Was a network correspondent back in the good old Nam days, attached to the Pacific fleet. Nam was a correspondent's paradise."

"My father was in the Navy in Vietnam."

"Name and rank?"

"Chester Cohan. Petty Officer Third Class."

He thought for a moment, and then shook his head. "Heard of a Chester Nimitz. But he was a World War II guy. Any relation?"

"No way. Why"

"Same name—Chester, eh?"

"Chester was my dad's first name."

"Har! Har! Har! Easy mistake to make. You know how the Navy is—calls everyone by their last name first. Used to call me Jolly Roger. I was the greatest news pirate on the Mekong Delta. Boom, boom, boom! Damn the torpedoes, full speed ahead! Jolly good show! The press corps nicknamed me Admiral Jolly and somehow it stuck to this day."

"So you work for the News Department?"

"Har! Har! Har! I am the News Department! Fact is: I command the good ship USS-TV!"

"So what are you doing up a tree?"

"You'll always find Admiral Jolly where news is breaking, eh?"

"So what's breaking now?"

"A riot! Jolly good shows! Make wonderful specials. Viewers love riots. Climb up and join me?"

"But the branch might break."

"Break? The branch of a mighty oak? Wouldn't dare. Not with Admiral Jolly on board. Good news hounds can't afford to be afraid." He reached down with his free hand and helped pull me up on the tub. "You can see much better from here. Right?"

"Right," I said, shinnying up the skinny trunk to his branch. My view was partially blocked by his bulk, but whenever he laughed the tree would shake, swaying enough for me to get fleeting glimpses of the picket lines. "What song is that catchy tune they're singing now?"

"Everything's Coming up Roses,'" he said.

"What show's it from?"

"*Gypsy.*"

My hackles stood on end. "*Gypsy*? Are all the other songs from *Gypsy*?"

"Right! Har! Har! Har!"

"Oh, no!" I lost my grip on the branch and started falling backwards, but he caught me by the back of my shirt and pulled me back up next to him.

"You're not playing the game, right?"

"Right, right," I groaned.

"Sick?"

"Just a little dizzy."

"Afraid of heights?"

"No way. It's just that I don't know what they're protesting."

"Haven't been able to figure that out myself, laddie. But the signs they're carrying say 'Down with Cohan' and 'Kill Cohan.' Probably a bunch of Sondheim fans out to get George M. Cohan."

"No way. They're a bunch of marketing Gypsy terrorists out to get Andrew H. Cohan."

"Andrew H. Cohan? Pardon my French, laddie, but who the hell is he?"

"Me."

"You? What have the Gypsies got against you, laddie?" He scrutinized me through the wrong end of his telescope. "You're rather small for your size, but you look like a pleasant lad to me."

"I was," I admitted. "But there's this girl, Melanie Schultz ..." and I went on to tell him everything, why I wanted to become president of USS-TV, how I thought up my invention, how Hedda Nichtwahr helped me perfect it, my casual meeting with Al and Mo who took me to a GYP Preview Theater to meet Raymond Solmar the Wizard, and how he put the Gypsy curse on me, and I rubbed the lucky rabbit's foot Madam Solmar gave me, and the GYP theater burned down, even how I decided to tell Melanie the truth, the whole truth, and nothing but the truth just as soon as I saw her at the morning coffee break.

When I finally finished, he grinned and said, "What a wonderful story—just filled with human interest: boy meets girl, boy wants to get ahead so he can marry her, dreams up a wonderful invention that will revolutionize the TV rating system, but evil Gypsy marketing terrorists move in to thwart his dreams. It has everything a slick story needs: a protagonist with a goal, antagonists to stand in his way, plot hindrances and furtherances, a darkest moment, and a final solution! Right?"

"Right," I agreed. "But like, I have no idea what the final solution will be."

"That's what creates the suspense. When we can't guess the ending until the story ends. Right?"

"Right. But what should I do now? The mob could kill me and I'll never see Melanie again."

"Be a man. Stand up and fight for your rights! You've got as much right to demand your rights as those damned Gypsies. Right?"

"Right, right, right," I said standing up on the branch.

He took a small bullhorn from one of his jumpsuit's zipper pockets. "To hell with all Gypsies!" his voice boomed out over the Plaza, amplified tenfold by the bullhorn.

"Tell them to go back where they came from," I urged him on.

"Go back where you came from, you dirty marketing terrorists!"

As the echo of his words resounded off the towering walls of the buildings facing the Plaza, a stunned silence fell over the protesters. The picketers stopped singing right in the middle of "Together", halting in their tracks as they did, turning more than a thousand pairs of fiercely burning eyes in the direction of the tree where I stood on the branch next to Roger Jolly. Then the silence was broken when, from somewhere below, I heard Cheetah's voice screech, "God, I totally don't believe! It's the geek, Andy Cohan!"

"Oh, Andy! Andy!" Melanie's sweet voice cried out bravely.

"Hang on, Andy!" Seymour Stone shouted.

"Andrew, dahling, what are you doing up there?" Hedda Nichtwahr's voice demanded from across the Plaza.

It was wonderful, knowing my friends were nearby. I longed to see their happy faces, so I stretched as far out on the branch as I dared, but they were lost among the sea of protesters. But I did see one familiar face standing by the main entrance to the USS-TV building: the Wizard, Raymond Solmar, who was hopping madly about on one foot atop the roof of a pink GYP sound truck, his face twisted in that perpetual sneer. "The Gypsy curse on you, Andrew H. Cohan!" His curse boomed out over the sound truck's five giant speakers. "Curse you, Andrew Cohan! Curse you!"

"Down with Cohan! Down with Cohan!" Al and Mo and a gaggle of Gypsy thugs circling the sound truck began to chant. "Kill! Kill!"

"Har! Har! Har! It's going to be a terrific riot! Wonderful!" Roger Jolly put the bullhorn to his lips again. "To hell with you! You're all a bunch of marketing terrorists!"

It became a battle of sound systems. On my side, I had the booming voice of Roger Jolly and one small, battery-operated bullhorn. On the Wizard's side, a five hundred watt sound truck backed by a thousand voice Gypsy chorus. It soon became obvious to the crowd which side was going to win the verbal tug-of-war.

"Down with Cohan! Down with Cohan!" everyone in the Plaza began to chant, throwing in their lot with the Gypsies. "Kill! Kill!"

"Good show! Good show!" Roger Jolly shouted at me above the crowds' roar. "Wonderful! Wonderful! See what happens when one man stands up for what's right?"

Right!" I agreed, hanging onto the trunk of the scrawny oak for dear life. The crowd below, now a howling, screeching mob with the smell of blood in their nostrils, began to violently rock the tub the scrawny oak was planted in, trying to shake us from its branches. "What do we do now?"

"Never fear, Jolly's here!" He unzipped another of his jumpsuit pockets and pulled out a Very pistol and held it above his head, firing it three times. Three brilliant orange flares flashed up toward the heavens. "Won't be long now, laddie. Help's on the way, eh?"

"I can't hold on much longer! The trunk's snapping."

"Don't give up the ship!" Roger Jolly pointed at the sky above our heads. "Here come the Marines!"

I looked up and saw an orange helicopter, with the words USS-TV News lettered across its nose, whirling down toward us, a rescue harness dangling by a steel cable from its belly.

"Too late!" I screamed, feeling the mighty oak starting to give.

"Damn the torpedoes, full speed ahead!" Roger Jolly shouted, grabbing the harness. "Har! Har! Har! Here we go! Up, up and away!"

There was an ear splitting crack as the scrawny oak tree broke and fell away from my feet. In a desperate lunge, I caught hold of Jolly Roger's black patent leather combat boots just as the helicopter started to reel him in. I found them extremely difficult to cling to. "I'm slipping!" I cried out.

"Courage, laddie! We'll beat those damned Gypsy marketing terrorists yet. Right?"

"Right," I gasped, feeling my fingers slipping down to the heels of his boots.

"Don't let him get away!" the crowd below shrieked.

"The Gypsy curse on you, Andrew Cohan!" the wizard's voice boomed up at us from the GYP sound truck's loudspeakers.

By now, I was hanging on by one bootlace more than fifty feet above the Plaza. "I don't think I can make it!" I shouted up to Roger Jolly.

"Don't give up the ship, laddie! Har! Har! Har! You'll make it!"

"Help!" I screamed as the bootlace broke.

"You've lost the battle, not the war!" Roger Jolly shouted down at me as I tumbled toward the crowd below. "Good show! Good show!"

"Down with Cohan! Down with Cohan!" the mob below chanted as I fell.

I frantically rubbed the rabbit's foot Madame Solar had given me long ago to protect me from Gypsy hexes.

It's strange, like how slowly time seems to pass when you're falling from a great height. I remember gazing down as if in a dream and seeing the Wizard's sneering face suddenly turn pale as he saw me plummeting down on him. Fortunately for me, he partially broke my fall, and I bounced off the roof of the sound truck onto the gaggle of thugs standing alongside it, knocking them to the ground in a mad tumble of sprawling bodies. Using what wits I had left, I grabbed Mo's fedora and leaped to my feet, shouting, "Down with Cohan!" at the top of my voice and, "Get him!" fingering the hatless Mo, who was dazedly struggling to its feet.

"Down with Cohan! Kill! Kill!" The mob shrieked, swarming toward him.

It was totally horrendous the way they turned on him, so awful in fact, I couldn't bear to watch, and I turned away as they swarmed over him, finding myself between the mob and the main entrance to the USS-TV Building. Taking advantage of the confusion, I made a mad dash for the revolving doors and safety. But if my wearing Mo's hat had fooled the mob, it certainly didn't fool my friends. Cheetah stood in front of the doors, blocking my way, and in her right hand she clutched a large paving stone.

"Aha!" she screeched, throwing the stone at me. "Cohan's a totally big fat pain in the ass!" Fortunately, her aim was not good. The stone merely knocked Mo's hat off my head.

"Ha, ha, you missed me!" I happily shouted, dodging past her. But one should never brag about good fortune, for Lady Luck has a way of turning on those who boast of her favors, and my brief exchange with Cheetah gave the Gypsies the time they needed to recover their wits and regroup.

"It's Cohan!" the Wizard boomed over the sound truck's loud speakers.

"Don't let the bum escapade!" Mo yelled struggling away from his attackers.

"Escape, idiot!" Al corrected him.

"Down with Cohan! Down with Cohan!" the Wizard continued to shout.

"Kill! Kill!" the crazed mob started chanting again. They let fly a volley of water bottles and rocks that whizzed through the air about me, crashing through the glass windows of Studio A.

"Good show! Good show!" Roger Jolly's voice boomed over the crowd as the orange news helicopter hovered above them, its HDTV camera crew videotaping the melee.

"Run, Andy! Run!" I heard Melanie shout at me from somewhere in the crowd.

I looked toward the sound of her voice, but all I saw was Hedda Nichtwahr running toward me shouting, "Make love to me, dahling!"

"I can't! I'm saving myself!" I shouted back, and I leaped through the shattered glass windows of Studio A and sprinted to the lobby where I bounded into one of the high-speed elevators and pushed the twenty-third-floor button. The ugly shouts of the mob in the Plaza quickly faded as I was whisked upward to the comparative safety of the data processing center.

CHAPTER 12

▼

Believe it or not, today was my lucky day. When I arrived at the data processing center shortly after nine-thirty I found it completely deserted. After everything I'd been through that morning, you're probably asking yourself how a little thing like that could possibly make me think it was my lucky day. Let me explain. For one thing, I was over half an hour late for work, and my department head, Homer Hardwick, could be a real stickler when it came to being punctual. Of course, he might have overlooked my tardiness that morning, since I'd never been late to work in two months. But only the day before I'd left the data processing center at noon for my lunch date with Hedda and Seymour and never returned, and I doubt very much that a stickler like Homer could have forgiven me for two such flagrant offenses in a row. So I have to think it lucky that he was not there to fire me.

Considering the state I was in, I'd have to say it was lucky that none of the other programmers and technicians were there to witness my arrival. Imagine how embarrassing it would have been, having all of them staring at me as I rushed in, wild eyed and frantic, my shirt covered with blood from the small gash on my forehead where Cheetah's poorly aimed stone had merely grazed my skull. I would've felt like a complete fool if anyone had seen me that way, nerves shattered, hiding behind my console, trapped like a rat in an air-conditioned, electrostatically filtered trap.

So I was totally fortunate that all my fellow employees were down in the plaza protesting my existence. But at the same time, I don't want to give you the impression I thought it was all a lark. Like, how anyone couldn't be concerned after hearing the way they shouted "Down with Cohan!" and "Kill, kill!" I was in a state of extreme mental anguish, imagining all sorts of horrible things the pro-testers might do if they ever caught me. Unless you've had an ugly mob riot against you, you have no idea how worried one can be about his own safety.

Luckily, I remembered what my mom always said when she caught me fret-ting about some childish little thing, like, why none of the other kids would play with me. "Andrew," she'd say in her loving way, "when a boy starts worrying about himself it's a sure sign he needs more work to keep him busy." Of course, she was always right. So I knew what I needed was some work to keep my overly imaginative mind off my troubles But truthfully, in the state of mind I was in, the only work I felt up to was boiling a cauldron of molten lead and pouring it onto the mob down on the plaza. Like, the way Lon Chaney, Jr. did it when that mob was after him in the *Hunchback of Notre Dame*. But I'd no idea where the prop department kept its cauldrons and lead.

Then I had one of my sudden inspirations. Why not work out my problems on the computer? In a way, it would be like killing two birds with one stone. Working would keep my mind off my problems, and once the computer came up with a solution, the problems would no longer be problems. I thought it was totally brilliant, a plan worthy of a mind like mine. Besides, it certainly would be more interesting than simply playing three dimensional chess and tic-tac-toe, working electronic crossword puzzles, or calculating the odds of blackjack, stud poker, or other games of chance. It was totally against company policy to use the computer for personal business. Only two weeks before, a programmer named Mildred Greenberg had been fired for using it to balance her checkbook. But no one was there to catch me, and it was something I'd always wanted to do, pitting two great brains—mine and the computer's—against real problems! So I man-aged to pull myself together and sit down at the keyboard of my console.

I still had to decide which problem to attack first. There was that small, nag-ging problem I was having with my Video Ion Refractor. Like, I'd worked on its every detail in my mind, right down to the cost per unit. But the problem of fig-uring out exactly how it should be built still remained. So I thought that might be something worth considering. On the other hand, events of the past two days had left me wondering if the device was really worth going on with, for what good would it do me to perfect it and use it to gain the presidency of USS-TV so I could marry Melanie Schultz, if in the end it meant the two of us would have to walk the road of life together, fighting off bands of Gypsy marketing terrorists and mobs of my fellow employees? Like, there had to be a safer road to happiness for Melanie and me. To find that road was the problem, a problem certainly worth solving. However, at that moment, it seemed very unlikely that Melanie and I would ever walk any road together, because at any second I expected that insane mob to pour into the data processing center and cut my head off or something even worse. So under the circumstances, I decided first things had to come first. The problem I had to solve now was how to stop the mob from killing me.

Realizing I didn't have a second to lose, I flexed my long, artistic fingers, the way a great concert pianist does before he begins to play, and set about building a decision tree. Now, I don't want to bore you with a lengthy, technical dissertation on the finer points of building a decision tree. But since there are still those who mistakenly believe a computer can't really make a decision, that all it actually does is store up facts and read them back, leaving the final decision up to the programmer, let me digress long enough to explain in simple, layman's terms exactly how the programmer and the computer work together to nourish little seeds of thought until they flourish into giant decisions.

Just for the sake of illustration, say you had to make a decision between taking a February vacation in Miami or Fairbanks. You would start your decision tree growing by cross pollinating known, simple facts. The secret is to start with a pair of known facts, one negative and one positive. For example, the mean February temperature in Miami is 70° versus the mean temperature in Fairbanks of—2°.

That alone is not enough information to make anything but a snap decision, because, as I'm sure you realize, I left out a vital piece of information just to show you how one, small error can affect the growth of a decision tree. You probably caught it right away. I didn't state what temperature scale I was using. Like, if the computer had been programmed to figure temperatures on the centigrade scale, it would've prematurely decided that Fairbanks was more ideal for a February vacation, since Miami's 70°C would be over 155° Fahrenheit, far too hot for anyone to enjoy, while the Fairbanks—2° Centigrade would be a more livable 28° F. So a programmer must weigh all the pros and cons, fairly and objectively, not simply half-truths. For example, say I did enter the temperature scale as Fahrenheit. The computer would instantly know that it was warm and pleasant in Miami and that it was unbearably cold in Fairbanks. Yet it couldn't make a decision based on that information alone. For all it knows, you might prefer cold weather to hot. So you would have to enter more information like: Miami Beach is famous for balmy weather, Gold Coast hotels, water sports, beautiful women in bikinis, deep sea fishing, sunbathing, and nightlife; while Fairbanks is famous for cold weather, gold mines, winter sports, horny guys, hunting, eternal night, and northern lights

At this point, your decision tree is growing, but it still needs more factual nourishment before it can bear fruit. For the computer doesn't know if you like warm weather or cold weather, Gold Coast beaches or gold mines, water sports or weather sports, beautiful women or horny guys, fishing or hunting, water sports or winter sports, sunbathing or eternal night. So the programmer has to be skilled at entering preferences without bias.

This is where the intelligence and skill of the programmer really come into play, for even though you fed the computer all the available facts, and the decision tree is growing, there are still some areas of doubt that must be pruned away, allowing the decision tree to bloom full flower. The negatives and positives begin to cancel each other out. If you hate cold, Miami gets a point; but enjoying Gold Coast hotels and wishing you had a gold mine end up a draw; and you love girls, but that doesn't mean they like you, so being a guy, you might enjoy the security of a man's country and Fairbanks gets a point; water skiing and snow skiing might cancel each other out; so might ice fishing and deep sea fishing; the fear of skin cancer caused by too much sun and your fondness for the dark could score another point for Fairbanks. Computers, fortunately, are not troubled by logic. They deal in facts. Or, as they say, garbage in, garbage out. And it has millions and millions of digitalized bits of information to draw upon, so in the end the fruit your decision tree bears may not be what you expected. And you can only sit and watch with fascination as the great electronic brain types out its final conclusion:

> DANGER! There are grizzly bears in Alaska. Avoid Fairbanks. Danger! Danger! There are man-eating sharks in Florida waters. Don't go to Miami. Stay home and read the April issue of *National Geographic*, a special vacationland issue.

Once again, the computer made a decision that can save you countless dollars and valuable time, and your life as well, all at the speed of light. In just the time it took me to tell you this, I fed the computer the information it needed to build a decision tree that would solve the problem of what I was to do when the mob broke into the data processing center. And its integrated circuits clicked and blinked happily away at the problem. I knew it was coming to the right decision, for having been trained to the decision tree technique at Michigan State, I knew I'd programmed it perfectly. In the twinkling of an eye, the computer came back with its decision:

Down with Cohan!

CHAPTER 13

▼

"Why? Why? Why?" I kept asking myself as I hid in the maintenance closet across the hall from the Data Processing Center, seated on a galvanized scrub pail, my face buried in the strands of a damp mop, my body shaking and trembling, listening to the high-pitched squeals and joyful screams of the mob as they trashed the computers. "Why did the great electronic brain turn against me?"

No matter how I racked my overwrought brain, I couldn't find a logical explanation for such a traitorous act. Like, you learn to expect such behavior from your fellow employees and Gypsies. They are, after all, only human. But from a computer? Never. A computer is perfectly inhuman, with no id or ego or libido. Computers are simply heartless, electronic brains that can neither love nor hate. So how could it come to the decision it did: DOWN WITH COHAN!

Those three simple words had to have a hidden meaning. I was positive that after all the beautiful decision trees I'd programmed, the computer had to have been trying to tell me how to save myself. But what did it mean? What? Then, suddenly, as I sat there, pondering the question in the traditional thinking position, an elbow on my knee supporting the hand my chin rested upon, the closet door was thrown open, and there, to my complete horror, stood my marketing terrorist Gypsy foe, Mo.

"Ohhh!" I screamed, so terrified my voice slid up a full octave.

"Oops!" he grunted. "Sorry, lady. Thought this was the men's libratory."

"Lavatory!" I corrected him.

"Yeah. That's what I meant."

"It's down the hall!"

"Gee, Sorry, lady. Truly, I am."

"Get out! Get out!" I cried, kicking him sharply in the shins.

"Yowee, yow, yow!" he shouted, hopping about on one foot. "I'm going! I'm going!" And he slammed the door shut, leaving me in the dark again.

That was a strange encounter, I told myself. Mo had obviously been looking for the men's room. But he had to be looking for me, too. Everyone was. Yet when he opened the closet door, he failed to recognize me. And why did he refer to me as *lady*? Was he playing some sort of waiting game, pretending he hadn't recognized me in order to put my mind at ease, so that when he finished his business in the men's room and returned with Rudy to kill me, I would still be there? Or was it possible he had really somehow mistaken me for a woman? Of course, it was dark in the closet, and when Mo opened the door, I must have remained in the shadows. And he could have mistaken the strands of the mop hanging over my face for long hair. Then I remembered my scream had been a high falsetto.

I had to laugh at the absurdity of it all. Mo had been looking for the men's room, and when he opened the door to the closet and saw me sitting on the pail in the traditional thinking position and all—well, he must have thought he had bungled his way into the ladies room. No wonder he had that sheepish look. And while I sat there, chuckling to myself, I saw at last what the computer had been trying to tell me. When it came up with DOWN WITH COHAN! it wasn't being traitorous. It was telling me to change my identity. Brilliant! If I did away with Andrew H. Cohan, like, by changing my persona, the mob would do me no harm. "Eureka!" I shouted, leaping to my feet. "Down with Cohan!"

I found the light switch and snapped it on. Once my eyes adjusted to the glare, I began to look about the cluttered closet for some sort of disguise. Again I was in luck. I found a scrubwoman's dress hanging from a hook behind the brooms and a floor waxing machine. It was a pretty frumpy frock, a flowered print with very little style. But beggars can't be choosy, so I rolled my pant legs above the knee and pulled the dress on over my head, stuffing rags into the top to form a bosom. I removed the mop head from its handle, and using the small, cracked mirror nailed to the back wall, put it on like a wig, carefully arranging it in a coiffure that covered half my face with long, flowing strands of string. Considering how makeshift the disguise was, I thought it quite good. Not perfect, of course, but I was sure no one would ever recognize me. And I only intended it to be temporary, like, just something to get me past the mob.

Taking one last look in the mirror, I removed my glasses, thinking their tinted lenses might give me away. I put them into their case and tucked it safely away in my bosom. Then I inhaled deeply, a Yoga breathing exercise designed to calm the nerves, picked up a mop and pail, and bravely stepped out into the hall.

What a mad blur of color greeted my myopic eyes! With the data processing center destroyed, the mob was in an almost carnival mood. Scores of happy USS-TV employees were dancing arm in arm with their newfound marketing terrorist Gypsy friends, singing *You'll Never Get Away From Me*, while a squad of security police did their utmost to bring the situation under control, playing streams of cooling water upon the dancers from the emergency fire hoses.

"Down with Cohan!" I shouted to show the mob I was with them. The security police greeted me with a blast of cold water that toppled me from my feet. "Police brutality!" I wailed, sliding along the wet floor on my back

"Tools of the oppressors!" someone shouted.

"Terrorist assholes!" the security men shouted back, giving me another blast with a fire hose.

"Police brutality," I wailed again, my long slide ending at a pair of shapely legs. I looked up and saw Hedda Nichtwahr smiling down at me.

"Don't hurt her, dahlings," she said, helping me to my feet. "She's only a poor, old cleaning person, doing her job."

"Help!" I screamed, happily clutching the makeshift wig to my head.

Mo came out of the men's room, his furled umbrella raised above his head like a sword. "Get the fuzz!" he cried, taking command.

"Down with Cohan!" I shouted.

"End police brutality!" Mo yelled, charging down the hall. "Get the fuzz!"

"Get the fuzz! Get the fuzz!" the mob chanted, charging after him.

"Call out the National Guard!" the head of security screamed as the mob swarmed over the police in one, great wave.

"Quick, dahling, this way." Hedda took my hand and hurried me to the stairwell at the far end of the hall.

"Down with Cohan!" I shouted as we escaped down the stairwell.

"You are absolutely marvelous," Hedda told me as we ran down the stairs. "Make love to me!"

"I'm only a cleaning lady," I told her.

"Don't be ridiculous dahling," she said, throwing her arms around my neck as we reached the landing two floors down. "You are my shy little genius, Andrew Cohan."

"You saw through my disguise." I sank onto the steps.

She sat next to me, patting my knee. "I'd know those cute legs of yours anywhere."

"Be serious," I said, rolling down my pant legs.

"But I am, dahling. Absolutely serious."

"The mob wants to kill me."

"So? After last night, I wanted to kill you, too." She began to unbutton the back of my dress. "Why did you leave me?"

"I was saving myself."

"For your ridiculous little Melanie Schultz? She could never make love to you the way Hedda could."

"I'm engaged."

"You are absolutely adorable. So old fashioned. Your Melanie is very lucky to have such an old fashioned boy."

"What'll she do if they kill me?"

"What will I do if they kill you?" She ran her hand inside my dress, trying to unbutton my shirt. "What will the world do?"

"The world?"

"If the mob kills you, your secret will be lost to the world forever. An absolute tragedy!"

"I'm not sure the world is ready for my secret."

She nuzzled my neck with her cheek. "My poor little genius. Don't you realize that is the way all great inventors feel? Tell me, dahling, where would the world be today without fire, or the wheel, or the atomic bomb? You absolutely must tell me your secret, Andrew. So it won't be lost to the world if you die before your time."

"I wish I could."

"Then tell me, Andrew. You can tell Hedda everything."

"No way."

"But why, dahling?"

"Because I haven't had time to work out all the details."

"My poor little genius. We must see that you have time to complete your work."

"But how? If the mob recognizes me, they'll kill me."

"That's it! You need a better disguise."

"I do?"

She ran her hand up under my skirt and patted my knee. "Your cute legs gave you away, dahling. This time, we'll disguise you all over. I know where we can get you the most marvelous costume."

"Where?"

"Down in wardrobe on nineteen." And with that, she tore off my dress.

CHAPTER 14

▼

Hedda was right. You should see all the wonderful costumes down in wardrobe, literally thousands of them. One that caught my eye right away was a very realistic ape suit. Who would ever guess the brilliant mind of a genius lurked beneath the receding brow of an ape? I always had this strong urge to swing from trees. Except for the incident in the plaza earlier that morning, I'd managed to suppress the urge. But if I were an ape, I could swing through the trees to my heart's content, and no one would think it the least bit odd, for people expect to see apes swinging from trees. So while Hedda was rummaging through the wardrobe boxes, I put the ape costume on and silently stalked up behind her. Fiercely beating my chest and rolling my eyes, I roared in her ear, "Agarahhh!"

"Oh, Andrew," she cried, clapping her hands like a happy child, "you look so animal!"

"Like it?"

"I love it, dahling. It brings out the beast in you. But of course, you can't wear it. It's absolutely out of the question. The National Guard would shoot you on sight. You know what happened to poor King Kong."

"Right, right."

While she continued rummaging through the boxes, I came across a familiar cowboy suit. I held it up for her approval. "Look! Lone Ranger costume. It's got a mask and everything. Heigh, ho, Silver! Away!"

"Forget it, Andrew. All he ever loved was his horse."

"And Tonto."

"Put it away!" She took a Gypsy costume off the rack. "This one is absolutely perfect, Andrew. Put it on and you could melt right into the crowd."

"Gypsies don't dress like that anymore."

"But of course they do, dahling. I know a little Gypsy bar down by Tiger Stadium, and all the waiters dress in costumes like this. If anyone asks, you can always say you came up to Southfield to join in the protest."

"I don't know—"

"Gypsies make absolutely marvelous lovers. Everyone knows that. Try it on, dahling."

"But I don't look like a Gypsy."

"You will after I make you up."

Hedda had been so nice, I didn't want to offend her taste, so I put it on, and let her make me up. She did a beautiful job, coloring my skin a deep, nut brown, then drawing a long, terrible looking scar on my right cheek, adding a few ugly pockmarks here and there for good measure. Then she pasted a huge, thick, black mustache on my upper lip, and hung a big gold ring from my left ear. As a final touch, she put a red and white bandanna on my head, tying the knot in back in the accepted Gypsy fashion.

When she finished, she let me take a look at myself in the dressing table mirror. The effect was amazing. I not only looked like a Gypsy, I felt I was one. "Aha!" I shouted at my image in the mirror, giving myself the evil eye. "Ze Gypsy curse on you Andrew H. Cohan!"

"You look absolutely marvelous!" Hedda said, admiring her handiwork.

"Aha!" I shouted again, throwing her down on the dressing room couch. "And who are you, my lovely laydee?"

"Oh, Andrew, you're an absolute animal!"

"I make love to you now," I said, unzipping the back of her dress, and kissing her neck.

She began to giggle hysterically. "Oh, Andrew! Stop! Please stop!"

"There's no stopping now, babee," I said, putting my hand down the front of her dress.

"Please, Andrew! You have no idea how ticklish I am. I mean, really! What's come over you?"

"Make love to me." I pressed my body down on hers and kissed her hard on the mouth.

"Oh, Andrew, dahling!" She gasped. "You are absolutely marvelous! A wild beast! But of course, I can't make love to you—"

"No?" I said, pulling her dress down from her shoulders.

"No, no!" she whispered frantically, her white breasts straining excitedly against her Wonder Bra. "Not here. I mean, it's against corporate policy—making love in the headquarters building—absolutely against policy. Even Harmon P. Harper can't do it here."

"Well, if eet ees against ze policy," I said, starting to get up.

"To hell with policy!" she cried.

"No, eet would be wrong," I said, zipping her dress back up.

"Let's do it! Make love with Hedda!"

"Not here, my little pigeon. Not if eet ees against ze policy."

"My place, then! Come to my place. Now! Oh, God, I am so hot!"

"You go. I will follow."

"Promise?"

"Would I lie to you, my pet?" I blew her a kiss.

"Hurry, dahling. Please hurry!" she panted, rushing from the wardrobe room.

I know I should have kept my promise, but then you know how Gypsies are, they never tell the truth. That's why I never wanted to assume the identity of a Gypsy in the first place. Like, when I left for work that morning, I'd made up my mind to tell Melanie the truth, the whole truth, and nothing but the truth. How could I expect her to believe me if I were a Gypsy? So as soon as Hedda was gone, I began to look about for something more me.

It took about five minutes of hunting through the racks and shelves to find exactly what I was looking for—an old stovepipe hat, a simple cape, a black suit. Quickly wiping away the Gypsy makeup Hedda had so artfully applied, I glued on chin whiskers and pasted a mole to my cheek. The resemblance was startling. I looked so honest no one would dare question anything I said. "Four score and seven years ago…." I began to practice my new identity.

There was no need to go further. For the first time in my life, I felt this was the real me. Donning my stovepipe hat, I opened the door and stepped into the hall, confident that Melanie would respect and believe in me. My only problem now was to find her. I looked at my watch. It was only a little after 10:30. Riot or no riot, I knew she'd be in the cafeteria with Cheetah, for neither rain, nor hail, nor sleet, nor snow could stay those two from their morning break.

CHAPTER 15

▼

Considering the extent of the rioting earlier that morning, I found the cafeteria surprisingly normal. Melanie, Cheetah, and Seymour were sitting at our usual table, drinking their coffee and making small talk as if nothing out of the ordinary had occurred that morning. But even if everything did appear normal, I was still afraid of what might happen if anyone recognized me, so instead of joining them, I seated myself at the table next to them.

"Oh, God, don't look now," Cheetah said as she saw me sit down. "The geek's back."

"Andy," Melanie gasped, "where have you been? Everyone's looking for you."

"Thank God, you're safe," Seymour said, moving from their table to mine. "But why the ridiculous getup, Andy?"

"Abe," I informed him.

"Listen to the geek," Cheetah said.

"Four score and seven years ago," I began.

"Don't you remember us? Andy, we're your teammates." Melanie moved to the chair next to mine.

"Why do you all insist on calling me Andy?"

"Because that's your name," Seymour said. "Andrew H. Cohan."

"Cohan's dead," I told them, gently as I could under the circumstances.

"Oh, God! The rioting has really, really affected his mind," Melanie gasped.

"What mind?" Cheetah asked.

I pointed an accusing finger at her. "You killed him. You hit him with a rock."

"The rock missed, Andy. You said so yourself." Seymour said.

Melanie nodded. "Yes, you shouted, 'Ha, ha, you missed me!' Don't you remember?"

"Four score and seven years ago ..." I began.

"Maybe we should get him to a shrink," Seymour said.

"Our forefathers brought forth unto this continent a new nation," I went on.

"The geek's faking," Cheetah said.

"Andy, are you faking?" Seymour asked.

"Conceived in liberty and dedicated to the proposition that all men are created equal."

"His mind has really, really snapped!" Melanie gasped.

"Has your mind snapped, Andy?" Seymour asked.

"Abe," I reminded him, clinging to my new identity. "Honest Abe."

"Oh, God!" Melanie wailed.

"Your mind can't snap if you don't have a brain. All that's between the geek's ears is a big, empty vacuum," Cheetah snarled.

I gave her an icy stare "Are you speaking of the departed Andrew H. Cohan?"

"Yeah, you—the geek," she retorted.

"Never met him," I returned. "Understand he was a genius."

"What a load of crap!" Cheetah snapped.

Seymour said, "Andy was a genius. Too bad he was such a coward."

"Coward?" I said.

"A really, real coward," Melanie agreed.

"Yellow!" Cheetah added.

"No way!" I said.

"Andy ran out on his teammates," Seymour said..

"Andrew H. Cohan desert his team mates? Like, I admit I never met him. But I know his type. He'd never let his teammates down."

"Then why did he leave us to face Harmon P. Harper alone?" Seymour asked.

I didn't understand. "Face Harmon P. Harper alone? What do you mean?"

"We got the word fifteen minutes ago," Seymour said, pulling out a blue USS-TV inter-departmental memo.

I put on my glasses and read it:

To: Cheetah

    M. Schultz

    S. Stone

From: Harmon P. Harper

Subject: Andrew H. Cohan

There will be a short meeting in my office today at 11:30 a.m. Be there.

Seymour said, "You've got to go with us. HP is obviously upset about the demonstration this morning. And we don't even know what it was all about."

"You can't let us face him alone," Melanie said.

"We're your freaking teammates, geek," Cheetah said.

"It wouldn't be right," I told them

"Why?" they all demanded.

"I wasn't invited."

"But you're the subject of the meeting," Seymour said, jabbing at the memo with his forefinger. "See? 'Subject: Andrew H. Cohan.'"

"He's dead," I reminded them.

Melanie said, "You really, really are Andrew H. Cohan."

I smiled sympathetically. "Sorry for your loss. My name's Abe."

"Abe, Schnabe," Cheetah snarled. "You're the geek!

"Honest Abe. Four score and seven years ago," I began again.

"Oh, God! What's wrong with him?" Melanie asked Seymour.

"I'd say he doesn't sound completely all there," he said.

"The geek's a real psycho," Cheetah agreed.

"Are you mentally ill?" Melanie asked me.

"No. Honest Abe."

Seymour said, "He refuses to accept his true identity. Undoubtedly, he's had some traumatic experience."

"Yeah, he was born a geek," Cheetah said.

"You've got to help him. You're his agent," Melanie told Seymour.

Seymour thumbed his iPhone. "According to the Freudian concept, most cases like this are the result of some sexual frustration. We've got to get him to open up and tell us what sort of a traumatic sexual experience frustrated him."

"The geek probably doesn't know what a sexual experience is."

"I do so. I had one yesterday."

Seymour said, "Tell us about it."

"It's too embarrassing."

"You have to be really, really honest and tell us everything," Melanie said.

"Everything?"

"The truth, the whole truth, and nothing but the truth," Seymour said.

A little bell went off in my head. "I was with a woman. Like, in bed, you know?"

Melanie gasped. "You were?"

"I guess so. At least, when I woke up there was a woman in bed with me."

Seymour noted that in his iPhone. "Now, you're sure she was in bed with you when you woke up? It's a very important point, Andy."

"Why?"

"Because if she was there when you woke up, it couldn't be a dream. Dreams are very important to the Freudian concept."

"Ha!" Cheetah laughed. "It had to be a dream. What woman would jump into bed with a geek like him?"

"Who was she?" Melanie demanded.

"A gentleman never tells on a lady," I told them.

"Gentleman?" Cheetah said. "What a crock!"

"Was it Hedda?" Seymour asked.

"Hedda?" Melanie wanted to know.

"Nichtwahr," Seymour answered. "Head of the USS-TV Research Department. We had lunch with her yesterday. To tell her about Andy's invention."

"She's very beautiful," I said, wanting to make Melanie even more jealous than I knew she already was.

"So it was Hedda in bed with you," Seymour said, adding that fact to his iPhone.

Melanie cried, "I hate you, Andy! How could you jump in bed with another woman?"

"Actually, like, I think she went to bed with me."

Seymour jotted that down and asked, "Why did she go to bed with you?"

"To help me."

"Help you?" Melanie said.

"Perfect my idea," I told her.

"And did she actually help you perfect it?" Seymour asked.

I nodded. "She said I should add yes and no buttons to my Video Ion Refractor."

"Why yes and no buttons?" Seymour asked.

"So we can ask people questions."

Seymour said, "Excellent suggestion. And that's what frustrated you, isn't it? You let Hedda climb into bed with you, thinking all along she wanted you to make love, but in truth, she only wanted to tell you about the yes and no buttons."

"No way! She really wanted me."

"Oh, Andy!" Melanie cried.

"Don't listen to the geek!" Cheetah told her. "It's all a crock. He's trying to build his super stud reputation. He probably pads his Jockeys with old socks to impress the chicks."

"You questioning my honesty?" I asked her.

"No, just your freaking sanity."

"She wanted me!"

"Oh, God! Listen to the geek," Cheetah said. "She was so freaking hot for his skinny bod she completely went ape."

"No. That was later."

"I see," Seymour said. He thought for a moment and nodded, like he actually understood. "That's very revealing."

"Totally," I agreed. "We didn't have any clothes on."

"Now we're getting down to the bare facts!" Seymour said.

Melanie asked, "Did you? I mean, you know—what did you really, really do next?"

"Locked myself in the bathroom."

Seymour thumbed that into his iPhone. "And that's what frustrated you, isn't it? Being locked in the bathroom that way. Did your mother ever lock you in the bathroom when you were a child?"

"It didn't have a lock."

Seymour said, "So you were frustrated at being locked in a bathroom, because as a child, you were never locked in a bathroom. Correct?"

"No way. I wanted to save myself for Melanie!"

"Oh, Andy!" Melanie said, squeezing my hand. "Was that really, really why you did it?"

"Uh, huh."

"The important thing is that you finally remembered your true identity. You just answered to the name Andy," Seymour said.

"A slip of the tongue."

"Do you really, really love me?" Melanie asked.

"Yo! Like, that's why I'm saving myself for you."

"If you really, really love me, admit who you are. Actually, I mean."

"Honest ... Andy Cohan," I finally confessed.

"I knew it!" Seymour shouted

"The all American geek," Cheetah said.

"Great!" Seymour pocketed his iPhone. "Now we can go see Harmon P. Harper."

"And he's going to fire us all!" Melanie wailed.

Seymour grinned and shook his head. "No, way. Oh, I admit at first I thought he might be going to fire us because we're Andy's teammates. But that can't be it. If HP wanted to fire us, he'd have our department heads do it. That's what department heads are for, handing out bad news. No, this has got to be good news. Hedda must have told him about Andy's idea and HP's probably going to reward us for being on his development team."

"You really, really think so?" Melanie asked.

"Absolutely," he said. "We're all team players, aren't we?"

"Haven't I always said we're on your team, Andy?" Cheetah purred.

"Yeah, right. You always said I was a geek."

Melanie said, "Actually, geek can be a term of endearment. I mean, look at Bill Gates. He's a geek and everybody loves him."

"I'm so lucky to have teammates like you guys," I said.

"Then you'll go to the meeting with us?" Seymour asked

"Like I said, I'd never let my teammates down."

▼

CHAPTER 16

"Maybe I better not go in there with you," I told Seymour as we all waited in the anteroom to Harmon P. Harper's six-window corner office suite on the thirteenth floor, waiting for his secretary to tell us we could go in. "Like, if Mr. Harper wanted me at the meeting, wouldn't he invite me?"

"Not necessarily," Seymour said. "Besides, we're all in this together."

"It's one for all and all for one," Melanie said.

"We're a team," Cheetah said.

"Maybe I should put on my Honest Abe costume," I said.

"You're too old for security blankets," Seymour said.

"You look just fine just the way you are," Melanie told me.

"Except for all that dried blood on your shirt," Cheetah said. "Ugh. Some people are born slobs."

"If you hadn't thrown that rock at me, I wouldn't have dried blood all over my shirt."

"Come on, Andy, she missed you," Seymour said.

"Then how did I get this cut over my forehead?"

"Duh! Maybe you cut yourself shaving your eyebrows," Cheetah said.

"I never shaved my eyebrows."

"Then what happened to them?" Melanie asked.

Seymour said, "I've been meaning to ask you that very question. It could be a significant point."

"The geek probably plucked them," Cheetah said.

"No way!"

"Yeah, sure, they magically up and disappeared in a puff of smoke," Cheetah said.

"That's it. They must've been burned off in the fire," I said.

"When were you in a fire?" Seymour asked.

"Last night," I said.

"The geek and the Hedda broad were probably smoking in bed," Cheetah said.

"Oh, Andy, how could you?" Melanie sniffed.

"I don't smoke. They tried to kill me last night—like, in this theater—"

"Who tried to kill you in what theater?" Seymour asked, taking out his iPhone.

"Oh, God, here we go again. John Wilkes Booth and his gang, in Ford's theater. Right, Abe?" Cheetah said.

"No. Not John Wilkes Booth," I said. "The Wizard—"

"Wizard?" Melanie asked.

"Yeah, right. Now the Wizard of Oz is after him!" Cheetah said.

"Wizard of Oz," Seymour thumbed it into his iPhone.

I shook my head. "Not the Wizard Oz. Just the Wizard. His real name is Al Solmar. Actually, it was his twin sister, the Great Madame Solmar who saved me from him and his marketing terrorist Gypsies."

"How'd she do that?" Melanie asked.

"She was a Gypsy fortune teller who read my palm when I was a little kid. She gave me my lucky rabbit's foot to fend off curses and hexes."

Seymour said, "Obviously, that's why you have this delusion that marketing terrorist Gypsies are trying to kill you. Don't you see? The rabbit's foot's some kind of a sex symbol. Your subconscious probably thinks that by giving you the rabbit's foot, Madame Zola emasculated all Gypsy males, preventing them from carrying out their nefarious plans. It all fits. You have a deep-seated guilt complex."

"God, Rock, you sound so intelligent," Cheetah said.

"But it actually happened. They tried to kill me," I insisted

"Extreme paranoia," Seymour said.

"Oh, Andy!" Melanie sobbed.

"Always knew the geek was a nut case," Cheetah said.

"Do you often feel people are out to get you?" Seymour asked me.

"Sometimes," I admitted.

"Give us an example."

"Well," I began, hesitatingly, "this morning, when everyone in the plaza was shouting, 'Down with Cohan!' and 'Kill, kill!' I felt a little intimidated."

"I see," Seymour said, adding that fact to his iPhone. "Now, tell me—and this is very important, Andy—did you ever have these feelings of persecution before you thought up your Video Ion Refractor?"

"No," I admitted.

"That's the root of your problem," Seymour said, pocketing his iPhone. "Bottling up this secret inside has imposed a great strain on your mind. It's a wonder you haven't had a complete mental breakdown. You've got to unburden your subconscious, Andy—let the secret out—now, before something snaps."

"Oh, please, Andy, unburden your mind. Tell us your secret before it's too late!" Melanie pleaded.

"If you ask me, it's already too late," Cheetah said.

"Well, I was born in Albert Lea, Minnesota," I began. "That's about a hundred miles south of—"

Harmon P. Harper's secretary interrupted: "Mr. Harper will see you now."

"Oh, God!" Cheetah gasped.

"I feel faint!" Melanie sighed.

I groaned and said, "I feel like throwing up."

"It's all in your mind," Seymour said, cheerfully. "Remember, I'm your agent. Relax and let me do all the talking. I'll really give your idea the old hard sell."

*   *   *   *

Harmon P. Harper's secretary led us into his private inner sanctum and then left, closing the massive gold inlaid bronze doors behind her, leaving the four of us just standing there, staring at our feet. At least I was staring at mine. Like, I was too nervous to look up to see if my teammates were staring at theirs, too. You can imagine how I jumped when I heard the shrill voice of my old nemesis Ray Solmar shout, "A curse on you, Andrew H. Cohan!"

I whirled toward the voice to see the Wizard jump angrily to his feet from the red velvet cushions of a Louis XV *lit de repos* where he had been seated beside three tanned and neatly trimmed executives, unobtrusively attired in dark, summer-weight suits, well cut with narrow lapels, no padding in the shoulders, white, broadcloth button-down shirts, bright paisley ties and French cuffs that sported round gold cufflinks with the initials USS-TV engraved on them, the mark of a vice president.

"Cohan? Cohan?" I heard a hearty, omnipotent voice say from somewhere above and behind me.

I turned again and saw a rather muscular young man, only a few years older than I, with prematurely graying brown hair styled with the slightest suggestion of a pompadour wave. He was seated on a modern copy of a Seventeenth Century State Chair, upholstered with crimson velvet appliqué and gold lamé, his long legs primly crossed, his unrevealing icy blue eyes looking down his aquiline nose at us from behind a Louis XVI *bureau plat*, an exquisitely rendered flattop desk inlaid with intricate brass designs and a veneer of tortoiseshell. The huge desk was strategically positioned atop a three-foot high platform, its pyramid-like steps carpeted in a deep purple plush pile, so that the desk and the man behind it dominated the entire room from on high.

"Is one of you Andrew H. Cohan?" he asked. "*The* Cohan who's been causing all of us at USS-TV such anguish?"

"Tell him I need to change into a clean shirt," I told Seymour, almost knocking down a black and gold Nubian slave statue as I turned and started toward the massive gold and bronze doors.

Seymour grabbed me by the arm to keep me from escaping. "Yes, sir, Mr. Harper, sir, this is that Cohan."

"A real geek, if you know what I'm saying," Cheetah added.

"Oh wow, isn't this just sock!" Harmon P. Harper exclaimed, happily, placing his elbows on the arms of the state chair, and lacing the fingers of his hands together under his square jaw.

"It's really sock, Harm," the three vice presidents all agreed.

Harmon P. Harper said, "Here I have everyone who is anyone go-going all over the place, eyeballing for booby baby here. And what does he do? He surprises us by making the scene himself."

The Wizard was still hopping about on one foot. "That's the damnable firebug who burned down my beautiful theater!"

"The geek was always a little buggy," Cheetah said as Seymour began to frisk me.

"I didn't burn down anything," I defended myself.

"He's clean, sir," Seymour said after he finished his pat down.

"Mark my words, Andrew H. Cohan, you've burned down your last theater," the Wizard ranted, wagging a bony finger under my nose.

"Oh, Andy, you really, really shouldn't burn down theaters!" Melanie gasped.

"My theater," the Wizard said. "My beautiful GYP Theatre."

"Then you must be Ray Solmar," Seymour said. "The amazing Wizard who owns the Market Research Institute—the world's largest marketing research organization."

"I am that Wizard."

"He's a marketing terrorist," I warned Seymour.

"Andy, I think you owe Mr. Solmar an apology. First you burn down his theater, and then you call him a terrorist."

"He is a marketing terrorist," I insisted

"Shame on you, Andy!" Melanie cried.

"Racist geek," Cheetah snarled.

"I'm leaving. I know when I'm not wanted," I said,

"Not wanted?" Harmon P. Harper said. "I'm ecstatic that you're here, booby baby. You have no idea how ecstatic I am."

"But I wasn't invited," I said, forgetting for the moment that I was supposed to let Seymour do all the talking.

"Isn't he terriff?" Harmon P. Harper exclaimed. "Our young genius says he wasn't invited! Of course you were, booby baby. You're the subject of this meeting. We just didn't know where you were or how to find you. Am I right?"

"Right, Harm," the three vice presidents echoed.

"Let me assure you, booby baby," Harman P. Harper continued, "had we known you were available, you most certainly would've received my memo. But because of the disastrous rioting in the data processing center, we had no idea where to find you—or even if you were still alive—so we invited your friends to the meeting, hoping they could shed some light on your whereabouts. I do hope you do understand, booby baby."

"Tell him I understand," I told Seymour.

"He under—"

Harmon P. Harper cut Seymour off with a snap of his fingers. "Shall we get down to business, booby baby? Mr. Solmar's been telling us about your Video Ion Refractor. It's a boffo idea. An absolute smash!" His ice blue eyes darted to his vice presidents. "Don't we all agree it's an absolute smash?"

"Absolute smash!" the vice presidents agreed.

"Smash him! Smash him!" the Wizard screamed. "A curse on you, Andrew H. Cohan! A curse on you and your damnable ideas!"

"Ray, please, there are ladies present." Harmon P. Harper turned his ice blue eyes on Melanie and Cheetah. "Hope you will excuse Mr. Solmar. You do understand, don't you?"

"Oh, perfectly," Melanie said.

"We're totally understanding," Cheetah said.

"You're beautiful. Aren't they beautiful?" Harmon P. Harper asked his vice presidents.

"Beautiful, Harm," they agreed.

"Oh, God! They think we're beautiful!" Cheetah purred.

"I'm going to faint," Melanie said.

"Behind every beautiful idea is a beautiful woman," Harmon P. Harper said. "And what a smashing conceptualism your beautiful idea is, booby baby! At long last, someone has dreamed up a completely foolproof method of measuring contemporary consumer likes and dislikes, eliminating all random factors and error percentages, so the success or failure of market research is no longer attendant upon mere sampling, but a survey of the complete respondent base. Now every man, woman, and child in America can contribute to our completely objective data base. In other words, booby baby, your idea is a wow. Isn't it a wow?"

"A real wow, Harm!" the vice presidents agreed.

"Wow!" Seymour said.

"Oh, wow!" Cheetah said

"Andy, I'm so really, really proud of you," Melanie said

I whispered to Seymour, "Tell Harm it's nothing."

"It's—"

Harmon P. Harper snapped his fingers again. "I'm sure you'd like USS-TV to expedite your idea with broad contingency plans. Right, booby baby?"

"Tell him that's right," I told Seymour.

"That's—"

"Mr. Solmar informed me of your desire to become president of USS-TV," Harmon P. Harper went on.

"My crystal ball sees all and hears all," the Wizard said.

"So you can marry Miss Schultz, as I understand it," Harmon P. Harper said. "A noble ambition. Isn't that noble?"

The three vice presidents nodded in agreement.

Harmon P. Harper leaned back in his chair, putting a hand to his forehead, assuming the executive thinking position. "But as I see it, there's just one flaw in your plan—I have no intention of stepping aside for anyone, booby baby. So, what to do? That is the question." He took his hand away from his forehead and began to drum his fingers on his *bureau plat.*

I whispered to Seymour, "Tell him he could—"

"Shh! Harm's thinking," the three vice presidents said.

"God, I can almost feel his thoughts," Cheetah said.

"Isn't it beautiful?" Melanie said.

Finally Harmon P. Harper sat up, snapping his fingers. "Got it!"

"He's got it!" we all shouted at once.

"I'm just talking off the top of my head, mind you, but it seems to me the solution for our little dilemma requires a dichotomization of the alienated parties."

"Brilliant!" the three vice presidents all shouted at once.

"Brilliant!" Seymour agreed. Then to me, in a low whisper, he asked, "What do you think he means?"

"He's going to separate us," I said.

"Break up our team?" Seymour asked.

"Fire us," I told him.

"Thank you for positioning my position," Harmon P. Harper said.

"You lousy little geek! Now you've gotten us all canned!" Cheetah screamed at me.

"Oh, Andy, how could you?" Melanie said.

"Afraid you're going to have to get yourself a new agent," Seymour told me.

Harmon P. Harper placed the tips of his fingers together and looking up his aquiline nose at the ceiling said, "On the other hand, booby baby, there might be a more equitable solution. I'm not a harsh man. Actually, I've been told I'm a sweetheart of a guy." He lowered his eyes to his vice presidents. "Wouldn't you say I'm a sweetheart?"

"Definitely a sweetheart!" they all agreed.

Harmon P. Harper pulled a sheaf of papers from the drawer of his *bureau plat.* "Just so happens I've had some papers drawn up. Agree to sign them and you can all stay at USS-TV."

"We'll sign! We'll sign!" Seymour, Cheetah, and Melanie shouted, rushing up the deep purple carpeted steps to his desk.

"Who's got a freaking pen?" Cheetah asked.

"Here," Seymour said pulling a ballpoint from his inside coat pocket.

Harmon P. Harper shoved the papers across the desk. "Sign by the Xs next to your names and it's a done deal."

Seymour turned to me. "You sign first, Andy."

"No way," I said.

"Oh, Andy, you've got to sign," Melanie said.

"Sign, geek, or I'll break your freaking arm!" Cheetah screamed.

"My mom told me never to sign anything without reading it first."

"Did you hear that?" Harmon P. Harper exclaimed, clapping his hands. "Booby baby's mama told him never to sign anything without reading it first. Isn't that beautiful!"

"Beautiful!" The vice presidents agreed.

The Wizard shouted, "Sign or I put a curse on you, Andrew H. Cohan!"

Harmon P. Harper waved his hand soothingly. "Now, now, Ray, let bygones be bygones. I think it's cute of booby baby not wanting to sign the papers before he reads them. Unfortunately, in today's global business world, we can't afford sentimentalities. Sign the papers, booby baby, before I forget that I am a sweetheart of a guy"

"Not until I know what they say."

"Okay, booby, if you want to be a baby, guess I'll have to be big about it and play the game your way. The papers say you agree to assign the rights to your Video Ion Refractor to USS-TV for ten million dollars—"

"Ten million!" Melanie gasped.

"As your agent, I urge you to sign, Andy," Seymour said.

"Why do my teammates have to sign, too?" I asked Harmon P. Harper. "It's my invention."

"Your team has to agree that they will never divulge your concept to anyone. Period. Now, booby baby, is that too much to ask for a cool ten million?"

"What are you going to do with my idea?" I asked.

"Destroy it!" the Wizard shouted.

"For the good of Corporate America and the Global Economy, booby baby. Can you imagine the havoc your beautiful idea would wreak on an unsuspecting business world? It could be the end of market research as we know it. Soft data would become hard data. Facts would become facts. Non-decisional situations would become decisional. A crisis of non-choice would be created. Imagination and creative activism would be stifled. Traditional dialectic motivational research would give way to creative thinking. The dynamic, unidirectional, ever-varying, human element of group think would become passé. It could be the end of bottom line motivation. Corporations could lose billions. Millions of middle class working stiffs would lose their jobs. The result would be World Depression. That could ruin us all. You don't want to ruin a sweetheart of a guy like me and all your teammates, do you, booby baby?"

I took the ballpoint from Seymour and signed the papers.

"It's a done deal!" Seymour shouted signing by the X next to his name.

"Oh, booby baby!" Cheetah was so excited after she signed, she threw her arms around my neck and began kissing my cheek. "I love you, geek!"

"I really, really love you, too!" Melanie said signing next to her X. "Let's fly out to Atlantic City or some other romantic place and get married this afternoon."

Seymour clapped me on my back. "Bet you're glad you've got a Yale man for an agent, Andy. Wow, we're in the money!"

"Really, really big money. Just think of all the things we can do with ten million dollars!" Melanie said.

"Start by building me a new GYP theater to replace the one you burned down last night! The original cost five million. Considering inflation, six million should take care of it," the Wizard said.

Harmon P. Harper folded up the papers and put them back in the drawer of his *bureau plat*. "Of course, the contract says you will reimburse USS-TV for all the damage you caused, booby baby."

"Ask him how much that will be," I told Seymour.

Seymour began, "How much—"

Harmon P. Harper snapped his fingers. "My best guesstimate is somewhere in the neighborhood of five million, plus or minus a hundred thousand. I'll let you know the final numbers as soon as the bean counters give them to me. Okay, booby baby?"

"My agent handles all my business affairs," I told him.

Seymour took out his iPhone and did some fast calculations. "The way I figure it, after Andy pays back the money he owes Mr. Solmar and USS-TV he'll be a over a million dollars in debt!"

"Roughly, that's it. But we're not here to sandpaper this thing down to a fine toothed comb. The bean counters and lawyers will work out the nitty-gritty money details." Harmon P. Harper said.

"Tell him I haven't got a million dollars," I told Seymour.

"Andy hasn't—"

"Not to worry, booby baby. You and your friends still have your jobs. I'm sure something equitable can be worked out. How about paying us back at the rate of five hindered dollars a week?"

Seymour did some fast figuring on his iPhone. "It'll only take you something like thirty-eight years to be debt free, Andy."

"I'll wait for you, Andy" Melanie said.

"Guess that wraps up everything here," Harmon P. Harper said as he leaned back in his state chair, clasping his hands behind his head. "Is it a wrap, or is it wrap?" he asked his vice presidents.

"It's a wrap, Harm," they agreed.

"I hope you're all as ecstatic about this as I am," Harmon P. Harper said.

"Oh, God, are we ecstatic!" Cheetah said. She turned to Melanie. "Let's bounce! The further we get away from the geek, the better off we'll be."

"Thank you for not firing us, Mr. Harper, sir," Melanie said, curtseying to him as she backed toward the gold and bronze doors.

"You're beautiful," Harmon P. Harper told her.

"Oh, God!" she said.

"I've got to e-mail the MRI board and give them the good news," the Wizard said. He shook Harmon P. Harper's hand. "We'll always look upon you as a friend."

The three vice presidents got up, heading for the huge bronze doors. "You're a sweetheart of a guy, Harm," they chimed in unison.

"I promise you, sir, Andy will pay back every cent he owes you," Seymour said.

"Even if it takes thirty-eight years,' I said.

"One more thing, booby baby. Did you tell anyone else about your Video Ion Refractor? If you did, I've got to know. We can't afford a leak on a thing like this."

"Just Hedda Nichtwahr," Seymour answered for me.

Harmon P. Harper winked one of his ice blue eyes at him. "Don't think we have to worry about Hedda spilling the beans. She's very loyal to me, if you know what I mean."

Seymour winked back. "Yes, sir, I understand."

"Oh, I did tell someone else," I suddenly remembered aloud.

"Who?" Harmon P. Harper demanded.

"Har! Har! Har!" the friendly laugh of Roger Jolly boomed as he marched into Harmon P. Harper's office. "Harm, I'm going to preempt ninety minutes of prime time tonight. We put together a wonderful special on the riot—it'll be a Jolly good show!"

"Him," I told Harmon P. Harper.

CHAPTER 17

▼

"Har! Har! Har!" Roger Jolly laughed, his droll little mouth drawn up in a bow. "Well, well, well, I see you already know my young friend, Cohan, Andrew H. Was going to tell you about him, Harm. Brilliant lad. Absolute genius. Has invented a device that could revolutionize our business. Right, Cohan?"

"Right."

Roger Jolly winked his good eye at Harmon P. Harper. "Better watch out for him, Harm. Wants your job. Might get it one of these days, too." He eyed Seymour, and then turned back to me. "Who's your friend, laddie?"

"Stone, Seymour, my agent."

"Good, good! Talent always needs a good agent." Roger Jolly put an arm over Seymour's shoulders. "Stone, you and I have some important business to discuss. Right?"

"Say right," I told Seymour. "Everyone always says right when he says right."

"And snap to attention when you say it. And say it fast. Right?"

"Right," Seymour said.

"That, my boy, was one of the fastest rights I ever heard. Stone, you're really going places."

"I went to Yale."

"Okay, let's talk turkey. How much do you want for the rights to laddie's Video Ion Refractor?"

"Afraid it's out of my hands now, sir," Seymour said. "We just sold all the rights."

"You must be joking." Roger Jolly turned to me: "You didn't sell out to those damned marketing terrorist Gypsies, did you, laddie?"

"No way. I'd never sell out to them."

"Good, good. Knew a bright young man like you wouldn't sell out to those thieves. Why, if I know the Gypsies, they'd just sit on your idea. Destroy it. They hate progress, you know. Right, laddie?"

"Right."

"Good. Now, Stone, who'd you sell laddie's idea to?"

"One of TVs most powerful HDTV providers."

For once Roger Jolly didn't laugh. "Not to one of our competitors. That'd be high treason. We'd have to string you up from the highest yardarm. As Founder-Chairman of USS-TV, I dedicated myself and my company to public service. Right, Harm?"

"Right, Admiral. We all respect your dedication to public service. It really makes us look socko in the FCC's eyes. That's why I bought the rights to booby baby's Video Ion Refractor. I saw all its public-service programming possibilities."

"You're beautiful, Harm. That's why I picked you to be president of USS-TV. Had to have a beautiful front man to suck up to all the advertisers and their agencies. Right?"

"Right, Admiral."

"So we bought all the rights to laddie's Video Ion Refractor? A stroke of genius, Harm. Didn't think you had it in you. But you've fooled old Roger Jolly before. Guess you know what to do when a brilliant idea comes along. Right?"

"Right," I said. "He's going to destroy it."

Jolly Roger didn't laugh again. "You're doing what, Harm?"

"Oh come on, booby baby!" Harmon P. Harper said, looking down his nose at me. "You know I just said that to appease Ray Solmar. Didn't I just say that?"

"I think I heard you say that, Harm" Seymour answered for me.

"Well, of course I said that. I had no choice, Admiral. Ray was here demanding all kinds of things. He said if I didn't buy booby baby's Video Ion Refractor and sit on it, his marketing terrorist Gypsy protest in the plaza would go on and on. And wouldn't that be just teriff—our halls filled with rioting marketing Gypsy terrorists? What would the agency people and their clients think? So I told Ray I'd destroy Cohan's Video Ion Refractor, just to get the Gypsies off our backs. But it was only a gentlemen's agreement. I never meant to keep it. Not a word of it."

"So I don't owe the marketing terrorist Gypsies and USS-TV eleven million dollars," I asked.

"No way, booby baby," Harman P. Harper said. "Let's call it a draw. You don't owe us anything and we don't owe you anything."

"Har! Har! Har! I'm really proud of you, Harm boy. Damn the torpedoes, full speed ahead!"

"You'll be ecstatic to know that's exactly what I said to myself," Harmon P. Harper said. "The moment Ray told me about booby baby's Video Ion Refractor, I told myself it was a beautiful concept! It's a damn the torpedoes, full speed ahead kind of idea—an idea we have to expedite in broad contingency plans—and to hell with the marketing terrorist Gypsies!"

"That's what I admire about you, Harm. You think like me. No matter what, public-service comes first at USS-TV! I can see it now. We'll FedEx one of laddie's Video Ion Refractors to every TV household in this beautiful land of ours. Absolutely free of charge, of course. We can write the whole thing off anyway. Har! Har! Har! Think of the shows we can create. We'll build a Blockbuster Public Service Show around it this fall just in time for the elections. Everyone of voting age can vote for the candidate of their choice the night before the election. What a scoop! We'll be able to predict the exact outcome. Just like that! Those damned marketing terrorist Gypsy pollsters will look like idiots after this. Right?"

"Right, Admiral," Harm and Seymour echoed.

"Right," I agreed, "but there is a problem."

"Like what, booby baby?" Harmon P. Harper wanted to know.

"Like, my Video Ion Refractor isn't perfected yet."

"Minor detail, laddie. With your brains and USS-TV's money and resources behind you, we can't lose. How much time will it take?"

"Well, I planned to work it out on the Data Processing Super Computer, but the demonstrators smashed it to pieces this morning."

"Damned marketing terrorist Gypsies," Roger Jolly grumbled. "They'll stop at nothing to prevent your idea from being perfected, laddie. But to hell with them! This is war. We've got to put this under a secret crash program. Let's call it Operation Torch! If it was good enough for Ike, it's good enough for USS-TV. Right?"

"Right! Operation Torch." Seymour thumbed the code name into his iPhone.

'We'll send laddie to Hollywood!" Roger jolly said. He can work there in absolute secrecy at our Reality Development Division."

"You'll just love the geeks out there, booby baby. They're way-out creative types like you."

"Brilliant people, all of them, and very secretive. Har! Har! Har! Why, even we don't know what the hell they're working on. Right, Harm?"

"Right, Admiral, no one does."

"Andy will need a project manager for this," Seymour suggested. "Someone with a fantastic combination of business acumen and creative talent, a mover and shaker who can cut through the red tape and command all the resources of the company to push this project through on a crash basis."

"You're really thinking now, Stone. Right, Harm?"

"Right, Admiral."

Seymour went on, "He's got to be a people person. A tall, handsome guy with a winning boyish grin. Above all, he's got to be a team player, someone who's worked with Andy on this project from the very beginning."

"Good thinking, Stone. The fewer new people we bring into Operation Torch, the easier it will be to keep it top secret. Right, Harm?"

"Right, Admiral."

"Even more important," Seymour continued, "he's got to be someone who can handle all the administrative details so Andy's mind can be free to create. Yet, he and Andy must be real friends, so they can work together like bosom buddies."

"Har! Har! Har! Anything else we should consider?"

"He should be a Yale man," I volunteered.

"Like me," Seymour said, humbly.

"Stone, sounds like you're the perfect choice. I order you and laddie to fly out to L. A. on the company jet this afternoon. You have a blank check to get Operation Torch up and running before the fall elections. It's damn the torpedoes, full speed ahead!"

       *   *   *   *

Just three hours later, Seymour and I were flying at fifty-two-thousand feet over Chicago, the contrail of our USS-TV Gulfstream V Bizjet streaking west toward L.A. at almost the speed of sound.

"I feel terrible," I confessed to Seymour.

"You're beautiful, booby baby," Seymour said, sounding exactly like Harmon P. Harper. "Here we are, winging our way to glamorous Hollywood with a blank check to complete Operation Torch before the fall elections and you feel terrible. I don't get it. What's bugging you now?"

"I didn't have time to say goodbye to Melanie."

"Take my advice, booby baby. Forget her, at least for the time being. You'll find lots of fantastic chicks in Hollywood—beautiful, sexy ones—maybe even a movie starlet. Wouldn't that be socko?"

"I'll always be true to Melanie."

Seymour shrugged, put on a pair of Maui Jim wrap-around sunglasses, reclined his leather executive chair, and began to sing:

"Hooray for Hollywood,
"That screwy, ballyhooey Hollywood!"

THE MIDDLE—CALIFORNIA

CHAPTER 18

▼

Three weeks later, on a balmy, light smoggy Saturday just before noon, Seymour and I were having brunch—breakfast for him, lunch for me—on the outdoor patio by the pool of Le Coq D'or, a storied apartment-hotel modeled after a Loire Valley chateau tucked into the Hollywood Hills just north of Sunset Boulevard. Its luxury apartments and free-standing French-style bungalows offer celebrities and moguls a private sanctuary on its secluded, rambling grounds.

Seymour said, "Andy, this town is the greatest. You should've seen the talent I had last night. She was"—he stopped forking his pink grapefruit and tried to describe her figure with his hands— "well, you had to see her. After dinner we went to her place for a drink. She changed into something more comfortable—a filmy little thing with a zipper down the front. Can you imagine? A filmy little thing with a zipper—"

"Listen to that," I said, not really listening to him.

"What?"

"A mourning dove. You can tell by the mournful coo."

"Oh, sure, Andy," Seymour said, sipping his Bloody Mary. "A mourning dove. Now this talent—"

"Last night I heard a nighthawk. They're related to the whippoorwill, you know. Only they have a more nasal call, sort of a *pent, peent*—"

"The talent I had last night had a fantastic mating call. Sort of a *pant, pant*!"

"Don't think I've ever heard so many different kinds of birds. Not even in Michigan in the spring."

"Amazing," Seymour said, wiping the lenses of his Maui Jim's.

"Hollywood's for the birds. Listen. Did you hear that? A Phainopepla. You don't hear its call very often. Like, Phainopepla nitens are totally shy birds."

"Andy, you're the shy bird."

"Me?"

"Hasn't it occurred to you that there's more to Hollywood than mourning doves and phaino-whatevers?"

"The flora's quite interesting, too. Like, last night when I walked down to a Seven-Eleven on Sunset for a Coke, I counted forty-seven different types of plant life in just one block. And you should smell the night blooming jasmine. It was like—"

"I was thinking more along the lines of fauna."

"Fauna?"

"Chicks."

"Oh, I could never allow myself to think about girls. I'm—"

"Saving yourself for Melanie. I know, Andy, but she's almost two thousand miles away. Forget her."

"I can't. I think of her all the time."

"And look at what it's doing to your work. Do you realize we've been out here over three weeks, and you're not any further along with your Video Ion Refractor than you were the day we left Southfield?"

"I wouldn't say that."

"No? What would you say?"

"Like, we've made some progress. Don't forget, we built a prototype."

"Oh, sure. Some prototype. How retro can you get? It has ninety-two vacuum tubes, weighs over a hundred pounds, is bigger than a bread box, and it cost thirty-six thousand dollars. And you call that progress? Andy, this thing has got to be no bigger than a polka dot, and it's budgeted for twenty five cents a unit—installed."

"I admit we still have miniaturization and cost problems to solve. But at least, we proved the principle of the thing."

"I don't know how much longer I can stall the Admiral and Harm. They're businessmen, Andy. They expect results. And you know perfectly well they want your Video Ion Refractor perfected before the fall elections. So, for God's sake, stop mooning about Melanie and get down to work."

"I'm trying."

"Try harder."

"If only Melanie were here."

"How many times do I have to tell you—you can't let anyone, not even Melanie know that we're out here working on this. It's top secret, Andy, remember? If one word of Operation Torch leaks out, Hollywood will be swarming with Gypsies. Want them marching up and down the Strip protesting you?"

"No way!"

"Then forget Melanie."

"I can't.

"Know what you need, Andy? You need someone to make you forget, that's what you need. Someone so beautiful, intelligent, winsome, fetching, graceful, and charming you'll stop thinking about Melanie and get down to work."

"You mean a girl?"

"Not just an ordinary chick, Andy. A *talent*."

"Talent?"

"Sure, Hollywood's loaded with talents."

"What do they do?"

"Commercials, mostly. Sometimes they get a guest appearance on a network show. They're awesome, Andy. Beautiful! And once a talent finds out you are a TV executive, they'll do anything for you. Anything. Take the chick I had last night, Dawn Day. Now there's a talent that is a talent. A real rising star."

"Like the morning Sun?"

"Right! Really hot. And she has lots of talent friends. I'll ask her to get you a hot date."

"She'd have to be wholesome."

"Wholesome?" He knitted his brow in concentration. "Okay, Andy. We'll get you a chick who does soap commercials."

"What kind of soap?"

"You name it—laundry detergents, household cleaners, high sudsers, low sudsers, dishwashing liquids, shampoos, facial or bath soaps—"

"I'd be embarrassed to go out with a talent who does bath soap commercials. Like, they don't wear any clothes, do they?"

"Know what your trouble is, Andy? You're afraid of chicks. Well, booby baby, when you're afraid of something, you've got to face it. Stand up to it. Take the old bull by the horns. Look sex straight in the eye." He took out his iPhone. "And I'm going to help you do it. I'll get you a date with a talent that does the sexiest bath soap commercials on the air."

"She's got to be wholesome, too."

"What's wholesome, Andy? Clean. So what could be cleaner than a talent who spends every working hour immersed in water?" He thumbed a number into his iPhone.

"But what would Melanie say?"

He held up a hand to silence me and cooed into his iPhone, "Guess who, baby? Right,"—he winked at me— "how's the world's most beautiful bod this morning? All rested up? Wonderful! Afraid you might've thrown your hip out last night. You're so wild, baby—the wildest." He laughed. "Well, you are, baby. You know you are. What about tonight, baby? Ready for another wild time with your tall, handsome, TV executive?" He covered his iPhone with his hand, giving me a sly smile. "She says I really know my vices." He went back to her. "Well, what's an executive for, baby? We have to be experts on everything. It's a management rule."

"I never heard of that rule," I told him.

He covered the iPhone again. "I'm just making small talk, Andy. Chicks eat it up." He winked at me and went back to her. "Is someone with me? You must be psychic. No, I'm not kidding. A person has to be psychic to know something like that." He shook his head "Nooo, it's not another woman. Didn't I tell you I am a one girl guy?" He winked at me again. "As a matter of fact, baby, it's an old friend—a real electronic genius. Andy Cohan. You must have heard me mention Andy. Everyone says he's going to be president of USS-TV someday. He's that brilliant." This time he didn't cover his iPhone when he spoke to me. "She says she wants to meet you."

"I don't know—"

"He wants to meet you, too. Isn't that wild, baby?" Pause. "Oh, wow. You read my mind. You are psychic. I was sure you could get Andy a date. He's crazy about talent, especially ones who do soap commercials." Pause. "You've got a friend who does them? Jordan Lee? Sounds like a fun chick, but is she—well, wholesome, if you know what I mean? She is? Terrific! Andy's really into clean, wholesome, sexy chicks."

"I never said sexy," I told him

He cupped his hand over his iPhone again. "What did I just tell you? The only way you can conquer your fear of sex is to stand up and face it. Take it from me, Andy. When it comes to chicks, the only thing you have to fear is fear itself."

"Yeah, right. I'll try to remember."

"Jordan sounds cool," he told Dawn. "In a clean, wholesome way, you know."

I could hear her laughing over Seymour's iPhone clear across the table from him. "What's so funny?"

"I'm a master of small talk," he reminded me. "Any ideas for tonight?" he asked her. "I'm in the mood for something really different." He listened for a moment, and then his face lit up. "Really—a rally! In the hills? Awesome! Oh, baby, of course we'll go. We're really into rallies. See you at eight." He closed his iPhone, grinning across the table at me. "We're in, Andy. Really in. She's taking us to a rally in the hills tonight."

"A what?"

"Rally. It's like a—well, you'll find out. But take my word for it, Andy. It'll be awesome. We're really in. Here we've only been in Hollywood three weeks, and we've been invited to a rally. In the hills! And you've got a date with a talent! How lucky can you get? I'll make a deal with you, Andy. If you don't forget Melanie tonight, I'll personally fly back to Detroit and bring her out to L.A."

"You're a true friend," I told him.

CHAPTER 19

▼

"You're cute," Jordan Lee told me as we sat in the back seat of Seymour's rented Mercedes convertible as it wound its way up the hairpin curves of Laurel Canyon.

"You, too," I told her. "Are you Chinese?"

"Oh, my gosh! No way. I'm an all American girl—born in San Francisco. So were my parents and grandparents and great-grandparents."

"Awesome."

"My friend Dawn says you're going to be president of the USS-TV someday," she said, sliding across the seat to me as Seymour wheeled around a particularly sharp curve.

"Right."

"You must be brilliant."

"I'm a genius."

"I just love geniuses," she whispered, snuggling closer. "They're so—well, so intelligent. Don't you agree?"

"Totally." I put my arm around her to keep her from sliding back across the seat. Like, I didn't want her to get hurt.

"And strong." She rested her head on my shoulder.

I could smell her silky black hair, which she wore perfectly straight, flowing down almost to her waist. It had a fragrance as sweet as night blooming jasmine. "Gee, you smell good," I told her.

"I did a Pantene commercial today."

For a moment we rolled along in silence while I tried to think up some clever small talk to amuse her. Remembering how my mom always told me to compliment a woman on her clothes, I finally said, "I like your suit."

"It's not a suit, silly. They're harlequin pajamas."

"Pajamas?" I suppose if I had followed women's fashions a little more closely, I would know that. The outfit was a one-piece nylon affair, brightly colored, in bold patterns of yellow, magenta, and red, with a voluminous bodice, full sleeves drawn tightly at the wrists, and harem-like pantaloons. The whole thing was so sheer you could see right through it. "Isn't that a little daring? I mean, like wearing pajamas to a rally?"

"Everyone wears pajamas to our rallies."

"They do?"

"Of course. Pajamas are the symbols of our party."

"Party?"

"The Freedom Party. We believe the world's problems could be solved if everyone was free to do what they want to do. 'Stop War, Party More'—that's one of our slogans."

"Oh, a political party. Like, the Love Party back in the Sixties and Seventies. 'Make Love Not War,' was their battle cry. How often does your Party party?"

"Every week. Except when it rains."

"Does everyone wear pajamas you can see right through?"

"The Party has nothing to hide."

"But I can see your skin!"

"You just think you can, silly," she said. "I'm wearing a body stocking under my pajamas. See?" She put my hand upon her waist. "Feel it. It's like a nylon stocking, only it covers my whole body."

"I see," I said, feeling the body stocking.

You have no idea how relieved I was, and not just because she was wearing a body stocking. Like, when Seymour told me we were going to a rally, and that the rally would be wild—well, to tell you the truth, I had no idea what I might be getting into. I suspected we might be going to one of those wild Hollywood parties you hear about, the kind where everyone gets high on pot and Ecstasy and goes skinny dipping in the pool. But once I discovered we were going to a political rally, I began to relax. Politics have always fascinated me. So, there I was, on my way to what I was sure would be a totally interesting and educational evening, seated next to a beautiful girl—a wholesome, clean talent—with the heady smell of Pantene and night blooming jasmine in my nostrils, actually enjoying myself for the first time since I left Detroit.

"What's a nice girl like you doing commercials?"

She sat up, looking hurt. "What's so bad about making commercials?"

"Well, you know. Sitting in the bathtub, while a film crew shoots you in high definition."

"I wear a body stocking."

"Right. I forgot."

After a moment she asked, "Think I'm pretty?"

"Yo!"

"How pretty?"

"Very."

"Beautiful?"

"Totally."

She put one of my hands to her cheek. "Feel my skin. How does it feel?"

"Soft."

She moved her face closer to mine, and whispered, "See any wrinkles?"

I studied her face very closely. "Just a few tiny ones around the eyes."

"Oh, no!" She took out a bottle of moisturizing lotion and started dabbing it around her eyes. "Whatever happens tonight, please don't make me laugh."

"You don't want to be happy?"

"I love being happy."

"Then why don't you want to laugh?"

She put the bottle of lotion back in her purse and said, "Because I laugh with my eyes."

"My mom used to laugh with her eyes."

"Did it give her wrinkles?"

I nodded, remembering the way my mom looked. "She had awesome laugh wrinkles."

"Laugh wrinkles are the worst thing that can happen to a talent."

"They are?"

"Did you ever see a talent with laugh wrinkles in a commercial?"

"I can't remember seeing a girl with any kind of wrinkles doing commercials."

"See? Then please don't let me laugh again tonight. I don't want to go back to working in a lab."

"Lab?"

"Research lab. I used to be an electronics engineer."

I could hardly believe my ears. "An electronics engineer?"

"What's so unusual about that? Some girls have brains, you know. I have a Master of Science degree from Cal Tech."

"Cal Tech, really?"

"I won a scholarship to the school of my choice in the Miss America Pageant."

"You were a contestant in the Miss America Pageant?"

"Miss California, second runner-up. It was the first time a runner-up asked to go to Cal Tech."

"You must be brilliant."

"I'm not sure if I'm a genius like you, but I do have a brain."

"We sure have a lot in common."

"We do."

We rode along in silence for a moment, with the wind whistling in our ears, before I came up with some more small talk. "What a waste," I finally said.

"Waste?"

"I can't imagine someone with, like, all your brains wasting her time doing commercials."

She began to giggle. "Oh, please, don't make me laugh."

"Sorry. I didn't mean it to be funny."

"But it was. Terribly funny. You see, I met this agent who told me I was wasting my time working in a lab." She rested her head on the back of the seat, looking up at the stars glowing thorough the smog. "Oh, my gosh! He sure was good looking—in a nice way, you know. He took me out to dinner almost every night for a month. Of course, I fell in love with him. I think all the girls in Hollywood fall madly in love with their agents. Anyway, the next thing I knew I was doing commercials. Now I can't afford to stop. I make too much money."

"Who needs money?"

"I do. Lots of it. I have to pay my agent for one thing. He has a wife and three kids to support, you know. And I just can't let him down. Oh, my gosh! He's such a marvelous guy. Really he is."

"Yeah, right."

"And, of course, I need money for clothes. You have no idea how many clothes a talent has to have, really expensive ones. Would you believe these pajamas cost over five hundred dollars?"

"They look like a million on you."

"Then there's the Party. I give ten percent of my residuals every year to the Party, before taxes, of course. It's deductible!"

"You must really believe in the Party."

"The Party is the hope of the world. You just wait and see. We're going to take the government away from the politicians and give it back to the people. Then there'll be no more wars and everyone will party and make love all the time. Think how beautiful the world would be then."

"It must make you feel good, working for a better world."

"I believe a person has to think about the future. I mean, why kid myself? I can't go on in this business forever, you know. Why, I'll be twenty-five in September. Can you imagine—twenty-five! A quarter of a century old!" She put a hand to her cheek. "Oh, my gosh! I think I just felt a new wrinkle. Do you ever feel wrinkles popping out on your face?"

"Not that I remember."

"You don't know how lucky you are. Really, it's terrible! I feel new wrinkles popping out on my face all the time." She took a compact out of her purse and studied her face. "I know there must be a new one there somewhere."

I looked at her closely. "I don't see a single new wrinkle."

"But someday I'll be thirty and old and wrinkled. Then I'll have to give up doing commercials."

"You can always go back to electronics."

"No way. I could never work in a lab again. Engineering is such a chauvinistic profession."

"Like, working in Hollywood isn't?"

"It's different. At least the guys here appreciate talent when they see it. At Cal Tech they were always putting me and my ideas down."

"Like?"

"One of my profs challenged my class to come up with a way to transmit electricity without wires. All the other students thought it was an impossible assignment. But I mulled it over in my mind for a couple a days and came up with a solution."

"I think I saw on the Internet that an MIT team claimed they could do that a couple of years ago."

"Uh huh, the MIT team claimed they could recharge cell phones and lap tops without wires. Big deal. My method could power just about anything that runs on electricity—cars, planes, ships, whatever."

"Really? How?"

"You'll laugh at me, just like my prof and the rest of the class."

"No way."

"It's really simple. I'd broadcast a musical note—say like a note of the so-called American Standard pitch, which takes A in the fourth piano octave to have a frequency of 440 Hertz—and use banks of receiver electronic tuning forks to amplify it and generate electrical energy on site anywhere."

I didn't have any idea what she was talking about, so I shrugged and said, "I'm not, like, really following you."

"Guys never do. So forget I ever said it."

"Don't be pissed."

"I'm not. Let's just say I'd rather do commercials than work in electronics, knowing the circuitry and designs I create could end up as part of the guidance system for an atomic warhead or something terrible and leave it at that. Okay? When I give up commercials I'm going to devote my life to the Party—working full-time to transmit freedom and love to the world!" As she contemplated that happy thought, her lips began to part.

"Don't smile!" I warned.

"Oh, my gosh! Thanks," she said, gratefully.

Seymour turned the Mercedes off Laurel Canyon onto a steep gravel drive.

"We're almost there," Dawn announced over her shoulder to us. "Just time to touch up your makeup, Jordan. Say, how are you two getting along back there?"

"Marvelously," Jordan said, taking one last look at herself in her compact. "We're very compatible."

"We discovered we have a great deal in common," I confessed.

"That is *marvelous!*" Dawn said with a happy laugh.

Dawn is so fortunate," Jordan whispered into my ear. "She doesn't laugh with her eyes."

CHAPTER 20

▼

Following Dawn Day's instructions, Seymour made a right turn onto a gravel road just below Mulholland Drive and turned off the lights and ignition, letting the Mercedes coast to a stop in front of the ghostly ruins of a burned out Georgian mansion.

"This is kind of a lonely place to hold a political rally," I told Jordan as we climbed out of the back seat.

"We have to be very careful," she said.

"Why?"

"Police."

"Police? It's not illegal to park here or anything like that, is it?"

"Of course not. But they're part of the military/industrial complex, you know. They keep trying to shut down our rallies, that's all."

"What have they got against Freedom Party parties?"

"The establishment has been afraid of People Power since way back in the Sixties," Dawn told us as we followed her and Seymour down a path through the bushes.

"Well, I'm not, baby," Seymour said.

"Shh!" Dawn hushed him. "We have to listen for a contact."

"Contact?" I said.

Jordan put one of her soft fingers to my lips. "We have to be very careful," she whispered.

Dawn cupped her hands around her mouth and cooed like a mourning dove, then whispered, "Shh. Listen."

It was like a spy movie. We all stood absolutely still next to a big rock in the moonlight, listening, and then I heard a mournful coo coo return from the lower branches of a rather shaggy cedar tree a few yards beyond the rock.

"Mourning dove," I whispered in Jordan's ear.

"That's our contact," she whispered back.

By the light of the full moon, I saw the lower branches of the cedar part, and a bearded face peered out at us, looking pale and ghostly.

"What's a four letter word for fornication, baby?" he whispered.

"Love," Dawn returned.

"You got the word, baby," the bearded face returned. A tall, gangly young man swung down from the lower branches of the cedar clad only in black silk pajama bottoms and L.A. Gear running shoes. Parting the branches for the ladies, he held out his hand to Seymour and said, "I'll nest the Mercedes for you, brother. The Party party's round the pool outback."

"You do a very good imitation of a mourning dove," I told him and turned to Dawn. "You don't coo quite as well as he does," I had to tell her. "Try again, a little more mournful, like this: coo coo."

"Hey baby, you know we don't allow nut cases in at Party parties," he told Dawn. "It could ruin the Party image."

Seymour clapped me on the back. "Coo coo! Isn't that awesome girls! Andy, you've got such a great sense of humor."

"He's going to be president of USS-TV," Jordan told the contact.

"Coo coo! Ha, ha! You got a great comic style, brother. Here—" he handed me a large plastic shopping bag. "Put these on."

I opened the bag. "Pajamas?"

"Just the bottoms, brother," he said, handing Seymour a bag. "No one gets in unless they're properly dressed."

I took my pajama bottoms out of the bag. "They're made of paper."

"Isn't it marvelous," Jordan said. "The Party thinks of everything."

Seymour and I went behind the cedar tree and changed into our paper pajama bottoms.

"Hope they don't tear easily," I said.

"Who cares, booby baby? As long as they get us in."

We put our clothes in the plastic bag and asked the contact to put them in the back of the Mercedes.

"Sure thing," he said. He held out his hand to Seymour. "Keys, brother."

Seymour hesitated for a moment. "Be careful with it. It's a Mercedes, you know."

"Not to worry," Dawn said. "All our attendants are bonded."

The contact slid behind the wheel, started the engine, slipped it into reverse, and stepped on the gas, raising a cloud of dusty gravel as it sped backward toward a line of oleander bushes. There was a muffled crashing sound as the contact found a nesting place for the Mercedes.

"My car!" Seymour gasped.

"Don't worry, honey," Dawn said. "As I said, our parking attendants are bonded."

"And it's only a Budget car," I reminded Seymour.

Seymour shrugged, and Jordan and I followed Dawn and him as they picked their way across the charred rubble of the burned out ruins of the Georgian mansion.

"Look. A male holly bush," I told Jordan, pointing out a small shrub growing out of the rubble.

"How do you know it's a male?"

"The leaves aren't prickly."

"Ouch! Seymour cried out, stumbling into another bush.

"Only the females have prickly leaves," I told Jordan.

We came to a high brick wall covered with tangled vines and followed the path next to it for a hundred feet or so until we came to a huge oak gate with rusty iron hinges. Dawn knocked softly on the gate.

A peep hole in the gate opened, and a low whisper asked, "What's an eleven letter word for love?"

"Fornication," Dawn whispered back.

"You got the word, baby!" came the reply from the peep hole.

The gate creaked open and down below I saw an Olympic swimming pool surrounded by white marble Grecian columns. The lighted pool sparkled in the gloom of the night like a blue Adriatic lagoon. The gatekeeper, like our first contact, was attired in black silk pajama bottoms, but unlike the attendant, he was clean-shaven with a shaggy mane of red hair so full of snarls it looked as if his head was full of snakes. "Twenty-five dollars a head," he said, stretching out his hand.

"Pay him," Seymour told me.

"A hundred dollars?"

"It all goes to the Party," Dawn told me.

I took five twenties from my money belt and handed them to the gatekeeper. He thrust a small wood berry box into Seymour's hands, saying, "Peace, brother."

"What's in the box?" I asked.

"Mushrooms!" Seymour said. "Oh, wow! How retro. Mom and Dad told me all about the magic mushrooms. Oh, baby, this is going to be a real Party party!"

"Why mushrooms?" I asked Jordan as we followed Seymour and Dawn down a long stone stairway to the pool.

"The Party believes mushrooms and peyote are the fruits of love," she told me.

"And they're a natural food," Dawn told me over her shoulder. "Way more natural than Ecstasy or Meth. And like peyote, they're not illegal. They're used in some religious ceremonies, so the Feds never outlawed them."

"Try one." Seymour offered me the box.

"Thanks but no thanks. My mom always warned me not to eat fresh mushrooms. You never can tell when you're going to get a bad one."

Seymour shrugged and turned to Dawn. "Want one, baby?"

"Not now, honey. I'll wait until refreshment hour."

"Anyone mind if I have one?" Seymour asked.

"Better wait until we find a place to lie down," Dawn warned.

We reached the overgrown lawn surrounding the pool and had to walk gingerly through it to avoid stepping on the couples reclining on the grass. Making a quick mental calculation, I estimated there were at least three hundred lying on the ground around the pool. Yet, it was unnaturally quiet.

"It's kind of spooky. Like, everyone's dead or something," I told Jordan as Dawn and Seymour finally found a place where we could lie down on the grass near the deep end of the pool.

"It's the meditation hour. You know, when you concentrate every fiber of your being on love."

"Oh, sort of like Qigong," I said.

"In a sexy sort of way," she said.

I sat on the grass next to her and started to fold my legs into the yoga squat.

She laughed. "Don't squat, silly." She patted the long grass. "Lie down. Here, next to me, so we can concentrate together."

"Can I try one now?" Seymour whispered. He was lying on the grass next to Dawn with the box of mushrooms on his stomach.

"Start with a small one first, honey," Dawn warned. "They're very potent."

"Don't worry, baby," he said, taking a large one from the box. "I went to Yale."

"This is kind of relaxing," I told Jordan, stretching out on my back next to her.

"Shh! I'm concentrating every fiber of my being on love."

"Don't feel a thing, baby," I heard Seymour tell Dawn as he finished the mushroom. "Sure these are the real thing?"

"Give it a few minutes, honey," she said.

"Are you concentrating on love?" Jordan asked me.

"No, I was listening to Seymour and Dawn."

"Concentrate. Only on us."

I tried to concentrate every fiber of my being on love for a while. But all I could think of was what Melanie would think if she knew I was lying on the grass in black paper pajama bottoms next to a beautiful talent like Jordan clad only in harlequin pajamas and a body stocking.

"Oh, boy, oh, boy, oh, boy!" Seymour's gasps interrupted my concentration.

I looked over and saw he was thrashing about on the grass clutching the box on his stomach with both hands.

"Think he got a bad mushroom?" I asked Dawn, who was lying on her side next to him, stroking his forehead.

"Oh, no," she answered. "He got a very good one. He's already on his way."

"To where?" I asked.

"He's on a trip, silly," Jordan said.

"But he's right there."

"Only his body. Spiritually, he's really gone."

"Hope he gets back before the rally starts. Like, he wouldn't want to miss the rally. Not the way he's been looking forward to it."

Seymour suddenly raised himself up on his elbows. "Oh, boy, oh, boy, oh, boy!" he shouted. "It's beautiful! Beautiful!"

"You know it," a man a few couples away, yelled.

"He's got the word, brother!" A woman shouted from across the pool.

"He's got the word! He's got the word!" everyone began to chant at once.

"Freedom! I'm free! I'm free!" Seymour cried out, leaping to his feet.

"Freedom. We're free. We're free!" everyone but me joined in.

"I'm free to love this whole, rotten, stinking world!" Seymour began dancing, a sort of weird, jerking ballet across the grass, leaping over row after row of reclining bodies.

"You got the word, brother! You're free! Free to love the whole, rotten, stinking world!" the crowd chanted.

Seymour danced up to one of the Grecian columns, threw his arms around it, and began kissing its flutes. "I love you, Grecian column!" Dancing away, he stretched out his arms and turned his face up toward the smoggy heavens. "I love you, sky!" He twirled around several times and dropped to his knees and kissed the grass. "I love you, grass! He rose to his feet again, and danced over to a holly bush. "I love you, bush! Ow!"

"Another female," I whispered to Jordan. "This is, like, totally weird. Seymour never showed any interest in nature before."

"Isn't it fabulous?" she said. "He's free at last to love nature."

"The Party needs more real believers like Seymour," Dawn said.

"I love you, water!" Seymour shouted, cannon balling into the pool, creating a mini-tsunami.

CHAPTER 21

▼

"Seymour can't swim," I cried out, struggling to my feet to save my friend.

"Don't worry, silly," Jordan said. She grabbed my arm and pulled me back down to her. "The Party takes care of its own."

I soon saw she was right. Two husky scuba divers wearing black silk pajama bottoms quickly pulled Seymour from the pool.

"I love you! I love you!" He shouted at them as they half-dragged, half-carried him back to where we were sitting, the crowd applauding and whistling.

"We love you, too, brother," one of the scuba divers told Seymour, fending off his kisses. "But no more free-style swimming. The rally's about to begin."

They laid him down on the grass next to Dawn, and she lovingly put her arms around him as he lay there, shivering in his dripping paper pajama bottoms. Another attendant brought them a blanket and Dawn wrapped herself and Seymour in it.

"Free at last! Free at last!" he whimpered softly.

"Shh," Dawn whispered softly. "Now, lie still. The rally's starting."

The lights dimmed and everyone around the pool began to cheer and clap, "Freedom! Freedom! Freedom!" they chanted.

"It's so fabulous!" Jordan said.

"The effect is very dramatic," I had to admit.

"Not the lighting, silly," she said. "Dawn and Seymour. They've got their love to keep them warm."

"And a blanket, too," I pointed out.

The pool lights kept dimming until they went out completely, and a hushed silence fell over the gathering.

"Hurry, honey!" Dawn whispered, urgently.

"I'm free … zing!" Seymour moaned.

"I love it! I love it!" Dawn cried.

A lone spotlight atop one of the Grecian columns came on, its beam shining down on the diving board, where a tall figure wearing a long, flowing white silk robe and Birkenstock sandals stood, his thin arms raised to the heavens, his hands stretched out, palms up.

"Brethren!" his rich bass voice greeted the crowd, breaking the hushed silence.

"Oh, Brother!" the crowd shouted exuberantly.

"Is that, him? I mean, is he?" I whispered to Jordan.

"Yes, it's him. Brother Freeman," she whispered. "The Party's beloved leader."

"Freedom!" Brother Freeman cried out, curling his long bony fingers into fists.

"Freedom! Freedom! Freedom!" The crowd chanted as one.

I couldn't believe my eyes and ears. "I remember his show, *Oh, Brother!* It was, like, the greatest comedy hour on late night TV. Freeman used to poke fun at all the politicians. When I was in high school, all the kids loved him."

"Right," Jordan said. "It was absolutely fabulous, the way he painted the White House black. I mean, verbally, you know, exposing the administration's lies and stupidity, and how they were taking away all of our freedoms."

"Yeah, right. So what happened to him?"

"The White House and all the politicians hated him. When the President called him a traitor and a terrorist and gay lover, both parties supported the Commander in Chief."

"I guess politicians don't have a sense of humor," I said.

"You know it. They sicced the FBI, CIA, and Homeland Security on him."

"Oh, wow!"

"But it was the IRS that did him in. They took away everything he had. His house, his car, all his stocks and bank accounts. HBO dropped his show. Even his wife and kids left him. It was absolutely tragic. And he was totally right about everything. The politicians were screwing everyone. So now Brother Freemen's out to get them. He wants to take the government away from the politicians and military industrial complex and give it back to the people!"

"Freedom is the hope of the world!" Brother Freeman shouted.

"Freedom is the hope of the world!" I shouted back with the crowd.

Brother Freeman began his speech. "Welcome brothers and sisters. We have given birth to a great new political party—the Freedom Party. The only American political party with its foundation rooted in the Ten Commandments of Freedom! Freedom from fear! Freedom of religion! Freedom of choice! Freedom of the press! Freedom to be different! Freedom to love! Freedom from war! Freedom from want! Freedom from politicians! Freedom from demagogy!

"You know it, Brother!" someone in the crowd shouted.

"We cannot rest until Americans are totally free! We cannot rest until the world totally is free!" Brother Freeman shouted. "A political party can survive only so long as it moves ahead. So tonight, I ask you to join me in a great crusade. A freedom crusade! The time has come for action! The time has come to spread the word!"

"Spread the word, sisters," all the males in the audience shouted.

"Spread the word, brothers," all the females screamed.

"God created us to be free!" Brother Freeman cried, raising his arms to the heavens.

"God created us to be free!" The crowd shouted back.

Jordan leaned over and whispered in my ear. "Oh, my gosh! Isn't he fabulous?"

"Totally," I had to agree.

"The Good Book tells us to love thy neighbor," Brother Freeman went on, lowering his magnificent voice to a pious whisper. "Isn't that what the Good Book says—love thy neighbor?"

"You know it, Brother!" The crowd answered.

"Love thy neighbor!" Seymour shouted, his head emerging from under the blanket.

Brother Freeman continued. "Now, I ask you, brethren, how many—how many of you truly love your neighbor? Come on now. Let's have a show of hands. How many?" He shaded his deep-set eyes from the glare of the spotlight with his hand and peered over the crowd. "Just as I thought. I don't see many hands out there. And I'm ashamed of you, brethren. Deeply ashamed. How can we ever hope to bring the gospel of love and freedom to the world if we don't start at home? So, if you believe in the Good Book, do as it says. Love thy neighbor. Be the first one on your block to start a good neighbor key club. Swap your door keys with all your neighbors. Let them know they can feel free to come to your home or apartment and make love to you at any time they have the urge."

The audience seemed too shocked to react.

"Just kidding," he said. "You know how I love to kid the establishment."

The crowd laughed.

"And they're great kidders, too. They say I'm just an old hippie crackpot who's high on grass and free love. Okay. I admit it. I'm high on grass—the grass roots of America—our hope for the future. And as for free love, join with me in singing the Party's theme song...."

Brother Freeman began to strum an electric guitar and the audience sang the theme song with him:

> The moon belongs to ev'ryone
> The best things in life are free
> The stars belong to ev'ryone
> They gleam there for you and me
>
> The flowers in spring
> The robins that sing
> The sunbeams that shine
> They're yours, they're mine
>
> And love can come to ev'ryone
> The best things in life are free

As the last guitar chord faded out, Brother Freemen asked, "So what's so wrong about free love? Peace and love were the theme of my Flower Child generation. What's the theme of yours?"

"Freedom! Freedom! Freedom!" the crowd began to chant again.

"Free the world for freedom!" Seymour shouted from under the blanket.

"Seriously," Brother Freedom went on, "it is time to spread the word. Reach out to your neighbors and form a neighborhood caucus. Let your neighbors know what the Freedom Party stands for—the Ten Commandments of Freedom—so they in turn can pass the word along to their friends and neighbors. It's in little ways like this that we'll get our great Freedom Crusade rolling. It's in little ways like this that we'll triumph over the power structure and the military industrial complex. If you do, the Freedom Party shall grow and prosper and in the end—we'll win! We'll take the government away from the politicians and give it back to the people!" He held up one of his bony hands. "Peace!"

The audience roared its approval. The spotlight went out and Brother Freeman disappeared in a cloud of smoke from the great finale of exploding fireworks.

"Wasn't he just marvelous?" Dawn asked when the finale was over.

"Awesome," I said.

"Have a mushroom," Seymour said, offering us the box.

"No way," I said.

"Go ahead," Dawn said, taking a small one from the box. "It's the refreshment hour."

"We don't need them," Jordan said. "We've got our love of freedom to keep us warm."

"Besides, she's a Baptist," I said.

Seymour shrugged. "Have it your way." He picked the largest, juiciest mushroom in the box and ate it. Then he took Dawn by the hand and the two of them sort of drifted off on the balls on their feet, heading toward the oleander bushes where it seems most of the party members had gone after the speech to get together in small groups of twos to caucus or something.

"Oh, my gosh! We're all alone," Jordan said, squeezing my hand.

"I know," I said, lying on my back on the grass, trying to pick Polaris out of the smog.

"Do me a big favor?"

"What?"

"Well, this darn body stocking is very uncomfortable. It's so tight, you know. Would you unzip it for me?"

Still searching the heavens for Polaris, I reached over and felt for the zipper at the back of her neck. "What happened to your pajamas?"

"Well, they did cost five hundred dollars, you know. And I didn't want them to get grass stained."

My heart skipped a few beats. "So?"

"I took them off, silly." She rolled over on top of me and I felt her round, soft, warm, bare bosoms pressing against my bare chest.

"There's Polaris," I gulped.

She reached down and tore my paper pajama bottoms off. "Isn't it fabulous that we have so much in common?"

"Yeah, right."

Seymour had described her perfectly at brunch that morning. Jordan was so delicate, so intelligent, so winsome, so fetching, so graceful, so charming, and so warm, I forgot all about Melanie. At least I did for the moment.

CHAPTER 22

▼

"Andy, I'm a changed man," Seymour happily told me as we sat by the Le Coq D'or pool having brunch the next forenoon.

"Me, too," I said, picking at my grapefruit with a spoon, not feeling at all like eating.

"I really saw the light last night."

"Wish it'd been light where I was."

"Suddenly, my life has meaning. Believe me, Andy, it's a wonderful feeling— suddenly discovering your life has meaning."

"I feel, like, terrible."

"I owe it all to the Freedom Party. The Party has finally given me direction— something to work for."

"Wish I were, like, dead."

"You may not believe this, Andy. Actually, I find it rather unbelievable myself, but last night I discovered I'm not really the person everyone thinks I am."

"Me too."

"I mean, take you, Andy. You probably think I'm suave and sophisticated—a cosmopolitan man of the world. Right? Actually, I can't blame you. Everyone thinks of me that way. Guess it's because I went to Yale or something. But they're all wrong. Let me tell you, Andy, that blasé worldly air of mine is just superficial. Superficial polish. Not the real me. Know what I really am? A square. A senti- mental, patriotic square. How do you like that? Me—Seymour Stone—a square."

"Everyone used to think I was square."

"You should have taken one of those mushrooms last night, Andy. You might have discovered the real you."

"I didn't need a mushroom. I discovered the real Andy Cohan last night anyway. And I hate what I found."

"Not a pretty picture?"

"Deep down I'm a monster—a lecherous monster."

"Well, that's life. Guess you're never what you think you are."

"You never said truer words."

"Now, take me. No one could have been more surprised than I was when I ate that first mushroomed and suddenly discovered how much I really loved nature. I never knew how much I appreciated all the wonderful things in the world around me. Listen. Hear that?"

"What?

"A mourning dove." Seymour said.

"I didn't hear it," I told him.

"Too bad. You don't know what you're missing."

"I used to hear them—before I discovered the real me."

"Life will never be the same for us, Andy. Know what I saw last night, right after I ate that second mushroom? A total revelation! Just as I bit into it, and all these rockets went off, it was so beautiful—the way the bombs burst in the air—but they weren't the kinds of bombs that hurt you, they burst into flowers, and the falling petals formed an American flag with the words *FREEDOM* spelled across it. Then I heard this stirring music—flutes and drums playing 'Yankee Doodle' and the 'Star-Spangled Banner' and 'God Bless America and America the Beautiful!'"

"All at once?"

"And in perfect harmony. It was totally unreal. I can describe it in a word—beautiful! Right then and there, I decided to dedicate my life to the Freedom Party."

"You're going into politics?"

"Not politics. I'm into freedom now."

"Like, you're going to leave USS-TV?"

"Not right away, of course. We have a moral obligation to see Operation Torch through. But as soon as you perfect your Video Ion Refractor, Andy, I'm getting out. I'm going to spend the rest of my life working for a better world. I want to help take the government away from the politicians and give it back to the people."

"A noble ambition," I said. "Makes mine look, like, small and petty by comparison."

"I'm sure you'll be very happy when you're president of USS-TV," Seymour said, sympathetically. "Personally, I'd rather be President of these beautiful United States of ours."

"I don't think I want to be president of USS-TV anymore," I said, dejectedly.

"Of course you do, Andy."

"No, like, I'm sure I don't."

"But what about Melanie?"

"She's just a delusion. It was that lecherous monster lurking inside me that was driving my ambition to have her. I only wanted to become president of USS-TV to gain control over her body."

"That's totally sick, Andy."

"Cheetah recognized the really, real me all along."

Seymour downed his glass of straight tomato juice in one gulp." Well, now that you know the truth about yourself, what are you going to do?"

"For one thing, stop living a lie. Like, I'm going to stop pretending I'm a square and live a life of lechery."

"That's a start."

"I'm going to reveal the monster living inside me."

You'll be much happier being yourself."

"I'll start by inviting Jordan over here this afternoon."

"Here? To your bungalow?"

"I'll entice her by telling her I want to show her the prototype of my Video Ion Refractor. That'll tempt her. She was an electronics engineer before she became a talent. Like, she has a Master of Science from Cal Tech."

"Better yet, tell her you're having problems with it. Chicks love to solve guys' problems."

"Yeah, right! I'll move it into the bedroom, so she'll have to work on it in there."

"Brilliant!"

"And when she's busy working on it, I'll sneak up behind her and grab her and throw her onto the bed!"

"Andy, I've got to admit it, you've become a true lecher!"

My appetite suddenly came back and I began to eagerly stab my grapefruit with a fork. "Like, I feel much better now that I know the real me."

"It's totally a relief when you stop living lies."

"Why don't you invite Dawn over? You can drag her into the other bedroom. It would be wild."

"I couldn't do that, Andy."

"Oh, I forgot you're the square now.

"But maybe I'll give her a call. I could drive her up to Griffith Park so she can hear the mourning doves."

"Cool. Or you can take her down to Venice Beach and look for jellyfish or something. I was down there last weekend, when I was still a square, and I found a Portuguese man-of-war that must have weighed ninety pounds. It was beautiful, all transparent, with long, pink tentacles."

"I don't know, Andy. Dawn's a real Party person. She might find stuff like that a little boring."

"Then, like, why don't you take her to Party headquarters?"

"Where is it?"

"I don't know. Jordan says they keep moving it around all the time, but it must be someplace in the L.A. basin."

"I could ask her to take me there. Maybe she could introduce me to Brother Freeman."

"Good idea! He can tell you what you can do for the Party."

"That's what I was thinking. Why don't you and Jordan come along?"

"No, I'd rather entice her to my bungalow and show her my prototype."

*   *   *   *

Jordan accepted my invitation and came to my bungalow later that afternoon. She arrived wearing a plaid mini-suit and a black patent leather cap, looking so cute I felt like grabbing her and throwing her down on the living room couch. Somehow, I managed to control myself for the moment.

"Gee, you smell good," I said, letting her in. I handed her a small gift box. "For you."

"For me? What is it?" She tore off the wrapping paper and opened the tiny box and looked up at me. "A key?"

"To my bungalow. I decided to be a good Party member and start a good neighbor key club."

"Oh, my gosh! That makes me so happy I want to laugh. Please don't make me laugh."

"Feel free to come here any time you feel the urge."

"You're so sweet." She gave me a peck of the cheek and took off her jacket. She had on one of those blouses you can see right through, and it made me feel even more lecherous.

"Now where is this device of yours? I'd love to help you with it."

"In the bedroom," I said, eagerly.

She followed me to the bedroom and I showed her the prototype of my Video Ion Refractor, which I'd cleverly put in the corner, just two feet from the foot of the bed.

"So, what's the problem?"

"Well, for one thing, it's too big."

"I see." She pulled out a pair of very fashionable glasses from a small holster at her belt and put them on. They made her look totally intelligent. "Well, circuitry miniaturization is my specialty."

I was just about to grab her and throw her on the bed, when she suddenly turned and asked, "Got a screwdriver?"

That caught me completely off balance. "Screwdriver?"

"I need to take the back off."

"Yeah, right. Like, you want to take the back off. Just a minute. I'll see if there's one in the kitchen."

"I should've brought along my toolkit. A girl should always come prepared," she said as I headed for the kitchen.

I rummaged through the drawers, but couldn't find a screwdriver. Why is it you can never find a tool when you really need one? "Will a table knife do?" I called back to her.

"If it's all you've got it'll have to do."

I brought her the table knife, and she began to work on the screws at the back of the refractor console, took the back off, and began poking around at all the wires and tubes inside, then looked up at me and said, "This is very crude circuitry, you know."

"Like, it's just a prototype."

"Who made it for you?"

"The USS-TV Brain Factory in Santa Monica helped me assemble it."

"That explains it."

"What?"

"The tubes and hand wiring. The geeks at USS-TV's brain factory out here are in the high-tech dark ages. The corporation imports all its really good stuff from China." She turned her back on me to take a closer look at the prototype's guts.

I knew this was my big chance, so I grabbed her.

"Whoa!" she cried as I struggled to throw her onto my bed. "What are you doing?"

"I'm going to make love with you."

"Oh, my gosh! Please don't. You might tickle me taking my clothes off. Then I'd laugh, and I can't afford to laugh, you know."

"Sorry."

"Don't be sorry! I thought you wanted me to help you with your device. So I wasn't mentally prepared, you know. You do want me to help you, don't you?"

"Right."

"Then sit on the bed and behave."

I sat rather dejectedly on the end of the bed and watched her as she lay on the floor between the legs of the prototype inspecting the wiring on the underside of the chassis. I almost went out of my mind, watching her work. Her skirt crawled, like, almost up to her hips. It was terrible, being a real lecher and not being able to reach out and touch her.

"What's this thing supposed to do?" she asked.

"It's top secret."

She peeked out from beneath the chassis. "How can I help you perfect it if I don't know what it's supposed to do?"

"True."

"Judging from the circuitry, I'd say it's designed to post-amplify and read a magnetic wave input signal. But why?"

I decided to go ahead and tell her something, anything, no matter how secret Operation Torch was. "It's supposed to be, like, a device you attach to an HDTV set, so the networks can see what shows the audience watch."

"If someone's watching cable or satellite TV, the networks already know what shows they're watching. And what are the little buttons on the front for? Power and volume controls?"

"They're, like, yes and no buttons."

"So you can ask the viewers questions?"

"Something like that."

"You're building a device to pry into people's lives? The Party's very much against that, you know. The government's prying into people's lives is what led Brother Freeman to form the Party."

"We wouldn't exactly be prying."

"What would you call it?"

"Research."

"Just another name for prying."

"No way. If we know exactly what kinds of shows people like, we can give them the kinds of shows they really want."

"Most people don't like commercials. Want to put me out of work?"

"We wouldn't use it to research commercials. We already know people hate commercials."

"I love commercials. They're my bread and butter."

I could tell by her tone she was a little pissed, so had to think fast. "Can I trust you not to tell anyone if I tell you the real reason I invented it?"

"You know you can," she said, sitting on the end of the bed next to me.

"Like, I designed it to help the Party! It's a new way to poll voters."

"Big deal! The politicians and media all have their own pollsters. So what makes you think yours is any different?"

"It's totally different. It doesn't, like, just poll a sample target audience. It can poll the entire viewing audience."

"Oh, my gosh! That is different, Andy. But how can that help the Party?"

"USS-TV plans to unveil it in the fall, like, just before the national election. As part of a big nationwide promo, we'll send one of my devices to every registered voter in American and ask them to cast their ballots on TV the night before the election. Like, it won't be just another voter sample or even an exit poll. We'll know all the election results before anyone actually votes. And it'll be totally accurate, with absolutely no margin of error."

"So, how will you know you're polling registered voters?"

"I haven't worked out all the details of that yet. So far we've only gotten to the yes and no button technology."

She turned back to the prototype. "Actually, the circuitry is very simple—almost simplistic, if you know what I mean." She stood up and began pacing the floor in front of the prototype. "Oh, my gosh! I think I've got it! We could include some kind of scanning device—say a fingerprint scanner or iris detector."

"That's what I was thinking."

"Gee, Andy, we have so much in common, we actually think alike, you know. So, how big do you want this device to be? I mean, you said you had a miniaturization problem. What's your size goal?"

"Like, a polka dot?"

"Polka dots come in lots of sizes."

"How about a quarter? Can it be reduced to the size of a quarter?"

"No problem. Miniaturization's my bag. How many units do you need?"

"Depends on the cost per unit."

"The bigger the order the lower the cost."

My great brain did some fast calculating. "Let's say fifty million."

"There's gotta be more registered voters than that in America."

"Like, a hundred million?"

"Oh, my gosh! I don't know." She went to my laptop and did a few calculations. "This is just a rough guesstimate, you know—somewhere in the neighborhood of thirty-seven cents a unit, give or take a penny or two."

I grabbed her and gave her a big kiss on the mouth. "You're a genius!"

"I know. Like I said, we have so much in common. But before I commit myself, tell me more—about how it can help the Party."

I rose to my feet and began thinking out loud, "It could help the Party take government away from the politicians and give it back to the people."

"No, way!" She was so excited she pushed me back onto the bed and leaped on top of me. "How?"

My great brain was really rolling now. "If everyone had one of these devices attached to their TV sets they could actually vote on any issue, right in the comfort of their own homes. Like, couldn't they?"

"Fabulous! I love it!"

My mind raced on. "That way, we could practically eliminate the politicians we elect to represent us. Like, if you can vote on any issue in your own living room, who needs all those politicians screwing up everything?"

She leapt off the bed. "Brother Freeman must be told of this immediately!"

"Not yet." I reached out and pulled her back down on the bed. "We can't tell anyone, like, until we're absolutely sure the device is perfected."

"Right," she said, snuggling up to me. "Let's work out all the bugs before we tell anyone."

"Great!" I said, unbuttoning her blouse.

"Lecher," she whispered, kicking off her shoes. "Oh, my gosh! Just don't make me laugh."

CHAPTER 23

▼

Five days later, after Jordan and I had demonstrated a bug-free working proto-type of my Video Ion Refractor for Seymour and Dawn. They were so impressed Dawn set up a meeting with Brother Freeman.

"Your invention does seem to have possibilities," Brother Freeman told us as we watched him hack a squid apart with his Bowie knife at the Party headquarters for that day, the Venice fishing pier. "It's wild." Hack. "Mad." Hack. "Crazy." Hack. "Completely whacko." He stopped hacking and began baiting each of his hooks. "That's why it appeals to me—it's my kind of free spirited idea."

"We hoped you'd like it," Seymour said.

"Like it? I love it!" Brother Freeman cast his line into the swells some thirty feet below, clipped his spinning rod onto the pier rail, propped his Birkenstocks up on a Coors Beer cooler, and gave Jordan a pat on her behind. "Sister, I love you. I really do. You're a credit to the Party—a true Party girl. Let me take another look at that wild thing of yours."

"It's not my thing," she said, handing Brother Freeman a small, black, half-dollar-size working prototype of my Video Ion Refractor. "Oh, my gosh. I mean, it was Andy's idea. I simply helped him execute it."

"So you say," he said, looking up at me appraisingly through the frayed brim of his straw hat. "The Party needs brilliant young people like you, Brother Cohan. That's the beauty of the Party. We accept men and women for what they are. Egghead or moron, makes no difference to us. All that counts is that he or she loves freedom and his or her fellow man or woman." He gave Dawn, a loving pat on the behind.

"The Republicans and Democrats should be so liberal," she said.

"Even the Green Party," I said.

Brother Freeman asked, "Exactly how does your Video Ion Refractor work, Brother Cohan?"

"Tell him how simple it is," Seymour told me.

"You place it anywhere near a TV set—but at a distance of no greater than ten feet—and it feeds on the free ion light waves that radiate from the video screen. Free ions are, like, groups of atoms that have acquired a net electric charge by gaining or losing one or more electrons."

Brother Freeman nodded. "So?"

"The Video Ion Refractor, or VIR as I call it, captures the electric charge, reads it, and bends it back on itself, sending the re-coded ion charge back into the video screen where it returns to its source of origin."

"Interesting," Brother Freeman said, turning the VIR unit over in his bony, squid-slick hands, examining it more closely.

I went on, "As you can see, there's a digital scanner pad and two buttons on top of the unit. Simply lick your finger, touch the scanner pad, and it instantly reads your DNA, digitalizes it, and the digitalized free ion information is fed at the speed of light by satellite to USS-TV's Master Ion Interceptor computer, which instantly confirms who you are and if you're a registered voter."

"Mm. And what about the green and red buttons?" Brother Freeman asked.

"They're yes and no buttons—green for yes, red for no—so the registered voter can vote for or against any candidate or legislation."

Brother Freeman scratched his chin whiskers thoughtfully. "But can hackers screw up the results? The power structure will pounce upon any flaw in your system—perceived or otherwise."

"Hackers can only hack into Internet sites. The VIR and Master Ion Interceptor aren't connected to the Web. Like, it's totally new technology that intercepts and interprets free ion emissions, and therefore, it's totally hack-free."

"Okay, but most liberals—including almost every member of the Party—object to surrendering even infinitesimal amounts of their personal DNA. That's what the Party's all about, protecting privacy."

I smiled and said, "You've been spreading your DNA all over this pier this morning. Because it simply exists, do you feel violated in any way?"

"No, but I'm sure the goddam squid do."

"DNA is life itself. But the VIR only reads the voter's DNA to confirm if he or she is registered, then returns the data to the free ion state where it's impossible to reconstitute it."

"There's got to be a flaw in your concept. Touch screen voting is unacceptable to the politicians because it leaves no paper trail and hackers can screw up the results. Seems to me, your VIR has the same problem."

"No way," I said "Once the voter's DNA is read, it's liberated as unreadable free ions, so, unlike touch screens and punch card ballots, there are no hacking or hanging chad problems. The voter's secret ballot is recorded at the precinct level, and the anonymous results can be instantly available as hard copy print outs for error-free recounts on demand by any candidate or party."

"By God, Brother Cohan, you've thought of everything!" Brother Freeman cleared his throat with a hack and spat over the side of the pier. Then he reeled in his line a few feet to make sure all his hooks were still baited, and released the brake on the spinning reel, letting the line fall back into the swells. "What's the per-unit cost?"

"Not to worry," Seymour said. "We guarantee USS-TV will foot the bill, including all handling and distribution costs."

"Who's worried? Forget handling and distribution costs. How much is USS-TV willing to pay per unit?"

Seymour checked his iPhone. "A dollar twenty-five tops."

Brother Freeman turned to Jordan. "Tell me, sister, what are the per unit manufacturing costs?"

"Based on a two hundred million unit order, ninety-nine cents per unit give or take a penny or two," she said.

"Leaving the Party approximately twenty-five cents a unit profit." Brother Freeman whistled. "That fifty million could really fatten up the Party coffers!"

"Party coffers?" I hesitated. "Wouldn't it be better, like, to farm production out to an independent third party?"

"That's what the Party is, goddam it, an independent third party!" Brother Freeman said.

"Somebody has to mass-produce the units," Seymour said. "We could let the Party do it."

"Is that legal?" I asked.

"Why the hell not?" Brother Freeman asked. "We don't have the backing of the military industrial complex and all their fund-raising lobbyists. The manufacturing profits will make us more competitive."

"We could use dummy offshore corporations and Swiss bank accounts like all the other parties do," Seymour suggested.

"Marvelous!" Dawn said.

"Oh, my gosh! Think of all the fabulous rallies the Party could hold!" Jordan said.

"And the mushroom and peyote farms the party could invest in," Seymour said.

I was still hesitant. "I don't know, like, I still think we should subcontract it."

Brother Freeman let out a loud guffaw, blew his nose over the side of the pier, and snorted, "No fucking way!"

"Oh, my gosh, Andy. Somebody has to manufacture the VIRs. I certainly can't grow two-hundred million units in my bathtub. Why not let the Party do it? Political parties are nonprofit organizations, you know. It wouldn't be like some huge corporate entity was getting rich on your invention or anything like that."

"Actually, I doubt it'll matter to management who gets the production contract," Seymour said. "This is Admiral Jolly's pet project. And he's one of America's richest billionaires. As long as we keep per unit costs below a dollar twenty-five cents, he'll buy it, and we're well below that."

"Don't forget to include my expenses," Brother Freeman said.

"Your expenses?" I asked.

He popped open another can of Coors. "The head of a national political party has unbelievable expenses."

"Moving Party headquarters every day must cost a lot," I admitted.

"Actually, that's a minor expense, Brother Cohan. Consider all the rallies and speeches I have to make. Good speechwriters don't come cheap—not cheap at all."

"Who writes yours?" I asked.

"I do," Brother Freeman confessed. "You don't think I'd stoop to use other people's material, do you? No way I'd ever do that. Just wouldn't be me! Then there are all the little extra expenses. Take my wardrobe. I have to look humble to appeal to the masses. Any idea how much it costs to dress humbly in these days? Would you believe, I paid over two hundred dollars for the simple little tailor-made robe I'm wearing?"

"Gosh, I believe it," Jordan said.

"Me too," Dawn said.

"I don't see anything wrong with allowing Brother Freeman a little expense money," Seymour told me. "After all, he is the head of the Party. If he wants to compete in the major leagues of politics, he'll need a campaign bus."

"And a private jet," Dawn put in. "I mean, you have to fly around in a private jet to be accepted as a real candidate."

"Oh, my gosh! I'm just a talent, and I know how much keeping up appearances can cost," Jordan said.

"You're more than just a talent, Sister," Brother Freeman said, giving her another loving pat on the behind.

"I know," she said.

"We have so much in common," I said.

"It's almost like we're made for each other," Jordan said.

"I love you both," Brother Freeman said.

Seymour obviously wanted to get down to business. "We'd better create a time line."

"Right on, Brother Stone!"

"Management wants to have complete nationwide coverage in time for the elections this fall. That means our target launch date should be moved up to August one," Seymour said.

"Is it possible to have that many VIR units in place that early?" Brother Freeman asked Jordan.

"If my calculations are correct—and they almost always are—we should be able to produce something like ten million units a week. More or less, you know."

"That means we have to allow six weeks for production," Seymour said, setting up a flow chart on his iPhone.

"Six weeks?" Brother Freeman said, checking his fishing line again. "Why so long?"

"It'll take at least a week to set up our production facilities," Jordan explained. "We'll have to lease at least ten Olympic size swimming pools to grow that many units."

"Pools?" Brother Freeman said. "You mean plants?"

I shook my head. "No, pools. Like, Jordan grows the circuitry on copper wires dipped in her secret solution of silicon magnesium and filtered bromine conditioned water."

"She grew five hundred units in five days in her bathtub," Dawn said.

"I can grow a million units per week per pool," Jordan said.

"It's a revolutionary technique," I said.

"Revolutionary!" Brother Freeman seemed to savor the word; the way one savors fine wine.

Seymour checked his iPhone and said, "If you want to manufacture them offshore, China has hundreds of Olympic swimming pools left over from the Beijing Games."

"I love it!" Brother Freeman said. "The Chinks could make a hundred million units a week—" he suddenly caught himself, giving Jordan a shit-eating grin. "Oops! Sorry, honey, I meant Chinese."

"Why should I care? I'm an American."

"Okay. That brings our timeline start date back to mid July," Seymour said. "Personally, I feel very strongly that we should start our promotions by the Fourth. That way, we can kick the program off with a volley of patriotic publicity."

Dawn exclaimed, "With fireworks and everything."

"It would be fabulous," Jordan said.

"I don't know," I said. "We may not want to involve the Party in the pre-show promotions."

"Andy's right. It should be a USS-TV project all the way," Seymour said. "We can't afford to let the power structure know the Party's behind the project. USS-TV will totally support the campaign—with hundreds of spots urging registered voters to install the units by election eve."

Brother Freeman nodded in agreement. "If USS-TV puts enough commercials on the air, the stupid people could be convinced that it's their patriotic duty to install the units and register to vote."

"That's what we're hoping for," Seymour agreed.

"Everyone will do it," Dawn said. "Americans love to be patriotic."

Jordan said, "Oh, my gosh! I'll help any way I can. I could do some commercials myself—pro bono, you know."

"So could I," Dawn said. "I'm sure we could find all kinds of talent willing to donate their time to such a noble cause."

"USS-TV will pay talent at the standard SAG rates," Seymour promised. "We can't afford any union problems."

"Oh, my gosh! I forgot all about SAG," Jordan said. "The Screen Actors Guild will demand we accept the money."

"Then we'll just have to accept it, honey," Dawn said.

"Guess it's every American's patriotic duty to accept money," Jordan replied.

"You can always donate your residual checks to the Party. Gifts to political parties are deductible," Brother Freeman pointed out.

Neither Jordan nor Dawn said a word.

"Okay." Seymour looked at his watch. "That's it for now. Hate to run, but Andy and I have a plane to catch to Detroit. We'll see what top management thinks of our ideas. It'll be a tough sale, but I'll fight the good fight."

Brother Freeman raised his right hand in a gesture of farewell. "Peace. Make love, not war."

"Boffo! How totally retro!" Seymour said, pocketing his iPhone.

"Hope you catch a fish," I told Brother Freeman.

CHAPTER 24

▼

The next day Seymour arranged a demonstration of my Video Ion Refractor for Harmon P. Harper and Roger Jolly via a closed-circuit satellite hookup between the USS-TV executive boardroom in Southfield and the production department conference room at our Hollywood studios where Jordan Lee and Dawn Day were ready to help us with an on camera presentation of the IFR.

"This better be boffo, booby baby," Harmon P. Harper told me as I set up my laptop on the massive mahogany Nakashima conference room table.

"I guarantee it'll knock your socks off," Seymour promised.

"Har! Har! Har!" Roger Jolly laughed. "You don't wear socks, right, Harm?"

"Right, Admiral," Harmon P. Harper admitted.

"I'm sure it'll be a jolly good show. Right, laddie?" Jolly Roger said, showing his faith in my great brain.

"Right," I answered, as the video of Jordan and Dawn came up on my laptop and the boardroom HDTV monitor. I flexed my fingers over the keypad. "This will be a simple demonstration," I explained for the benefit of Roger Jolly and Harmon P. Harper. "I programmed my laptop to act as the master computer for this morning's presentation. Ready Hollywood?

"Oh, my gosh! Ready if you are, Andy," Jordan came back.

"Who's she, booby baby?" Harmon P. Harper asked.

"Jordan Lee," Seymour answered for me. "Andy's executive assistant. I arranged it. She has a Master's from Cal Tech in electronic engineering."

"Is she Chinese?" Harmon P. Harper demanded. "You can't trust the Chinese."

"She's an all-American girl," I said, "second runner-up in the Miss America Pageant."

"The Miss America Pageant? That's good enough for me!" Roger Jolly said. "Okay. Let's get on with the show."

"Are you a registered voter?" I asked Jordan.

She nodded and pressed the green button on the VIR in front of her. My laptop beeped and *YES* instantly flashed on its screen and the monitor.

"Prove it," I said.

Jordon smiled, licked her finger and pressed it firmly on the VIR ID pad.

REGISTERED PRECINCT 9007129 NORTH HOLLYWOOD CA flashed on my laptop screen and the monitor.

"Good show! Good show! Congratulations, Laddie! You did it!"

"I'm still not convinced, booby baby. You and the Chinese girl could have set this up," Harmon P. Harper said.

"You've got a point, Harm." Roger Jolly turned to me. "We need to test another subject, laddie."

"Are you a registered voter?" I asked Dawn.

"Yes," she said. "And I'm ready to prove it." She licked her finger and pressed the VIR pad.

REGISTERED PRECINCT 59120 ORANGE COUNTY CA flashed on my laptop and monitor screens.

"And who's she, booby baby?" Harmon P. Harper demanded.

"My executive assistant," Seymour answered for me.

"I still don't buy it," Harmon P. Harper said.

"Harm's right, laddie. We need an independent voter. Someone not connected with you two in any way. Right, Harm?"

"Right, Admiral. And I know just the guy." He took out his BlackBerry and punched in a number. "Jack, you in the office today? Beautiful! You don't know how ecstatic that makes me. Get your big ass down to the production department conference room. They're running a little test for the Admiral and me. We want to use you as a guinea pig." He pocketed his BlackBerry and turned back to me. "Jack Shipiro's our Executive VP on the Coast. I'd trust him with my life."

A few minutes later Jack Shipiro came into the production conference room in Hollywood and took a seat at the table across from Jordan and Dawn. He was a very small man with a very large shaved head that glistened in the lights.

"Okay, Harm, what can I do for you?" he asked.

"Booby baby here has a question for you," Harmon P. Harper said.

"Are you a registered voter, Mr. Shipiro?" I asked.

He hesitated for a moment before he asked, "What kind of test is this?"

"Just answer the question, Jack," Harmon P. Harper ordered.

Shipiro blinked and little beads of perspiration broke out on his polished dome. With a nervous shrug, he said, "Well, ah, of course I am."

"Prove it," Harmon P. Harper ordered.

"How? I don't carry my voter registration card around with me."

"Just lick your finger and put it on this little pad," Jordan said sliding the VIR in front of him.

"What's this? Some kind of sick joke?" he asked her.

"Do as she says," Harmon P. Harper said.

"Okay. If you say so, Harm." He licked his finger and placed it on the VIR pad.

Instantly my laptop buzzed and blinked *NOT REGISTERED*!

"You lied to us, Jack. Right?" Roger Jolly said.

Shipiro's face flushed and he bowed his huge head. "Right, Admiral."

"You're fired!" Harmon P. Harper shouted at him.

*   *   *   *

Seymour spent the next fifteen minutes using a PowerPoint presentation he downloaded from his iPhone to explain our VIR launch timeline to Harmon P. Harper and Roger Jolly. "After we've stunned America with our totally accurate election eve results next November, we'll set January 20th as our new reality show launch day. That night, in prime time, USS-TV will premiere the ultimate in audience participation shows. For the first time on TV anywhere, viewers can watch and debate the burning issues of the day live on TV, and then vote yes or no to pass or reject them from the comfort of their living rooms."

"Slow down, kiddo," Harmon P. Harper interrupted. "What's this about a new reality show launch in January? I only approved the election eve public service blockbuster. That's my only programming commitment to you and booby baby."

"It's Andy's idea," Seymour said. "He thinks it could be the most fantastic reality show of all time—the ultimate audience participation show. But if you don't like it … well, tell him about it, Andy."

"We call it *By the People,*" I began.

"Come on, booby baby. I don't care what you call it. Until the ratings numbers come in on the election night show, I'm not going out on a limb."

"You know, Harm, that's how laddie and I met—way out on a limb. That's what I like about him. He doesn't play games. When he's got an idea, it's damn the torpedoes and full speed ahead. You were that way once, when you were a rising young programming star. Now you're acting like just another bean counter. Right?"

Harmon P. Harper's face paled. "Oh, come on, Admiral. You agreed to leave entertainment programming to me. Public service and news is your domain."

Roger Jolly didn't laugh. "You forgot to say 'right,'" he snapped. "And you forgot you don't own USS-TV. I do. So I'm the boss, right?"

"Right, right," Harmon P. Harper said. "Okay, booby baby, let's hear your fantastic idea."

"Like, it's a reality show about government," I began.

"Like C-Span? Boring, boring," Harmon P. Harper said with a sarcastic snigger.

I shook my head. "No way! Not like C-Span. They just cover government. *By the People* will be a total reality government show. Like, the host and moderator is the virtual chief executive, and the people—all the registered voters in the TV audience—will be the legislative branch. Using the VIR, the Internet, or cell phones, the people can introduce new laws and vote to pass or kill them."

"I hate it," Harmon P. Harper said. "It'll never fly."

"So? I love it!" Roger Jolly cut him off. "It could show the people how rewarding government can really be. Right?"

"Right," Harmon P. Harper said. "What I meant to say is: it'll never fly if we don't have some big name celebs to build interest. And it's got to be a big giveaway show with super prizes and big money rewards!"

"Money's no object. This is a truly revolutionary idea. Who needs congresses or legislatures if the people can represent themselves? Right, laddie?"

"Right," Seymour answered for me. "That's the idea. Think of the possibilities. Eventually, if the show is as boffo as I think it will be, *By the People* could actually become a reality and take the government away from the politicians and give it back to the people."

Roger Jolly's good eye lit up. "We can get rid of all those political piss ants in Washington! By God, this is an investment in America's future! Damn the torpedoes, full speed ahead. We'll spend whatever it takes to kick off the show. Right, Harm?"

"Right, Admiral. Okay, booby baby, you've the go ahead. Produce a pilot and we'll screen it for testing. If it knocks the focus groups off their bonanzas we'll go national with it."

"To hell with pilots and testing," Roger Jolly said. "This is a public service project. So damn the torpedoes, full speed ahead. We'll kick it off nationally. Har! Har! Har!"

"Like, I don't think we should do that," I disagreed. "Maybe California should be the initial target market. California always leads the rest of the country. If *By the People* works there, we'll launch it nationally and the other states will follow."

"I like the way you think, laddie! The cable TV companies came up with C-Span as a public service sop. We could form a new public service network—call it G-Span or something with a little more pizzazz—"

"Like, VIRGIN?" I suggested.

"Virgin?" Harmon P. Harper asked. "Come on, booby baby. There are no virgins in government!"

"VIRGIN could be an acronym for Video Ion Refractor Government Network," I said.

"Brilliant!" Jolly Roger roared. "Har! Har! Har! It has a helluva lot more sex appeal than G-Span. We can sell anything with the right acronym. Okay. Go for it. Let's use VIRGIN to pre-empt all our satellite news and public service programming for *By the People* ninety-minutes a week in prime time. Right?"

"Right!" Harmon P. Harper's blinked as if a bulb suddenly turned on in his brain. "*By the People* could break down the stupid voters' faith in their elected representatives!"

"Har! Har! Har! VIRGIN and *By the People* are truly revolutionary ideas. Ones worthy of a creative mind like yours, laddie. I'd love to see all the political hacks thrown out of office. They only represent themselves. But what makes you think you can actually morph a reality show like *By the People* into true reality?"

"The Constitution of the State of California," Seymour answered for me, bringing up a copy of the document on his iPhone. "It's all here in hi-def digital color. If two thirds of all voters in the last election sign a petition asking for a change in the state constitution, the proposition has to go on the ballot at the next general election. And Brother Freeman says his party workers will go all out to get the petitions signed when and if we need them."

"Freeman's a total nut case," Harmon P. Harper said. "That's why HBO dropped his TV show."

"He's no worse than the nuts we call our leaders now. I'm with you, laddie. Damn the torpedoes, full speed ahead. *By the People* is a go! Right, Harm?"

"Right. And it has such a terif ring to it. *By the People*. So Lincolnesque. I'm totally ecstatic about your idea, booby baby. It'll be a smash. Absolutely boffo!

The show's a go-go!" He stood up and nodded at Seymour. "Come on down to my office, kiddo, and we'll work on the launch schedule."

✳   ✳   ✳   ✳

After Harmon P. Harper left, Roger Jolly took a Cuban cigar out of the gold humidor on his desk, lit up, took a deep drag, and blew out a huge smoke ring that circled above his head like a halo.

"Laddie," he began without laughing first, "you ready for a serious bit of advice from an old clown?"

"You're no clown," I objected.

"You know it, and I know it. But I've found it's easier to get what you want in the business world if no one thinks you're to be taken serious. So I'm sort of like a court jester. People laugh at me, but in the end I get what I want. Let's leave it at that. Okay?"

"Right."

"And forget the *right* B.S. *Okay*'s okay with me. At least for now." He sucked on the cigar and blew out another puff of smoke, coughed, snuffed it out in an ash tray, and tipped its contents into the waste basket beneath his desk. "Love Cubans—cigars, I mean. And hate 'em at the same time. That's the way life is, laddie. A series of love/hate relationships. You love what you hate, and hate what you love. What about that girl of yours? The one with the knees that smile at you. Still want to be president of USS-TV so you can marry her?"

"She's too good for a lecher like me."

Roger Jolly shook his head. "I'd laugh if it wasn't so sad. You used to say you were a genius, laddie. Now you're a lecher?"

"I guess."

"Doesn't matter. Don't care if you're a genius or a lecher. But you're my boy, laddie. Know why?"

I shook my head.

"You're what I call a Make Believer—you believe in your ideas, and you make other people believe in them. Very few people have that talent. Know what I mean?"

I shook my head again.

"Successful inventors have that talent. Take Edison, laddie. He believed he could invent a machine that could record and play back sounds. It was a simple idea. Too simple to work. But he made everyone believe his phonograph actually worked."

"Like, it did."

"Don't make me laugh, laddie. You honestly believe an electric magnet and a little disk of ferrous metal can produce all the sounds of a symphony orchestra? But we believe it works and it does in our minds. Never underestimate the power of the human mind. Take money. Our money is absolutely worthless. Not backed by anything but the universal belief that it can buy us anything. If society believes something works, it does. That's what creativity and invention are about, making people believe in what you dream up."

"Maybe."

"No maybes about it. Making the masses believe your ideas work is a form of genius. And by God, laddie, I really want to believe in your dream of taking the government away from the politicians and giving it back to the people. What this sick country really needs is healthy new political thinking. I love the idea of getting rid of our singular party system."

"Like, singular meaning out of the ordinary?" I asked. "Or singular, like one?"

"One."

"We have a two party system—"

"Don't kid yourself, laddie. Republicans and Democrats are identical twins, mirror images of themselves except for slight aberrations. But you are right, this country has a two party system of sorts—the In party and the Out party. The Ins want to stay in, and the Outs want to be in. That's what the American political system is all about. And that's why I'm for your new Freedom Party. It has the potential to be a true second party. But your Freedom party has one serious flaw."

"Meaning?"

"Brother Freeman. Harm said it, laddie. Freeman's a nut case. If the Freedom Party's to succeed, it has to build its leadership and image. Your current image is the Pajama Party. Get Freeman to drop the pajamas and play to the party base. People who want freedom from political idiots. If you can get your leadership to play to your base—voters who are truly fed up with the current political situation—I, USS-TV, and all my media companies will support your dream in any way we can. And we're damn good at making people believe anything we want them to believe. Hell, I'd run for president myself if I was born in this country. I'm a Canuck."

"Like, you're not an American?"

"Har! Har! Har! Course I am. Dual citizen of Canada and the United States. Any foreigner can buy U.S. citizenship if you've got a million dollars in hard cash. But to hell with all that. You've got to be nuts to be president of this country. Besides, I'd rather help you bring true democracy to this republic. Just do me one little favor in return, laddie."

"Like?"

"Give up your idea of becoming president of USS-TV. Presidents of corporations don't believe in anything but the bottom line. You're creative. Stick with your ideas and dreams and leave the nitpicking B.S. to executive types like Harm and your friend Seymour. Right, laddie?"

"Right. Like, I mean if it's okay to say *right* again."

CHAPTER 25

▼

It took just two years for the voters of California to put Proposition Sixty-Nine on the ballot to change the State Constitution, allowing the people to represent themselves as the State's new legislature. The Proposition and the Freedom Party won the election in a landslide. Brother Freeman was elected Governor and Seymour Stone was voted in as Lieutenant Governor.

"Oh, my gosh! Isn't the bus fabulous?" Jordan exclaimed the day after the election as she and Dawn and Seymour and I sat in the leather upholstered lounge aboard the Premiere Luxury Campaign Coach that Brother Freeman had purchased for his mobile Party headquarters with the royalties he'd made from my invention.

"Don't you love the luxury mood lighting?" Dawn asked Seymour. "It makes us all look so marvelously cool."

"And so it should. We are the beautiful people," Seymour said.

"Awesome!" Jordan said.

Governor-elect Freeman turned back to us from the driver's seat. "If you think that's awesome, listen to this!" He hit the Premiere Luxury Campaign Coach's triple air trumpets. "Isn't that glorious? Like Gabriel's call on Judgment Day."

"No one can say the Party isn't on the move," I said, watching the deliriously happy faces of the people lining the curbs on Sunset Boulevard flash by the lounge's tinted picture windows.

"It's Party time!" Governor-elect Freeman shouted into the microphone of his Bluetooth headset, his voice reverberating over the joyous throngs from the bus's external Bose FreeSpace speakers. "Peace! Make love, not war!"

"Peace! Make love not war!" the throngs of young people lining the curbs echoed.

"Ah, youth—the Party's base," Governor-Elect Freeman said, swerving the luxury campaign coach around the curve just east of Marmont.

"Who'd have thought when we met on the Venice pier two years ago we'd really take the government of California away from the politicians and give it to the people!" Dawn said.

Like all of us, she was still barely able to comprehend the completeness of Proposition Sixty-Nine's victory at the polls the day before.

Seymour was going through the congratulatory e-mails on his iPhone. "Listen to this one: 'Election Boffo! Knocked the politicos right off their bonanzas! I'm ecstatic!!! I'm jetting back for the inaugural show. Love and kisses from Monte Carlo!!! Harm.'"

"I'm glad Harmon P. Harper's ecstatic," I said.

"You can call him Harm now, booby baby. He retired to join the Party. He's one of us now," Seymour said.

"I forgot," I said, apologetically.

Jordan snuggled up to me. "Oh, my gosh! Now that he's one of us, maybe he can help me get a part in a series. I mean, he was president of USS-TV before he joined the party. He must still have lots of connections out here. I've always wanted to do a series, you know."

"You'd be perfect in a series," Dawn said.

"I'd rather you stayed on as Andy's executive assistant," Seymour said. "You've too much talent to waste it on a series."

"I'd like that, too," I said. "You're the best assistant I've ever had."

"She's the only assistant you've ever had," Dawn said.

"Oh, my gosh, Andy. You know I'd do anything for you. But I guess I'd rather be your partner than an assistant."

"Whatever," Seymour said, going back to the congratulatory e-mails on his iPhone. "I'm totally for freedom of choice."

Dawn threw her arms around Seymour's neck and kissed him. "You're such a marvelous, beautiful person. If it weren't for you, Proposition Sixty-Nine couldn't have passed," she cooed.

"True. I made *By the People* more than just another reality show. I made it a reality."

"At least in California," I pointed out.

"Brother Freeman will make a fabulous governor," Jordan said. "He's such a visionary visionary."

"Yeah, right," I said. "He really turns people on."

"Oh, my gosh! Look at them dancing in the street! It's awesome the way they love Brother Freeman," she told Seymour.

"Love your neighbor!" Brother Freeman shouted into his microphone as the bus was forced to stop at Sunset and Fairfax by a delirious mob that swarmed around it, kissing its stainless steel sides.

"Love your neighbor!" the crowd shouted back and they began kissing and hugging each other.

Brother Freeman leaned on his horn and the triple trumpets blasted a path through the people and we started east on Sunset again.

"That should be the new Party goal. Taking Congress away from the politicians and giving the power to the people," Dawn told Seymour.

"Changing the U.S. Constitution isn't that easy," Seymour said. "Congress has to initiate Constitutional amendments. I doubt U.S. senators and representatives will vote to eliminate themselves. And even if the House and Senate did, the amendment would have to be ratified by two thirds of all states. That could take years and years."

"There is another way," I volunteered. "Like, it's never been done before. But the states do have the right to amend the Constitution without the consent of Congress."

"You sure?" Dawn asked.

"Absolutely," I said.

Seymour brought up Wikipedia on his iPhone, and thumbed through the Constitution. "Andy's right. The states can amend the Constitution. It might take a few years to get it done, but *By the People* is the number one show in the California ratings, and now that we're going national, who knows what can happen."

Brother Freeman shouted back at us. "It's wild! Insane! I love it! An idea worthy of the Party, Brother Stone. I'll make it my next great crusade, kicking it off in my inaugural address."

"Marvelous!" Dawn said.

"The military-industrial complex will spend billions to stop us," Brother Freeman shouted. "But right will triumph over might!"

"What we need is a crisis—a terrorist attack, maybe—to unite the people," Seymour said.

"Americans always unite in times of crisis," Dawn said.

"It would have to be something really big," Seymour said. "Something that could threaten America's position as the world's only superpower. Give me time and I'll think of something." Seymour assumed the executive thinking position.

"Look at him think," Dawn said.

"Awesome," Jordan said.

"It makes me thirsty," I said.

"It's the air-conditioning, you know. It dehydrates you," Jordan told me.

I got up from my seat and headed for the entertainment bar at the front of the bus and opened the refrigerator door. It was filled with Coors and Diet Pepsi, but no water. I turned on the sink spigot and filled a glass with tap water.

"Don't drink tap water," Brother Freeman warned. "It's full of pollutants. Have a beer."

"I don't drink beer," I told him.

"If the Governor wants you to have a beer, silly, humor him," Jordan told me.

"He won't be governor until January," I reminded her.

"Oh, my gosh. Then have a Diet Pepsi," she said.

"No way. It's loaded with caffeine. Mom told me to stay away from caffeine. It keeps you awake."

I suddenly lurched forward as Brother Freeman braked to stop as a long line of senior citizens snake danced across Sunset at La Brea.

"Look's like everyone's heading for the Hollywood Bowl," I told him.

He stood on the triple air horns, blasting a path through the snake dancers. "Glorious! This will be the biggest Party party of all time. But if these damn boomers don't move, we'll be late for the rally." He blew the bus's triple air trumpets again.

"I can't believe it. California's seniors have been celebrating nonstop for almost two days," I said.

Brother Freeman laughed and blew the air horns again. "Crazy old boomers are reliving their youth. They were liberal as kids. Blamed everyone over thirty for the world's problems. Make love, not war—that was their slogan. They hated the power structure in the Sixties and early Seventies. But they changed as they became Thirty Somethings. When America's Bicentennial came along in 1976, they wrapped themselves in the flag and moved to the right. They came of age as a political force in the Eighties when they helped elect Ronald Reagan."

"What about Clinton?" I asked. "Like, he beat George H. W. Bush because of the economy, stupid."

"Economy didn't have a thing to do with it," Brother Freeman said. "The pundits and talking heads never did catch on to the real reason. Clinton won because old man Bush was supposed to be a World War II hero. And most Boomer guys were draft dodgers during Nam. Clinton was, too. So they related to him. He was one of them—a freaking draft dodger—and he beat the war hero's ass off. Same thing happened again in 2000 and 2004. Gore was in Nam and Kerry was a Nam hero. Georgie Porgie beat them both because he was a draft dodger the Boomers could relate to."

"You're such a great brain when it comes to political strategy," Dawn told him.

"Screw the Bushes and Clintons. They're history! We liberated the people!" Brother Freeman said as we turned north on Highland. "Before the Freedom Party, the people were slaves—slaves of their inhibitions. Now they're free. Free to make love and consummate the dreams of their youth."

"Like, the HIV vaccine helped make it possible, too," I pointed out.

"Look at the people lined up to get in the Hollywood Bowl to watch the stars make love!" Brother Freeman sounded the triple air trumpets at the couples queued at the entrance to the Bowl. "Love you!" he shouted into his microphone.

"Love you, too!" the crowd echoed.

"That was a marvelous strategy decision you made the day before the election, honey," Dawn told him.

"Which one, baby?" he modestly asked.

"Ordering Party workers to pour two hundred pounds of acid into the reservoirs," she returned. "It made everyone so happy."

"Acid? You mean, like, the Party polluted the reservoirs?" I asked.

"There are no pollutants in LSD!" Brother Freeman shouted.

"Acid is pure," Dawn said. "A marvelous psychedelic drug."

"And so totally retro," Seymour said.

"I can't believe it! Like, the Party drugged everyone in California to win an election?" I asked.

"Not everyone, Andy," Seymour said. "Just Southern California. And only as a last resort. We needed their votes to carry the State. And look what happened. After twenty-five years of HIV suppression, free love is finally back."

Jordan said, "Oh, my gosh. Acid's not like magic mushrooms or peyote. It's illegal."

"Who cares?" Brother Freeman said. "Free love is back."

"In the Hollywood Bowl?" I said, my mind still reeling.

"Anywhere to be different," Dawn said. "I can hardly wait until we get to Forest Lawn."

"Forest lawn?" I said.

"Where the big victory rally for Party regulars is being held," Brother Freeman said, turning off North Hollywood onto Cahuenga. "We're a hundred thousand strong in L.A. now. We need lots of lawn."

I tapped Brother Freeman's shoulder. "Stop the bus. I want to get off."

"On a freeway interchange?" Dawn asked. "It's against the law unless it's an emergency."

Brother Freeman shouted, "If we break a law the power structure will—"

"You're crazy!" I cried.

Seymour looked up from his iPhone. "Tell me, Andy, do you often feel your friends are crazy?"

"The whole world is crazy!" I cried.

"Thinking the whole world is insane could be a sign of insanity," Seymour said.

"Yeah, right. Like, I didn't drug millions of people to fix an election!" I shouted.

"Oh, my gosh, Andy! I'm totally with you. Stop the bus!" Jordan cried.

"But look how happy the people are," Dawn said.

"And free!" Brother Freeman shouted.

"Stop the bus!" I pleaded again. "Jordan and I want to get off!"

"You can't leave us. The Party needs you both," Dawn said.

"You're the only ones who know how to program the master computer to tally up the people's votes," Seymour said.

"Don't let the Party down!" Brother Freeman shouted.

"Don't let us down!" Seymour said.

I lunged at Brother Freeman and grappled with him for control of the wheel. The bus careened insanely under the freeway, heading northbound on Cahuenga.

"Just kidding about the acid!" Brother Freeman shouted, crashing his fist against my face, knocking me to the floor at his feet. "You know how I like to kid."

"You weren't kidding!" I shouted back from the floor, stretching out a hand, feeling for the emergency brake.

"Stop the bus!" Jordan screamed.

"No way! We're on a roll!" Brother Freeman cried, stomping his right foot down on the back of my neck.

I wrapped my fingers around the emergency brake handle. With all my strength, I yanked it back. The tires screeched. The bus swerved right, tore up a hundred yards of chain-link fence, and skidded back onto Cahuenga, zigzagging across the northbound lanes.

"We're free, free, free!" Brother Freeman shrieked, his voice rising an octave with each word. "Woweeee!"

The new stainless steel Premiere Luxury Campaign Coach hurdled off Cahuenga down onto the 101 Freeway just before the Barham Bridge. There was one final blast from the triple air horns followed by a long, ripping, tearing, crashing sound, then nothing.

CHAPTER 26

▼

The next sound I remember hearing was tinkling glass. Actually, it was a pleasant sound, like the Chinese window chimes my mom used to keep outside the kitchen window back home in Albert Lea. The first tinkling sounded rather far-off, but then it moved closer and closer until it seemed right at my side.

"Andy?" a voice whispered in my ear. It was a sweet voice, the voice of someone I knew and loved. But who? It had been so long since I'd heard the voice say my name.

"Mom?" I finally guessed.

"Oh, Andy!" the voice cried, and I felt the soft touch of a hand stroking my poor forehead. "Open your eyes. Please open your eyes."

I tried to do as the voice asked, but no matter how hard my mind urged my eyelids to open, they refused to obey. "I can't," I sobbed.

"You can. I really, really know you can," the voice said. "Try harder, Andy. Please try harder."

I really did try harder, but all I saw was a fluttering of light.

Then I heard another, harsher voice command, "Open your eyes, geek!"

That voice triggered some reflex action deep in my brain, and my eyes flicked open wide, and there, not less than six inches from my face, I saw an angel bending over me holding a glass of ice water. "Melanie," I whispered.

"Oh, Andy! You're really, really conscious again!"

"Again? Ha! When was the geek ever conscious?" The second, harsh voice asked.

I turned my head a little to the right and saw Cheetah standing right behind Melanie. "Where am I?"

"Oh, God! I knew the geek would come up with a corny line like that!" Cheetah snarled.

"Cheetah!" Melanie scolded. "Get Seymour and the doctor. Tell them Andy is conscious at last."

"Where am I?" I asked again, trying to raise my right hand to stroke Melanie's hair, but the intravenous tube taped to my arm made it too painful to move more than an inch or two.

"Hollywood Presbyterian Hospital," Melanie told me.

"How long have I been here?"

"Weeks and weeks. Seymour called and told us about the accident."

"Accident?"

"The Chinese sabotaged Party headquarters."

"Brother Freeman's new campaign bus?"

"A truckload of Chinese forced it off the freeway. Seymour told us all about it. It was a terrorist plot to wipe out the Party leadership in one blow." She offered me the plastic straw from the glass of water she held in her hand. "Take a sip. The way your voice sounds, your mouth must be really, really dry."

"Is that bottled water?" I asked, not wanting to be doped or poisoned by L.A. water.

"It's safe," she reassured me. "Southern California has been declared a disaster area and the Red Cross and FEMA shipped in truckloads of bottled water from all over the country. It was really, really terrible, the way the Chinese poisoned all the reservoirs."

"Did Seymour tell you that, too?"

"Yes. But he didn't have to. It's been on all the network news shows and Internet blogs. You have no idea how really, really incensed the American people are, Andy. Why, there's even talk of war with China. And who could blame us? I mean, after the assassination all—"

"Assassination?"

"They murdered Brother Freeman in cold blood!"

"Brother Freeman—murdered?"

"He was killed in the bus crash. And those poor innocent girls, Andy—"

"Jordan and Dawn? They were killed, too?"

"Oh, no. Just badly bruised. Poor things were going to be released from the emergency room when it happened."

"Like, what?"

"They kidnapped Jordan. Right out of the E.R."

"No way. Who did it?"

"Some talking heads say it was Al Qaeda. But Seymour's sure it was Triad terrorists."

"Triad? Like, Chinese? How can he be sure?"

"He was a witness. Jordan had just been discharged from the E.R. Seymour was wheeling her to his car when a Rolls Royce pulled up next to them in the parking lot. Four men with really, really stringy beards jumped out of the limo waving AK47s. They forced Jordan into the Rolls and sped off into the night. Seymour knew by their stringy beards they were Chinese. And the way the Chinese economy's booming, Rolls Royces are the Triads' preferred getaway limos."

I struggled to get out of bed. "They'll be after me next."

"Oh, please, Andy," Melanie said, holding me down. "You can't get up yet. You just regained consciousness."

I ripped the intravenous tube from my right arm. "I always thought you were different. But you're just like all the others. You only want me in bed—"

"Have you lost your mind, Andy?" she cried, pinning me to the mattress with her body to keep me from getting up. "I only want to help you!"

I shouted, "That's what they all say!" I managed to twist out from under her and rolled out of bed and onto the floor.

She leapt on top of me. "Oh, Andy, please get back into bed before you have a really, real relapse!"

You have no idea how weak I was after weeks and weeks in bed. I'd spent most all of my remaining energy just rolling onto the floor. Yet I had to escape. I let my body go limp, pretending to give up. "If you really, really want to help me, let me go! The terrorists will kill me!"

"You're safe here. Seymour has taken care of everything."

"Yeah, right!" I summoned the last of the strength I had left to push her away and staggered to my feet.

"Oh, God! Don't go!" she cried, tackling me before I could take a wobbly step.

The door burst open as we lay there, struggling on the floor, and I looked up to see the ugly face of my old nemesis, Mo, peering down at us.

"Mo!" I gasped, so shocked I began slapping Melanie's hands in a desperate attempt to break her grasp on my life.

"Hey, Al!" Mo called over his shoulder to another old nemesis. "Help me get the genesis!"

"Genius, stupid," Al snapped as the two of them charged into the room, furled umbrellas raised high.

"Oh, thank God!" Melanie gasped, panting at my feet. "I wasn't sure how much longer I could hold him down."

"Relax, lady," Al told her, hooking his umbrella handle under her arm and helping her to her feet.

Mo leered down at me as I huddled in the corner furthest from him. "We'll take care of him good—like regular angels of mercury."

"Mercy, stupid," Al snapped, eyeing me with his one good eye.

Mo and Al advanced on me with their umbrellas.

"Come on now, kiddo. Be a good little geek. We don't wanna hurt you. We're on your team now." Al hooked my ankle as I struggled to stand, yanking my legs out from under me. I fell into Mo's arms.

"Let me die on my feet!" I cried as they hoisted me onto their shoulders like a sack of potatoes and carried me back to the bed.

"You ain't gonna die with us around," Al said, and they dropped me on the mattress.

"Yeah, we're your buddyguards now," Mo said, strapping me down on the bed, his yellow teeth showing through his grin.

"Bodyguards," Al grunted.

Melanie rushed to my side. "Seymour hired them. He's taken care of everything."

"Seymour hired them? To take care of me?" I groaned.

"You catch on fast," Al said, checking the strap buckles to make sure they were snug.

Like, suddenly I remembered the Pavlov shockers in the chair's back at the GYP Preview Theatre, and I stiffened my body, waiting for the first horrible jolt of electricity.

Melanie gently stroked my rigid stomach. "Relax, Andy, you're in good hands."

Mo said, "Yeah. From now on, where you go we go. With us on the job, there ain't gonna be no more assignations."

"Assassinations," Al snapped.

"I don't understand," I said. "A few months ago you were protesting my very existence."

Al shrugged. "Times change, kiddo, and we change with them."

"Yeah, we joined the Party," Mo said. "So did Ray."

"But Gypsies have never been members of any body politic," I said.

"It's like the Wizard always says," Al said. "If you can't beat' em, join' em."

"So we switched sides for the deflation," Mo put in.

"Duration," Al corrected. "Until this Chinese crisis is over."

"Screw the Finks!" Mo shouted.

"Chinks," Al corrected. 'Those Commie Chinks ain't gonna kidnap no more innocent American girls."

"Yeah, or poison no more reservations."

"Reservoirs, stupid!" Al whacked Mo on the head with his umbrella.

"Yowee, yow, yow!" Mo howled, holding his head, hopping around the room on one foot.

"The Chinese didn't do it! We did!" I shouted as Seymour and Cheetah rushed into the room with the doctor.

"He's still delirious!" Seymour said.

"Hypocrite!" I shouted at him.

"Oh, Andy, how can you say anything so unpatriotic? Especially in a time of national crisis," Melanie cried.

"Geek's probably a Chinese mole," Cheetah said.

"The Chinese didn't kill Brother Freeman, I did. Tell them, Seymour."

He just stood there, coolly shaking his head. "You're hallucinating, Andy. You've had a severe blow to the head. You've been unconscious for weeks. A lot has happened while you've been out of touch with the real world. Now, cool it before you have a relapse."

"You had Jordan kidnapped!" I screamed, straining my body against the straps that were holding me down.

"Ring for the nurse," the doctor ordered Cheetah. "He needs a shot to calm him down."

"What the geek needs is a good shot to the head," she said, pushing the page button.

"Assassin," I snarled at her, closing my eyes to get her out of my sight.

A few minutes later I felt someone lift my arm, and I opened my eyes and saw an Asian woman bending over me. "You Chinese?" I managed to whisper.

"Vietnamese," she said, plunging a needle into my arm.

"Ow!" I cried.

"It's just a shot of Dilaudid," she said, rubbing my arm with an alcohol soaked wad of cotton. "In a minute you won't feel a thing."

"She's trying to kill me." I groaned as the room began to spin.

"No way," Seymour said. "She's a nurse. You just need to rest."

"Poor Andy. We all love you, you know. Close your eyes. You really, really need to relax," Melanie said, stroking my fevered brow.

I heard the doctor tell Seymour, "This young man needs rest now, and quiet. For his sake, I suggest you all leave. I'm sure he'll be fit as a fiddle in the morning."

"Let's bounce," Cheetah told Melanie.

"Be with you in a minute," she said.

"We've got to talk to him," Seymour told the doctor.

"Can't it wait until tomorrow?" he asked.

"No way!" Seymour said. "It's a national emergency. If I don't talk to him right now, this hospital might be crawling with Chinese terrorists by tomorrow. How would you like that? Hordes of Mongols killing the patients and raping the nurses!"

The doctor checked his watch. "You have five minutes."

Seymour turned to Al and Mo. "Stay outside the door and don't let anyone in," he ordered them.

After they left, Seymour and Melanie pulled chairs up next to my bed and she said, "Don't say anything, Andy. Just listen to us—"

"I killed Brother Freeman," I confessed with a yawn.

"Don't ever say that again, Andy. Don't even think it. The Chinese Communists killed him. Keep telling yourself that over and over again. It was a plot. A terrible Communist plot."

"Pot?"

"Plot!" he corrected. "Now concentrate. You've got to remember all this for your sake. For my sake. For the Party's sake. And for Melanie's sake. Got it, Andy?"

"For Melanie," I repeated, concentrating for her sake. "I'd do anything for Melanie." Just saying her name made me feel so melancholy for my happy past that I began to cry. "Don't let the Chinese kidnap Melanie," I pleaded, the tears streaming down my cheeks.

"Don't worry, Andy. I'll take good care of her."

"I'm so lucky to have a friend like you."

"And we're so really, really lucky to have a friend like you," Melanie said, stroking my hand.

"Friends in need are friends indeed," I sighed.

"Don't pass out on us yet," Seymour said. "Just listen. In three weeks I'm going to be inaugurated as the governor of the state of California—"

"Congratulations!"

"Thanks, Andy. I know you mean it."

"I do! I do!"

"It's going to be a really, really big show, Andy. I'm going to be sworn in on the first national telecast of *By the People*."

"Free the people."

"We will, Andy. That's why I'm doing this. I still want to free the world. But you can't have a revolution without crisis. To free the people, we've got to scare them first. And I'm going to scare the hell out of them, Andy. First I'll whet their appetites for freedom. Then I'll drop a real bombshell—"

"Boom, boom!"

"Boom, boom is right! If the people are in a panic about China now, just wait until *By the People* goes on all the satellite news networks and the Internet. And I need you there, Andy, at my side, working the Master Computer, tallying up the votes. I need you there. Melanie needs you there."

"America really, really needs you, Andy."

I had a brief moment of lucidity, just before the hypo put me under. I looked up at Seymour and whispered, "Promise you'll never let a lecher like me marry Melanie."

"I not only promise you that, Andy. I guarantee it. Melanie will never marry you."

"You're a true friend," I said.

Melanie squeezed my hand and smiled down at me. "Seymour and I were married almost a week ago."

The room spun faster and faster. Like, I was being sucked down in a whirl-pool, yet I managed to groan, "You married him? But you promised me—"

"That I'd marry anyone who became President. And Seymour may be the President of the whole U.S.A. someday." She laughed. "So, I did it. I really, really did."

A bomb burst in the air of my brain and I saw the spangled banner was still waving as the rocket's red glare rose up to the heavens, and then there was noth-ing but nothingness.

CHAPTER 27

▼

As much as I resented all the things Seymour had done since he decided to dedicate himself to the Party, I was there, ready to tally up the votes on the Master Legislature Console when *By the People* went on the VIRGIN full network in prime time the third Tuesday in January.

What else could I do? Like, I know Seymour. He'd really make poor Melanie miserable if I walked out on him. And I felt I owed it to my dear departed friends to be there. Brother Freeman and Jordan would have wanted me to work for the good of California, America, the Freedom Party, and the people. Actually, I had very little choice in the matter. Al and Mo had practically dragged me into the studio, and I knew they'd be waiting in the wings, ready to kill me if I failed to cooperate.

In spite of the danger, it was an exciting moment for me. I had first night jitters as I sat at the Master Legislature Control Console, my eyes glued to a battery of HDTV monitors, listening to the floor director's countdown while the live audience watched the second hands of the four time zone clocks sweep inexorably toward the zero hour—ten Eastern, nine Central, eight Mountain and seven Pacific.

"Five, four, three!" the floor director's shouts came from the control booth at the rear of the studio, "two, one! We're on the air!"

There was an expectant split-second of silence before a stirring trumpet and timpani fanfare began, and over it a happy, mellow-voiced announcer shouted, "And now, direct from Satellite City in Hollywood, the VIRGIN HDTV Network presents America's first reality TV government spectacular—*By the People!*"

The floor director hit a switch and giant cue screens flashed the audience with *APPLAUSE!*, the green and white letters blinking on and off at thirty times a second. The studio audience exploded on cue; their whistles, clapping, and stamping feet swelling to a thundering roar. The eighty-three-piece live orchestra swung into "California Here I Come." Two lines of gorgeous, long-limbed chorus girls in red, white, and blue bikinis and Uncle Sam top hats danced out from the wings waving miniature California flags.

The announcer continued over the roar, "This is a VIRGIN public service presentation with a cast of millions—you, the legally registered voter members of the California Legislature!"

The two lines of chorus girls met at center stage, did a precision crisscross, and drew open the gold curtain.

"Starring the talented people's choice, the Governor-elect of the great State of California—Seymour Stone!"

The audience went totally wild as Seymour, nattily attired in a sparkling gold-sequined tuxedo, casually strolled through the ever widening gap in the gold curtains, his suit glittering in the beams of the three spotlights converging upon him.

To the delight of the audience, the gorgeous, long-legged chorus girls squealed, "We love you, Gov!" and they swarmed Seymour, smothering him with kisses. An HDTV camera zoomed in for a close-up of the Governor-elect grinning from ear to ear, raising his arms for silence. The floor director pushed the *QUIET!* button and on cue a hush fell over the audience.

The dancers, high-kicking behind him, were still blowing him kisses. "Please, please, ladies! Control yourselves," Seymour scolded them with a wink. "I'm not the Gov yet."

The audience roared with laughter.

The chorus girls formed two counter-rotating circles around Seymour, singing an original song composed by *The Red Hot Chili Peppers* for the show's premiere.

Oh, say can you see
Now we are totally free
So it's time to celebrate
California's inaugurate

He's a man for us all
Standing firm and so tall
The man we elected
Our democracy perfected

Seymour Stone is our choice
To give freedom a voice

Yeah, it's time to go-go
Go-go on with the show
So let's start him off right
Yeah, it's time to go-go
Swear in the Gov tonight!

The chorus girls ended the song with "Whoopee!" and formed two lines flanking Seymour.

The stage behind them rotated, revealing a life-size set of the State Capitol steps in Sacramento where the Chief Justice of the California Supreme Court stood at a golden dais, his gold-trimmed black judicial robes flowing in the soft breeze generated by the chorus girls' high-kicking legs and by two off-stage fans. The spotlight turned on the Chief Justice.

The orchestra struck up "Pomp and Circumstance" and a respectful silence fell over the audience. Seymour slowly climbed the Capitol steps to meet the Chief Justice. When he reached the dais, the music faded to a soft snare drum roll. An HDTV camera moved in for a two-shot close-up of Seymour and the Chief Justice, who offered Seymour an original Gutenberg Bible VIRGIN had obtained at great expense for the occasion. Seymour solemnly placed his left hand on the great Book and raised his right hand. The Chief Justice cleared his throat, and in a high-pitched, almost squeaky voice, began to read from a Tele-PrompTer, "Repeat after me: I, Seymour Oliver Stone, do solemnly swear ..."

"I, Seymour Oliver Stone, do solemnly swear," Seymour repeated.

"That I will faithfully execute the office of Governor of the State of California."

"That I will faithfully execute the office of Governor of the State of California."

The floor director momentarily lost his place in the script and pushed the *APPLAUSE* button, and the studio audience erupted again on cue.

The Chief Justice waved a bony hand. "Order in the court! Order in the court!" The floor director frantically pushed the *QUIET!* button. The clapping and shouting quickly subsided. The Chief Justice cleared his throat and went on with the oath, "And will, to the best of my ability, preserve, protect and defend the Constitution of the State of California."

"And will, to the best of my ability, preserve, protect and defend the Constitution of the State of California," Seymour said.

"I now pronounce you Governor," the Chief Justice said, extending his hand to Seymour in a congratulatory gesture.

"I now pronounce you Governor," Seymour repeated, clasping the Chief Justice's hand in both of his.

The audience burst into laughter at what they obviously thought was a flub.

Seymour turned to the HDTV cameras, and after a short pause, grinned his boyish grin, quipping, "How do you like that? Here I've only been your governor for a total of two seconds and I've made my first big boo-boo."

The audience cheered their new Governor—America's first elected Reality TV Governor.

Clasping his hands above his head in the traditional victory salute of champions, Seymour strode down the Capitol steps, his gold sequined tux sparkling in the flashes of the audience's digital cameras, and happily made his way between the two lines of gorgeous, long legged chorus girls as they sang another original song written specially for the show.

> *He's such a dear sweet love*
> *And now that he's our Guv*
> *How happy we will be*
> *Voting with him on TV*
> *As he sits and mod-er-ates*
> *Our great po-lit-ical debates*
> *So let's go-go, let's go-go*
> *Let's go-go on with the show!*

Seymour strode confidently to stage front and center. The orchestra segued into a cancan and the line of chorus girls high-kicked their way into the wings, waving goodbye with their miniature California flags and blowing kisses to the audience.

The gold curtain closed behind Seymour, and an HDTV camera rose up from the orchestra pit on a boom to get a close up of him as he stood there, looking like a reincarnation of Will Rogers, his hands in his pockets, grinning his boyish grin, waiting for the applause to die down. When it finally did, he raised his arms toward the left and right wings, and asked, "Hey! Weren't the girls just fantastic?"

The applause rose to a thundering roar again, and he let it go on for a good half-minute before he raised his arms for silence again. "They make me wish I could be inaugurated every day!" He took a handkerchief and began to wipe the lipstick from his cheeks and laughed, "You know, I think I'm going to like this job!"

The floor director pressed the *LAUGH* button and the audience obeyed the flashing cue, laughing like Seymour was another Jerry Seinfeld.

"All kidding aside, folks," Seymour read from the TelePrompTer, "it really, really does feel great to be Governor of the great golden State of California. And before we go on with the show, I'd like to take a few seconds to thank all you good folks in California TV land who voted for Proposition Sixty-Nine, the nation's first high-tech electronic election. Guess it proves you Californians really want to take government away from the politicians and give it to the people."

The audience cheered.

"We threw the bums out, didn't we?" More cheers. "You know what one politician said to the other politician when they heard I was elected governor and you wonderful registered voters elected yourselves the State Legislature?" He grinned. "Well, that's show biz!" Cheers. "And that's going to be my first order of business as Governor of this great state: I'm going to prove to our vast American TV audience that from now on government is the showbiz of the people, by the people, and for the people!"

The audience roared its approval even before the floor director hit the *APPLAUSE* button.

"According to the pundits and the politicians, the passing of Proposition Sixty-nine and the election of all the Freedom Party candidates was the greatest political upset in history. And they're right. A lot of politicians are totally upset since you, the people of the great state of California, shocked the nation and the world!"

The audience exploded.

"Can't say I feel sorry for the politicians. They only have themselves to blame for the loss of their jobs. They could have raised unemployment compensation and the minimum wage when they had the chance. They could have provided Californians with universal health coverage. And they could have stopped pandering to big oil and the military industrial complex and their greedy lobbyists. But the corporations and their bagmen told them to vote for the status quo, and they did. Well, I've got just three little words for our nation's greedy politicians, corporate America. and your lobbyist naysayers—you are history!"

The studio audience exploded again, hooting and hollering, and stamping their feet with joy.

"You tell 'em, Gov!" someone shouted over the roar.

"We all love you!" a woman's voice cried out.

Seymour blew an HDTV camera a kiss. "God bless! And I love you, California!"

That was the cue for the stage lights to dim. The lyrics of "I Love You Califor-nia" were projected on a scrim behind Seymour. The orchestra began to play the state song, and the studio audience joined in, singing the chorus with Seymour as the lyrics scrolled down the scrim:

I love you, California, you're the greatest state of all
I love you in the winter, summer, spring, and in the fall.
I love your fertile valleys; your dear mountains I adore,
I love your grand old ocean and I love her rugged shore.

I love your redwood forests—love your fields of yellow grain,
I love your summer breezes, and I love your winter rain,
I love you, land of flowers; land of honey, fruit and wine,
I love you, California; you have won this heart of mine.

I love your old gray Missions—love your vineyards stretching far,
I love you, California, with your Golden Gate ajar,
I love your purple sunsets, love your skies of azure blue,
I love you, California; I just can't help loving you.

I love you, Catalina—you are very dear to me,
I love you, Tamalpais, and I love Yosemite,
I love you, Land of Sunshine, half your beauties are untold,
I loved you in my childhood, and I'll love you when I'm old.

When the snow crowned Golden Sierras
Keep their watch o'er the valleys' bloom.
It is there I would be in our land by the sea,
Ev'ry breeze bearing rich perfume,
It is here nature gives of her rarest,
It is Home Sweet Home to me.
And I know when I die I shall breathe my last sigh
For my sunny California.

While the audience and Seymour sang the state song, a small army of stage-hands produced a minor miracle behind the scrim. One crew whisked away the set of the State Capitol steps and the Chief Justice's dais, while another moved me and my Master Legislature Computer and a huge HDTV wide screen to cen-ter stage. A third crew erected a marble and paneled mahogany set below me that was patterned after the Roman Forum. A throne-like Governor's Chair stood at the center of the Forum, flanked by two slightly smaller chairs a step below it.

As the ring-out of the final note of the State Song slowly faded, the scrim parted and the lights on the set came up. With the audience cheering him on, Seymour turned and marched up the steps to his golden seat of power. He sat down and gave the audience a confidant thumbs up.

After the applause died down. The floor director punched the *QUIET!* button and the audience obeyed, sinking back in their plush seats to enjoy the show.

Seymour turned in his golden chair and looked up at me. "Master Legislature Computer up, Maestro?"

I flexed my long fingers and placed them on the keyboard. "Up and running. We're ready to tally the people's votes."

CHAPTER 28

▼

"I know how anxious all you California Senators and Representatives in the studio audience and out there in TV Land are to get down to the business of proposing and passing new laws for the good of the people of California. But first, for the benefit of our coast-to-coast audience, I'd like to explain the way *By the People* works. Okay? When I say go, I want you, the people, to vote yes or no on a motion to open the first session of the new California Legislature. Ready, Maestro?"

According to the script, I was to demonstrate how the Master Legislature Computer and Video Ion Refractor worked together to instantly check the DNA of the state's voters, and verify that they were officially registered.

I nodded that I was ready.

"One for the money, two for the show ..." Seymour began, then he hesitated, breaking into his boyish grin. "Just kidding, folks. I know all you new legislators are ready ... so go ahead, lick a finger, touch your VIR pad, and hit the green *YES* or the red *NO* button, and cast your ballots for or against the motion on the floor!"

The Master Legislature Computer hummed to life and the yes and no vote count flashed on the giant widescreen HDTV above my head. In less than a minute, the tally was complete:

12,697,482 YEAs
4,264,351 NAYs
2,314,986 no-account, non-registered deadbeats

"That's it!" Seymour said, pointing to the giant HDTV screen. "The yeas have it. The motion passes. I now declare this session of the California Legislature open for business."

The studio audience cheered.

"Okay. Let me explain how the new California Legislature works under Proposition Sixty-Nine: it still has two branches—the State Assembly and State Senate. But the voters no longer elect politicians to represent them. Now they can represent themselves—proposing, debating and passing legislation of their own. Registered voters between the ages of eighteen and twenty-nine are automatically elected to the Assembly; while registered voters thirty and over become members of the Senate. We've asked each political party to nominate their candidates for Speaker of the Assembly and Senate Majority Leader.

"In the last election, the elected majority of both Houses were members of the Freedom Party. So the leaders of the Freedom Party were given the privilege of appointing the Speaker of the Assembly. Their choice is a remarkable young woman. She's been called the All Afro-American Girl. Born in the San Fernando Valley, she graduated cum laude from the University of Southern California, and was a member of the U. S. Olympic track team in 2004. She's a legally registered voter, a superb organizer, and a leader of the Freedom Party. Let me introduce you to the new Speaker of the Assembly—the one and only Cheetah!"

The audience rose to its feet, chanting "Cheetah, Cheetah, Cheetah" as she strode out from the left wing in a simple but elegant, glittering gold gown by Farina. Happily waving to the audience and the HDTV cameras, she stood by the Speaker's Chair, just to the right of, and one step below, Seymour's golden seat of power.

"Welcome aboard, Madam Speaker," Seymour greeted her.

She shook his hand and turned to the audience and the TV cameras. "Yo! That's my boy!"

The audience cheered their new Speaker.

"And now," Seymour began after the cheers had faded, "I want to introduce the Party's choice for Senate Majority Leader. He's a man of the world and a long-time resident of California, a man who's famous for proving the difference between right and wrong, the Wizard of Decision Making, Raymond Solmar!"

The orchestra swung into *Gypsy* and the Wizard entered from the right wing, clasping his hands above his head like a champion, taking his place on the Forum, next to Cheetah.

"Welcome aboard, Ray," Seymour said, shaking his hand.

"Glad to be here," the Wizard said. He gave Cheetah a kiss on the cheek and a friendly pat on the behind. "You know, Governor and Madame Speaker, I'm a numbers guy. Always have been. Numbers are the name of my game. But tonight's numbers took me by complete surprise. When I saw the votes totaled up by the Master Legislature Computer on that giant screen a few minutes ago, I was amazed to see it was the largest voter turnout in the history of this great golden State of California!"

The audience gave that fact a standing ovation.

"We must be doing something right," Seymour shouted over the din, and he waved for order, then motioned for Cheetah and the Wizard to sit below him, and took his seat above them.

A camera moved in for a closeup of Seymour. The boyish grin left his face and he turned serious. "As everyone in California is aware, another man was elected to fill the chair I am now occupying—a man whose life was tragically cut short just a few weeks ago—giving me, California's newly elected Lieutenant Governor, the opportunity to fill his gigantic shoes and this chair. You all know I'm speaking of the founder and leader of the Freedom Party, the late, great Brother Freeman!"

The crowd began to clap and cheer, but Seymour raised a hand for silence. The floor director took the cue and pushed the *QUIET* button. The applause quickly subsided.

Seymour rose to his feet. "I ask you to stand with me and bow your heads for a minute of silence to honor the memory of this great man of the people, by the people, and for the people."

The second hands of the time zone clocks slowly and silently completed their 360° revolutions.

"And now," Seymour shouted when the tribute was over, "let's play *By the People!*" He paused for a moment to let the cheers subside. "But before you can play the game, you gotta know how to play it."

The giant HDTV above my head became the giant screen for Seymour's PowerPoint presentation.

"Okay. Our Rules of Order are simpler than Robert's," he began. The word *Simple* spun onto the screen. "Simple. Now there's a word most politicians never understand. Ask them a question that can be answered with a simple yes or no, and the words surge out of their mouths like a great tsunami. But let a real tsunami or floods come along, and they say nothing and do nothing.

"Now, I don't want to sound like a politician, so I'll keep this short and simple: To submit a bill to the legislature for its approval, simply fill in the Proposed

New Law Form you'll find at *bythepeople.gov.ca.* on your TV wireless VIRGIN net or Internet connection."

An official New Law Entry Form appeared on the giant HDTV screen.

"Or, if you don't have a TV or a computer with a secure VIRGIN or Internet connection, you can pick up a snail mail form at your nearest Secretary of State Office, or at any California Motor Vehicle Bureau. Electronic or printed, the forms are available in all three official California languages—English, Spanish, and Vietnamese. But be sure you use the correct form for your side of the Legislature—the Assembly or the Senate.

"Simply fill in the title of your proposed bill, and in twenty-five words or less, complete the following sentence: 'I think my bill would make a good law because …

"Could anything be simpler?

"To be considered for discussion by the Legislature, all entries must be received by midnight Pacific time the Sunday before the following Tuesday night show.

"Of course, only one person can sponsor a new bill, so in case of duplicate entries we had to devise a fair method of selecting the winner. At first we thought the Master Legislature Computer should judge the entries on the basis of originality and aptness of thought. But upon further consideration that idea was rejected because it might penalize the less educated. So it was decided that to be truly democratic the winning entries should be picked using an unbiased lottery.

"*By the People's* Master Legislature Computer's Decision Tree Program will sort and pick five hundred New Law entries to be printed out, and the hard copies will be placed in either the State Assembly or Senate New Law Lottery drum, depending on the sponsor's originating chamber."

The director cut to split-screen closeups of the giant Assembly and Senate gold rotating lottery drums and the two beautiful Hollywood starlets who would spin them.

"If your New Law entry form is selected by the Master Legislature Computer to be entered in either lottery drum, you'll win a $500 Prize! In the case of duplicate New Law entries, the first entry received by the Master Legislature Computer will be considered the winner.

"And here's where the big money comes in. Each Tuesday, the *By the People* lottery drums will be rotated, and our charming assistants will draw five New Law entries from the Assembly and Senate drums for you, the people, to discuss and vote on the floor.

"More good news. Each New Law entry selected to be debated on by the Assembly or the Senate will receive a ten day all-expense-paid vacation for two at the Hilton Hawaiian Village in Honolulu, round-trip first class transportation supplied by United Airlines, plus ten-thousand dollars in cash.

"And here's the really, really big payoff: if your proposed legislation is passed by both houses of the Legislature and Senate, and I sign it into law, you will receive one million dollars in cash! Tax free! How's that for big money? Do we give prizes, or do we get prizes?"

The audience cheered.

"Now, the producers of *By the People* realize there are two sides to every issue. If our democratic system is to be maintained, the other side has the right to be heard. So if you object to any proposed legislation presented on this show, simply file your objection by filling out an I Object form, telling *By the People* in twenty-five words or less why you object to the proposed law. The Master Legislature Computer must, however, confirm the objector is a registered voter before his or her objection will be allowed.

"*By the People* never plays favorites. There are big prizes for objecting to a bill. If your objection is selected for debate, the prize is exactly the same as the prize for a submitted bill—a nine-day all–expense-paid vacation for two at the Hilton Hawaiian Village in Honolulu, round-trip first class transportation supplied by United Airlines, plus ten-thousand dollars in cash. And if your objection defeats a bill when it comes up for a vote, or I veto it, and the Senate cannot override my veto, you could win our weekly Good Government Grand Prize of one million dollars!"

The audience erupted in another round of applause, cheers, shouts, and whistles.

The floor director pushed the *QUIET!* button and the audience brought itself under control.

Seymour continued, "As the elected head of the Executive Branch of your State Government, I am not only the Decider; I have the legal power to submit legislation to the Legislature–"

"Who gets the prize money if your bills are passed?" a planted heckler shouted from the audience.

Seymour grinned. "I'll turn all Executive Branch prize money over to the State Board of Education."

"We love you, Gov!" a woman's voice cried out over the applause.

CHAPTER 29

▼

"And now it's time to play *By the People!*" Seymour announced. "Since the State Assembly has traditionally been the chamber closest to the people, let's start by selecting a New Law entry from the Assembly Lottery Drum." He pointed to the drum to his right and said, "All right, ladies, let her roll!"

The two starlets in gold tights gave the huge drum a spin, chanting, "Around and' round she goes—"

"And where she stops, nobody knows," Seymour joined in.

A suspenseful hush fell over the audience as the drum slowly spun, first on its vertical axis, and then rotating horizontally like a carnival tilt-a-whirl. An HDTV camera zoomed in for a close-up of the New Law entries tumbling like concrete in a cement mixer. When the drum finally stopped spinning, the two starlets stepped aside, looking expectantly at Seymour.

"And now, Madam Speaker, please select tonight's first winning New Law entry."

Cheetah got up from her seat below Seymour and slinked gracefully to the golden Assembly Lottery Drum, opened the trapdoor at the top, reached inside, and dug deep down into the entries. Selecting one, she pulled it out, waved it at the studio audience, and exclaimed, "Oh, God. Isn't this exciting?"

"And the winner is?" Seymour asked.

Cheetah read the entry to herself, building the suspense, before handing it to Seymour.

He looked at the winning entry and broke out into a grin. "Our first New Law proposal was submitted by Mr. George Zimbleman—or I should say, Assemblyman Zimbleman. George is twenty-eight years old and he lives in Oxnard. The title of his proposed New Law is: The $40,000 Minimum Wage Bill."

The *APPLAUSE* cue sign flashed and the audience cheered.

"And here's why George says he's for it." Seymour began reading from the card. "'I think this is a good bill because everyone in California should be above the national poverty line.'" He counted the number of words on the form. "How's that for being succinct? Assemblyman Zimbleman used only eighteen of the twenty-five allotted words."

He looked up at me. "Okay, Maestro, is George on the line?"

I gave him a thumbs up, and punched the F8 key on the Master Control Console. The huge HDTV screen above me faded to black, and a close-up of Mr. Zimbleman appeared. He was a thin young man with a full head of greasy little black pomade peaks.

"Good evening, George. Are you at home?" Seymour said.

"Yeah, I'm here."

"Is your TV on?"

"Uh, huh. I can see you and you can see me."

"Then you know you're tonight's first prize winner. Are you married, George?"

"Yeah, ten years."

"And what's your lovely bride's name?"

"Shelley."

"Do you and Shelley have any children?"

"Yeah."

"Boys or girls."

"Both kinds."

"How many?"

"Too many."

The audience laughed.

"That's why I want my bill to pass," Assemblyman Zimbleman continued. "We can't live on anything less than $40,000 a year."

"Well, George, I've got good news for you and Shelley. You're both flying to Honolulu—transportation supplied by United Airlines—where you'll spend two glorious sun-filled weeks at the glamorous Hilton Hawaiian Village—courtesy Hilton Hotels. And you'll have $10,000 in cash to take with you and pay for your kids' babysitter. Isn't that great!"

"Yeah. So when do I win the million dollar prize?"

"Afraid you'll have to wait to see if your bill passes the Legislature and if I sign it into law."

The camera cut in for a close-up of Seymour. "Okay. You've all heard Assemblyman Zimbleman's proposed bill. Now it's time to hear from the opposition. Do any of you registered Assemblymen or Senators out there in TV land object to the $40,000 Minimum Wage Bill?"

The Master Computer began to beep, and strings of ones and zeros danced across the giant screen above my head, followed by a clickety-click-clacking as the Senate and Assembly laser printers filled the Golden Lottery Drums of both houses with five hundred opposition entry blanks.

"Okay," Seymour said when the flashing numbers and clickety-click-clacking stopped. "For the sake of expedience, let's consider tonight's session of the Legislature a joint session." He turned to Ray Solmar. "Mr. Majority Leader, would you please select the Senate's winning opposition winner."

Ray Solmar reached deep down into the Senate Drum and pulled out the winning entry and handed it up to the Governor.

Seymour read from the entry card: "Tonight's winning Senate objection is from Virginia Vaughan of Santa Barbara."

I pressed the F9 button on the Master Computer console and a closeup of Virginia Vaughan's face appeared on the giant screen. She had thinning gray hair that framed her deeply lined face.

"All right, Ms Vaughan," Seymour started.

"Senator Vaughan," she corrected him.

"Okay, Virginia, how old are you?"

"Old enough to know better."

The audience laughed.

"I need to know you age, Virginia, to determine if you're a member of the Assembly or the Senate."

Virginia bit her lower lip, and then shouted, "I'm eighty-eight years young!"

The audience applauded.

"All right, Senator, you've just won a trip to Honolulu—transportation supplied by United Airlines—where you'll spend two glorious sun-filled weeks at the glamorous Hilton Hawaiian Village—courtesy Hilton Hotels. How do you like that?"

"Keep the trip to Hawaii. All I want is the cash."

"But you're entitled to—"

"Don't need any more entitlements, sonny. Got too many already. What I really need is a new set of false teeth—implants. Know what I'm saying? The ten thousand should just about cover it."

"All right, Senator. What's your objection to the bill on the floor?'

"What floor?"

"The floor of the Legislature."

"Oh, that floor. What's the bill again?"

"The $40,000 Minimum Wage Bill."

"Don't like it. No, sir. Don't like it at all."

"Can you be more specific?"

"It'll bankrupt the State."

There was a smattering of applause from the studio audience.

"That's a legitimate objection," Seymour said.

"Sure is, sonny. If the State goes bankrupt, who'll pay my public assistance and Medicaid bills?"

"Good question."

"You bet."

There was another smattering of applause.

"Thank you, Senator Vaughan, for airing your objection. Of course, if the bill on the floor is defeated you could win more big money."

Seymour turned and looked up at me again. "All right, Maestro, bring up Assemblyman Zimbleman again."

I pressed the F10 key on my console and the giant screen split with the Assemblyman's image on the left, and the Senator's image on the right.

"Okay, George. Do you have a rebuttal to Virginia's objection?"

"Yeah. I still think my bill should be passed because no Californian should make less than $40,000 a year!"

The studio audience cheered and stamped their feet.

"And you don't think it would bankrupt the State?"

"No way! If people make more money they can pay more taxes—"

The audience booed.

"I'm against new taxes!" Virginia shot back.

The audience cheered.

The camera cut to a close-up of Seymour again. "Okay. It's time to bring the motion on the floor of this joint session to a vote. The Assembly will vote first. Are you for or against the $40,000 Minimum Wage Bill?"

I pressed the *ASSEMBLY VOTE* key on the Master Computer Control Console and the great electronic brain went into action, its hundreds of colored lights blinking on and off in time to the beep-beeping and clickity-clacking. In less than ten seconds, the numbers began to total up below Assemblyman Zimbleman's image on the giant screen..

Seymour waited for the numbers of yes and no votes to slow to a final tally before he read the numbers off the giant screen:

YEAS=4,797,343
NAYS=2,646,280

"The yeas have it!" Seymour shouted. "Okay. Now it's time for all you Senators out there to vote.

I pressed the *SENATE VOTE* key and the flashing lights, beep-beeping, and clickity-clacking filled the studio again as the votes totaled up below Senator Vaughan's image on the giant screen:

YEAS=5,535,915
NAYS=4,982,295

"The yeas have it!" Seymour shouted. "The $40,000 Minimum Wage Bill passed the Assembly and the Senate!" Seymour shouted.

Assemblyman Zimbleman raised his fist, joyfully shouting, "Yes!"

The audience roared its approval.

Senator Vaughan looked as if she was about to burst into tears. "Oh, Lordy."

"Sorry, Virginia, sometimes you win and sometimes you lose," Seymour said. "That's politics. But don't be discouraged. Keep playing *By the People* and next time you could win a million dollars."

"Can I keep the money for my new teeth?"

"Absolutely," Seymour said. "Goodbye and good luck."

That was my cue to cut her image from the big screen.

A camera cut in for a close-up of Seymour and his boyish grin as he stood looking up at the full-screen image of Assemblyman Zimbleman.

"I'll bet you're feeling good, right, George?"

"Right. Wouldn't you if you'd just won a million bucks?"

"Sorry, George, but you haven't won it yet. Your bill isn't a law yet, because I haven't signed it. So the question now is—" the orchestra played a few bars of suspense music "—will I sign the bill?"

The audience began to chant, "Yes! Yes! Yes! Yes!"

"What do you think, George? Should I sign your bill?"

"That's up to you, Governor. But I sure hope you do."

"George, I hate to tell you this—" Seymour paused for drama. George and the audience groaned. "Just kidding, George." He took out a stylus and signed the touch screen on his iPhone. "You and your lovely wife, Shelley, have won a trip to Honolulu—transportation supplied by United Airlines—where you'll spend two glorious sun-filled weeks at the glamorous Hilton Hawaiian Village—courtesy Hilton Hotels. Plus ten thousand dollars in cash. And ..." he paused to create more suspense. "You have just won a million dollars! How's that for one night's work as a new California law maker?"

The orchestra broke into *We're in the Money,* and the two lines of gorgeous, long-limbed chorus girls in red, white, and blue bikinis and Uncle Sam top hats danced out from the wings waving dollar bills to the delight of the studio audience.

CHAPTER 30

▼

In addition to the $40,000 Minimum Wage Bill, Seymour signed three more new bills into law the night of the first nationally televised broadcast of *By the People*.

The second bill was the California Pure Water Act proposed by a Senator from Orange County, which made it a crime punishable by death to pollute California's reservoirs, lakes, or waterways with any chemical or drug that could cause hallucinations. Strong opposition to the bill was voiced by a young Assemblyman from Berkeley who thought the death penalty was too severe. The bill barely eked through both houses after Seymour made an impassioned argument for the bill, declaring death was a just punishment for anyone who would stoop to drugging an entire population.

The third bill was the End the Pacific Time Zone Act, which was proposed by a San Francisco Senator, a Merrill-Lynch broker, who said he was tired of getting to work at six in the morning to be in sync with the New York Stock Market. He claimed the Pacific Zone was created by the railroads in 1883 and it was time to eliminate it. It was opposed by an Assemblyman from L.A., a student at U.C.L.A. who said he enjoyed staying up three hours later than his parents in New Jersey. The bill was supported by eighty-three percent of the legislators and Seymour signed it into law.

The fourth bill was the Brother Freeman Memorial Bill, which was proposed by the Governor and passed both houses of the Legislature with very little opposition. The bill renamed the Hollywood Freeway the Freeman Freeway, and it provided funds for a hundred foot rainbow granite statue of the Freedom Party's martyred founder to be erected in the hills above the world famous Hollywood sign.

The passing of the fourth bill gave Seymour a platform to provide the national audience with a Breaking News Story—the bombshell he had told me he was going to drop the night he talked to me in the hospital three weeks before the national launch of *By the People*. Like, I was under the influence of Dilaudid when he told me about it, so I'd completely forgotten about it.

His timing was perfect. He announced it as part of his closing monologue.

"Well, folks. How did you like the first show?" he asked, standing in the beam of a single spotlight, his hands in his pockets, grinning his boyish Will Rogers grin.

He and the show received a standing ovation. He let the clapping, cheering, and whistling go on for almost a full minute before he raised a hand for silence. "Let's hear it for the gorgeous *By the People* dancers!" he said, motioning to the left and right wings, and on his cue, gaggles of chorus girls danced out, crossing the set in two lines from wing to wing, waving California flags and blowing kisses to the audience.

Wolf whistles and cheers greeted the girls and they danced past Seymour and disappeared in opposite wings.

"Beautiful!" Seymour said. "And let's hear it for Madame Speaker and the Majority Leader."

Twin spotlights played on Cheetah and Ray Solmar standing on the forum. They bowed to the audience's applause. Then the spotlights converged on me.

"And let's not forget the Maestro of the Master Computer who tallied up your votes," Seymour said.

I waved to the audience and, like, they actually cheered me. Then the lights on me dimmed, then went out, and a camera moved in for a closeup of Seymour standing at center stage.

"Seriously, folks," he started. "You've witnessed a revolution here tonight—a revolution in self government—a totally honest-to-goodness grass roots government of the people, by the people, and for the people. A bloodless revolution that could only happen in the United States of America!"

As the audience applauded, the floor director ran out from the wings and handed Seymour a note.

Seymour read the note and raised his hand for silence. "Just a minute, folks. I've just been handed a breaking news bulletin." The camera moved in for an extreme closeup of Seymour's face. He stared directly at the camera as he read the note. "Beijing. The People's Republic of China has just announced that it is the first nation to give every Chinese citizen of voting age universal suffrage. According to a government spokesman, every TV set in China will be equipped with a Video Ion Refractor, allowing all Chinese over the age of twenty-one to vote on any proposal by the Politburo Standing Committee of the Communist Party of China. The Politburo claims this act to be the greatest breakthrough in universal suffrage in the history of the world!"

The audience sat in shocked silence, watching Seymour fold the note and slip it into his pocket.

"My friends," he said, in a low but firm, emotionless voice. "This is totally a blow to American prestige. We invented the tamper-free home TV ballot box and the first truly democratic form of government. And now the Chinese have stolen the idea from us. Yes, now we know why the Chinese assassinated Brother Freeman. And why they kidnapped Jordan Lee, the VIR inventor's executive assistant. They wanted to tear down our status as the world's only super power by intimidating the United Nations and the European Union into kowtowing to them by recognizing China as a second super power. Are we, the American People, going to sit idly by and let the Chinese win the battle of the ballot box?"

The audience shouted, "No! No! No!"

Seymour raised his voice. "Then I, as Governor of the great state of California, would like to submit a resolution to the Legislature. A resolution calling for a federal constitutional convention to specifically amend the Constitution of the United States of America to allow the people of this great nation to represent themselves in both houses of Congress, following the guidelines established by the state of California!"

"I second the motion," Cheetah shouted over the roar of the audience.

"And I second your second, Madame Speaker," Ray Solmar shouted.

"Okay," Seymour said. "It's time to put it to a vote."

I flexed my hands over the Master Computer's Control Panel and it lit up like a Fourth of July fireworks finale. The resolution passed both houses almost unanimously. Seymour signed it and donated his million dollar prize to the California school system.

WASHINGTON—THE END

CHAPTER 31

▼

"Hrumph!" I grunted after reading the handbill of the *Washington Post* editorial page. "Now the *Post* has labeled me the 'Mad Hermit' of Capitol Hill."

"Why don't you sue the crummy rag for libel?" Mo asked, swilling down the last of the pigeon soup. "Sure is a lie. Hermits live alone. You got Al and me to protect you."

I crumpled the editorial page handbill into a ball and added it to the scraps of paper burning in my Capitol office's cheery fireplace. "Doesn't matter," I said. "Like, no one reads newspapers any more. Wonder why the *Post* even bothers to publish this trash."

"Yeah," Mo agreed, rubbing his hands together over the flickering flames in my fireplace. "Personally, though, I hope the bums keep it up. We're running out of old Congressional recordings to burn."

"Records," Al corrected.

"Yeah, and when they're gone we'll f-f-freeze," Mo added, his uneven yellow teeth chattering uncontrollably.

I got up, stamped my cold-numbed feet on the marble floor to get the circulation going again, and went over to my grime-streaked window overlooking the National Mall. "Things will get better," I said, noting the touch of pink in the branches of the few cherry trees circling the Tidal Basin and the Jefferson Monument that hadn't been chopped down for firewood. "Spring's in the air. Like, the cherry blossoms are starting to come out."

"Why don't we go out and jog around the mall or something?" Al suggested.

"Yeah, we haven't been out of this stupid Capital for almost three years," Mo said.

"Has it really been, like, three years?" I asked.

"Yeah, and that's too long to be cooped up in this crummy mausoleum," Mo said.

"Mausoleum?" Al said.

"Yeah, an i-i-ice cold tomb," Mo said.

"You guys go out if you want to," I said. "There's nothing in the real world outside that interests me anymore."

"Guess you're right," Al said. "It's like one big slum out there now."

"That's because we're in a recession," Mo said.

"Depression," Al corrected.

"What time is it?" I asked.

Al looked out the grime-streaked window and checked the shadow of the Washington Monument. "Looks like it's around ten to one," he said.

I shrugged and said, "Guess I'd better get down to Master Computer Control. A Secret Service messenger delivered a note from the President. He wants to have a meeting with me at two."

"That bum coming over here again?" Al asked. "Whenever a problem comes up he rides his bike over here with his Secret Service detail to have you solve it."

"You should be, like, more respectful. Seymour Stone's our President," I told him.

"Yeah," Mo agreed. "When a bum's president, you should call him a more high-class name."

"Nincompoop," Al said. "What's the bum want this time?"

"Same as always," I said. "He wants the Master Computer to help him solve the nation's problems."

"Yeah. The power grid's been down for months. How can you run the Master Computer without power?" Al said.

"The President's generates his own electricity," I said.

*   *   *   *

I left my two bodyguards and started down the Capitol's cold and hallowed corridors to Master Computer Control, located in what you probably remember as the Rotunda. Like, you'd never recognize the interior of the nation's Capitol if you visited it today. The House and Senate Chambers were completely gutted years ago to make way for all the high-tech electronics that had to be installed to tally up the people's votes. You could say your nation's Capitol is one great electronic brain, but of course you'd be wrong if you did. Great electronic brains aren't all that great without the power it takes to run them. So there's only one great brain still at work here. Mine.

I reached Computer Control a few minutes early, so I sat down at the master console at the center of the great circular digital display to await my old friend and teammate, Seymour Stone, the President of the United States.

It's actually quite amazing, like, how quickly things can change in the United States in the Twenty-First Century. I mean, when you look back and think about all that's happened since the turn of the century. Take high-tech stuff. In 1999 practically no one had a cell phone. If you weren't at home or in your office you had to use a pay phone. Five years later, pay phones didn't exist, and people walked and drove around like they were born with a cell phone in their ear. And take books, newspapers, and radio. Fifty or sixty years ago, when my grandma and grandpa were my age, reading and listening to the radio were the people's only source for information. And people actually read novels! By the turn of this century, how-to books and celebrity memoirs were the only books people read. Then the Internet came along and it was more or less the end of books and the Fourth Estate. Like, I think that's why Americans became dumber and dumber. TV and the Internet robbed them of their imaginations.

You think I'm exaggerating? No way! When people read fiction and listened to radio sitcoms and dramatic shows, they had to use their minds. Because books and radio only give the reader or listener half the picture. There were no visuals to support the words. So people had to create the characters and picture locations and situations in their own minds. It was an exercise in creativity. Like, grandma and grandpa used to tell me they never enjoyed seeing a movie based on a novel if they'd read the book first; because none of the characters and scenes in the movie seemed anything like the characters they'd created in their minds.

So maybe that's where America went wrong. TV and movies and the Internet may be entertaining and filed with information, but everything's there for the viewer to see and hear in beautiful high definition color and surround sound, so people not only became fat physically; they also became fatheads. Reality became virtual reality, and most people never understood the difference between the two.

Understand what I'm saying?

In a way, I feel sorry for the country and Seymour. Like, when I look back over the last six years of his administration, and think of the high hopes we had for government of the people, by the people, and for the people—well, it's sort of like a Shakespearian tragicomedy

Like, Seymour's first year in office was very entertaining. *By the People* was the top rated show on TV the first year he was President. Actually, there was no real competition for the show. Roger Jolly preempted two hours of prime time every Thursday evening from nine to eleven—not only on the VIRGIN Network, but on all five hundred and seven-seven USS-TV satellite channels. And for the first time in history, the American people actually took an active interest in their government. Congress truly became the voice of the people, and the United States republic actually became what the politicians had always claimed it was: a democracy.

The country seemed back on track. Our prestige and image were rising around the world again. War, global warming, and the HIV virus appeared to be conquered. The CIA division of STRATCOM proved there had never been a democracy gap between the U.S. and the People's Republic of China. It reported the Chinese version of the VIR was just a cheap copy of mine—its only button was a yes button, so the Chinese couldn't vote against anything.

The legislation the American people passed that first year was the most liberal and forward looking since Roosevelt's New Deal. There were major tax cuts. As in the past, most of the cuts were mainly for the rich, since becoming rich was, as always, the great American dream, so the people didn't want to tax themselves if their dream came true, and they won a billion dollars in a state lottery or something. The Social Security system was modernized and universal healthcare finally became a reality. All branches of the Executive were streamlined. The Fourteen Cabinet Departments—Agriculture, Commerce, Defense, Education, Energy, Health and Human Services, Homeland Security, Housing and Urban Development, Interior, Justice, Labor, State, Transportation, and Treasury—were merged into one: STRATCOM.

It was sort of like deregulating the regulators, designed to produce a super efficient system of management, with only one department director reporting to the Commander in Chief instead of fourteen. Seymour's choice for director of STRATCOM was a very popular decision. Since I was the Maestro of *By the People's* Master Computer Control, and the people were used to seeing me perform on the show two times a week, I'd become a celebrity in my own right, so I was a natural for the job.

The second year was almost as exciting and productive as the first, but by the third year *By the People's* ratings began to slide. Three factors contributed to the show's decline.

One: If you count the five California years, the show had been on national TV eight years, and it's a well known fact that even the most popular TV shows begin to slip after three years, and eight years is usually the longest a top show can survive.

Two: The local Freedom Party rallies were beginning to compete for the viewers' attention, like, more and people were beginning to enjoy the reality of partying more than they enjoyed virtual reality.

Three: Audience participation and quiz shows seem to have an off and on cycle of twenty years or so, and the inflation of prize money seems to turn people off—like, in the 1930s *The Sixty-Four Dollar Question* was a top rated radio show. By the 1950s *The Sixty-Four Thousand Dollar Question* moved to the top of the TV ratings, but by the turn of this century *So You Want to be a Millionaire* was considered boring, boring.

Anyway, when *By the People*'s ratings began to slide, Roger Jolly summoned Seymour to Satellite City in Southfield to lay down the law to the President and tell him in no uncertain terms that he had to hype the show in the upcoming season or they'd move it out of VIRGIN prime time and turn it over to C-Span.

In a desperate attempt to breathe new life into *By the People*, Seymour and the writers turned it into the world's biggest reality TV giveaway show.

At first the people seemed overjoyed. The weekly prizes grew from an average of ten million dollars a week to over a billion. *By the People* gave away more money than all the state lotteries combined. And the people went wild, proposing more and more Freedom Bills. The Free Love Bill. The Free Food Bank Bill. The Free Money Bill. The Free Power Bill. The Free TV Bill. The Free Transportation Bill. The Free Education Bill. The Free Gasoline Bill. The Free Telephone and Cell Phone Bill. The Free Home Furnishing and Appliance Bill. Suddenly all the best things in life were, as Melanie would say, really, really free. I don't know what Seymour's legacy will be, but I'm sure future historians will label his administration the Carefree Era.

The age-old American dream had come true. People no longer had to work for anything. Goofing off and making love became the great national pastimes. But, like, in the cold light of really, real reality, it was a fool's paradise. No country in the world—not even the United States of America—could long afford to support a totally free economy.

Ironically, it was Seymour's attempt to hype *By the People* that actually drove the show off the air. Because the people weren't working, a serious parts shortage caused a breakdown of the national power grid which, in turn, meant the end of not only reality TV, but the end of TV, the Internet, cell phones and telephones, and all forms of high-tech transportation and commercial intercourse. So at a time when the nation needed a strong government to avert economic disaster, Congress and the voice of the people became impotent. By default, Seymour inherited almost dictatorial powers. But in the reality of the real world, he was virtually powerless. No one cared what he said or did, because no one knew what he said or did. Like, I'm sure if he'd been a stronger man, he could have made all the necessary decisions that were needed to keep the country from sliding into the Great Depression of the Twenty-First Century. But, sadly, Seymour was a born celebrity—a great actor and presenter of other people's ideas—but, like, he just didn't have it in him to be a practical thinker or great initiator.

And like I said before, it probably wasn't all Seymour's fault. Gossips inside the Beltline say the First Lady is giving him a hard time. I know for a fact that it's more than gossip. The President told me so the last time he consulted with me. Like, he complained Melanie finds fault with everything he does. You know, he doesn't pick up his underwear and socks, and she can't look at the afternoon soaps because the TV never works. He claims it's the little things like that that really, really piss her off. He confessed they sleep in separate bedrooms now. He says the biggest mistake of his presidency was listening to Melanie when she asked him to appoint Cheetah Assistant to the President and the First Lady's chief of staff so they could enjoy having their morning and afternoon coffee breaks together again. Melanie and Cheetah have become so close that Seymour thinks they may be having an affair. To make life in the White House even worse, he says the First Lady and Cheetah are constantly bickering with his Chief of Staff, Dawn Day, and he's completely fed up with their persistent catfighting. Like, he's so depressed about life in the White House he actually told me he thought anyone who aspires to be President has to be totally insane, literally. And he claims that's why the executive mansion has become a virtual nut house the past couple of decades.

And he told me things at Number One Observatory Circle, the Vice President's executive mansion, are just as bad. The Veep's wife, Hedda Nichtwahr, was so obsessed with Arnold Schwarzenegger's body when he was the Governator, that she bought the Veep, Harmon P. Harper, a Bowflex for his birthday, and the first time he tried it, he tightened the bow so tight it shot him through the exercise room's skylight, putting him in Walter Reed Hospital for almost two weeks.

I think that's why Seymour seeks my advice so often. Like, he apparently looks upon me as his last true friend, the only person he can talk to who listens to him and tries to solve his and the nation's problems. Whatever. All I know is that the President believes I can work miracles by building Decision Trees for him on the Master Computer. He doesn't seem to realize that the failure of the nation's power grid also resulted in the breakdown of the Capitol's great electronic brain. And, like, he has enough problems of his own, so I didn't have the heart to tell him high-tech just doesn't work anymore. So I did my best to humor him and scrounged around the Capitol, managing to cannibalize enough parts to generate enough electricity to power my laptop and use it to light up the Master Computer's giant LCD screen in the Rotunda control room. Only I can't power it up without the President's help, so I need him as much as he needs me.

✳   ✳   ✳   ✳

The President's echoing footsteps are approaching. It's time to get down to work.

"Hi, Andy, friend," President Seymour Stone greets me as he enters the Rotunda control room.

"Good afternoon, Mr. President. How's the First Lady?"

"Melanie? Oh, fine I guess. She asked me to tell you she sends her love."

"Love is the hope of the world."

"Yeah, right, Andy. How's the Master Computer today?"

"Hard to say until we power it up. Climb up on the Exercycle."

Seymour climbs up onto the Exercycle's seat. "That was a great idea of yours, Andy. Salvaging the Exercycle from the Senate Gym and hooking it up to the emergency lighting generator you scavenged from the Capitol subway."

"If you pump hard enough, you can generate up to twenty-four volts."

The President begins pumping away. "You're a genius, Andy."

"I know," I say, turning on my lap top. "Pump harder."

"Okay." Puff! Puff. "Somehow, I always feel better doing this." Puff. Puff. "This thing not only generates enough juice to run the computer." Puff. Puff. "It's great exercise."

My laptop is up and running, and for the first time in months I see the Wi-Fi Icon at the bottom of the screen light up. "Good news, Mr. President. We're on the Internet."

Puff. Puff. "Fantastic. What's the latest news?"

"Can't read it. It's all in Chinese."

Puff! Puff! "Damn Chinks and their wireless electricity! They're taking over the world."

My laptop screen flashes, *You've got mail!* "Keep pumping, Mr. President. I need to check something out."

Puff. Puff. "Okay. But make it snappy. I can only go about ten miles on this thing."

I double click the e-mail icon. I almost fall off my chair when I see the incoming mail is from jlee@china.org.cn. I blink at it twice and open it:

Hi Andy!!!

I've almost given up hearing from you. Oh, my gosh!!! I miss you so!!!
I don't know what you've been told about me, but the Chinese didn't
kidnap me. I defected!!! Can you believe it??? I thought I could bring
democracy to China if I gave them the secret of your VIR. Sorry!!!
Don't hate me for it!!! But the VIR didn't do much for the people.
The government only allowed me to create it with a yes button!!!
But the Chinese do listen to my ideas!!! Oh, my gosh!!! They used
my idea for transmitting electricity without wires to broadcast
a wireless grid throughout China!!! Everything here is Wi-Fi powered!!!
Cars, bicycles, buses, trucks, trains—even electric propjets!!!
Can you imagine!!! I'd love to defect back to the U.S., so I can
be with you again!!! And I know the Chinese government will
let me go!!! They want me to help you create a wireless grid
in the U.S. so the American people can buy Chinese electric cars
and stuff!!! Oh, my gosh!!! It would be so great to be with you
again!!! If you get this, please answer one question: after all these
years do you still want me????

Love,

Jordan

I press the reply button and send a one word answer: *Yo!!!*
Puff! Puff! "What's taking so long?"
"Sorry. Just a little glitch. Like, pump harder. So what do you need to know today?"
Puff! Puff! "Remember that last Decision Tree you made in the Southfield cafeteria? You know, when our team was trying to come up with a new virtual reality show to win one of Harmon P. Harper's prizes?"

"Not really. Like, I thought up so many new virtual reality shows. You guys didn't like any of them, so I more or less forgot them."

Puff! Puff! "You never totally forget anything. Remember? It was your *All American City* reality show idea." Puff! Puff!

"Oh, yeah. The one where we blow up an American City every Fourth of July."

Puff! Puff! "And the entire country gets together to rebuild it." Puff! Puff!

"Stimulating the economy?"

"That's the one." Puff! Puff! "I think the time for it has totally come."

"Yeah, right. But the power grid's down. If there's no TV, how are people going to watch the show?"

Puff! Puff! "Use your computer's great brain, Andy. Build me a decision tree that shows me how to get the power grid up and running." Puff! Puff!

I look at Jordan's e-mail again. "There may be a way," I say. "But I'm not sure the American people are ready to blow up their cities to stimulate the economy."

Puff! Puff! "I'm the Decider, Andy. And you're still director of STRATCOM." Puff! Puff! "Your Strategic Air Command and Office of Homeland Security Divisions are still up and running." Puff! Puff! "As Commander in Chief, they've got to do anything I say." Puff! Puff! "Get it done! That's an Executive Order!" Puff! Puff!

"Mr. President, I have a solution for the nation's problems," I say, pretending my laptop has used its feeble brain to come up with a decision tree. "Power is no problem overseas. I just got an e-mail from Jordan. Like, she's in China, you know, and she wants to come in out of the cold and help us build a national wireless power grid. I can order STRATCOM to renew her passport and bring her home."

Puff! Puff! "Think she can have the grid up by the Fourth of July?" Puff. Puff!

"Like, you know Jordan. She's worked miracles before."

Puff! Puff! "It's a done deal, Andy. If she can do it, this could be the most spectacular Fourth of July fireworks show since 1776!" Puff! Puff! "Now, get me off this freaking Exercycle!"

—30—

About the Author

Jim Gilmore
Lecturer Emeritus
College of Communication Arts & Sciences
Michigan State University

Jim Gilmore is a veteran of more than 25 years of experience in the advertising agency business, rising to Vice President/Creative Director and member of the Board of Directors of Leo Burnett in Chicago.

At the age of 47, Jim decided to make a major career change. He quit Burnett and moved his family to Santa Barbara to become a freelance writer. Two years later, he was interviewed by Phil Donahue on NBC's *Today* show. Donahue wanted to know why Jim gave up a high paying, highly successful advertising career to become a struggling freelance writer.

Jim may have been struggling, but he was having fun. He sold his first mystery novel and published short stores in *Alfred Hitchcock* and *Mike Shane* mystery magazines. He also wrote for *Santa Barbara* magazine and was one of the founders of *Islands* magazine.

Five Iron Cannons, an article he wrote for *Santa Barbara* magazine, revealed new archeological evidence in an age-old California controversy: Where in California was the bay Sir Frances Drake named Nova Albion during his round-the-world voyage in 1579? Jim's evidence indicated Drake's bay was in Santa Barbara, not San Francisco. The *Los Angeles Times* ranked his article among California's top ten news stories that year. As a result, he and marine archaeologist Jack Hunter were commissioned by the State of California to coauthor a fact book on their discoveries. *National Geographic* provided them with a grant to continue their research.

Caught in the middle of a bitter debate he created among Santa Barbara and San Francisco historians and academicians, Jim decided it was time to get back into the less competitive world of advertising. He signed on as the International Creative Director of Japan's Standard Advertising, and moved his family to Tokyo.

For the next four years, he created international advertising campaigns for many major Japanese clients: Nissan, Sony, Sharp, Canon, Honda, Minolta, Fuji Film, Olympus and Seiko. His campaigns ran in Europe, the Middle East, South America, Africa, Australia and Southeast Asia.

In 1987, Jim made another major career change. He joined the Michigan State University's College of Communication Arts and Sciences as Visiting Lecturer, teaching creative courses and mentoring students. After 19 years of visiting he retired in 2006.

Jim's new mystery novel, *Dead Rite*, was published by Contemporary Press, New York in 2005.

He is a licensed pilot, IFR rated, with over 3,000 logged hours; and he is certified for open ocean scuba diving.

978-0-595-71085-0
0-595-71085-9

Printed in the United States
95906LV00004BC/26/A